PLANETKILL

Exterminatus, the destruction of an entire world, is the last and most desperate weapon of the Imperium of Man. Witness the struggle of mankind in the 41st millennium as it strives to throw back waves of deadly aliens and the warping powers of Chaos. The forces of the Immortal Emperor, the stalwart Imperial Guard and the superhuman Adeptus Astartes are the galaxy's only defence against such foes. There is respite, no chance for a lasting victory. In the grim darkness of the far future there is only war!

Planetkill is a collection of short stories set in the Warhammer 40,000 universe featuring authors such as Graham McNeill as well as the best new talent.

Also available from the Black Library

WARHAMMER 40,000 STORIES

PLANETKILL

Edited by
Nick Kyme
& Lindsey Priestley

A BLACK LIBRARY PUBLICATION

First published in Great Britain in 2008 by
BL Publishing,
Games Workshop Ltd.,
Willow Road, Nottingham,
NG7 2WS, UK.

10 9 8 7 6 5 4 3 2 1

Cover illustration by John Blanche.

A CIP record for this book is available from the British Library.

ISBN13: 978 1 84416 550 6
ISBN10: 1 84416 550 7

See the Black Library on the Internet at
www.blacklibrary.com

Find out more about Games Workshop
and the world of Warhammer 40,000 at
www.games-workshop.com

Printed and bound in the UK.

IT IS THE 41st millennium. For more than a hundred centuries the Emperor has sat immobile on the Golden Throne of Earth. He is the master of mankind by the will of the gods, and master of a million worlds by the might of his inexhaustible armies. He is a rotting carcass writhing invisibly with power from the Dark Age of Technology. He is the Carrion Lord of the Imperium for whom a thousand souls are sacrificed every day, so that he may never truly die.

YET EVEN IN his deathless state, the Emperor continues his eternal vigilance. Mighty battlefleets cross the daemon-infested miasma of the warp, the only route between distant stars, their way lit by the Astronomican, the psychic manifestation of the Emperor's will. Vast armies give battle in His name on uncounted worlds. Greatest amongst his soldiers are the Adeptus Astartes, the Space Marines, bio-engineered super-warriors. Their comrades in arms are legion: the Imperial Guard and countless planetary defence forces, the ever-vigilant Inquisition and the tech-priests of the Adeptus Mechanicus to name only a few. But for all their multitudes, they are barely enough to hold off the ever-present threat from aliens, heretics, mutants – and worse.

TO BE A man in such times is to be one amongst untold billions. It is to live in the cruellest and most bloody regime imaginable. These are the tales of those times. Forget the power of technology and science, for so much has been forgotten, never to be re-learned. Forget the promise of progress and understanding, for in the grim dark future there is only war. There is no peace amongst the stars, only an eternity of carnage and slaughter, and the laughter of thirsting gods.

CONTENTS

VOIDSONG

Henry Zou

THE EVENING CHILL comes quickly to the mountains of Sirene Primal. Already, the twilight made shadow puppets of the rumbling vehicle column, transforming them into boxy silhouettes against an ochre backdrop.

Captain Gonan of the 8th Amartine Scout Cavalry heaved himself above the roll cage of his half-track, panning the pintle-mounted stubber across the deep shadows of dusk. His convoy was rolling through yet another orchard village. Another ruptured settlement of paperbark pagodas, the walls of straw rotting with mildew and the roof tiles bearded with moss. In some places curtains of overgrown tea orchard clung to the frames of empty buildings, hiding any sign of settlement before the Secessionist Wars.

It was the tenth village that the captain's column had passed that day. Through the smoky haze of dusk, boredom and weariness dulled his senses. It was little wonder that Gonan did not see the armoured figure lurking within a rough bank of myrtle reed.

He never saw the shot that killed his driver. The snapping hiss of a lasrifle was followed by a blossom of arterial blood that misted the windshield. The driver, an inexperienced young corporal, began to screech in shock and hysteria, ramming down hard on the brakes of his half-track. Immediately, the slithering file of a dozen vehicles collapsed into an awkward accordion as treads fought for purchase on the mountainous shale.

Above the shriek of brakes and throbbing engines Gonan began to yell. 'Contact! Enemy at left axis of advance!'

By then, the ambush was well and truly sprung. A scattering of lasrifles released their shots into the scout cavalry half-tracks. The AM-10 *Hammer Goats* indigenous to the Amartine 8th were two-ton buggies with rear caterpillar tracks and pintle-mounted heavy stubbers. Also dubbed AM-10 *Scapegoats* by virtue of soldierly cynicism, they were regarded as death traps for the two-man reconnaissance teams that operated them. Immediately, six Guardsmen were killed and two vehicles disabled before they could even react.

The second salvo of las-shots was followed by the thrumming war cry of fifty warriors erupting from ambush. Cold panic seized Gonan and for a moment he was paralysed by neural overload. In their full regalia of war, the secessionist fighters of

Sirene Primal were an awesome sight to behold. Three score were Khan-Scholars, tall, fierce-looking men, clad in hauberks of mosaic jade and armed with all manner of lance and flak-musket. Another dozen were pounding through the undergrowth in the tectonic armour of Symbolists, their salvaged lasrifles already discarded for spine sabres. Others still were Blade Artisans, charging with their robes of embroidered tapestry flared, like the wings of some great hunting bird.

Pandemonium followed. When the line of baying warriors collided against the left flank of the vehicle column, it did not in any way resemble the heroic battle murals so vividly brocaded on Symbolist robes. Instead, what unfolded before Gonan was the messy, ugly affair of men killing each other at close quarters.

An Amartine Guardsman was screaming and babbling as a Khan-Scholar beat him to death with the broken halves of his lance. A Guard sergeant grappled with a Blade Artisan for control of his halberd before sinking his teeth into the warrior's neck.

Captain Gonan had barely freed his bayonet from the AM-10's gun rack when a Khan-Scholar surged over the cowling of his vehicle. Gonan had never seen a more vicious predator. The warrior's mane of thick black dreadlocks flowed down to his calves and silver quills were threaded through his cheekbones. Around his torso was a hauberk of interlocking jade scales, worn brown-green in its antiquity, and that was where Gonan aimed his fighting knife.

He thrust thirty centimetres of steel just below the ribs, but the Khan simply stepped into the blow with a carnivorous grace and hooked with an open palm. The first strike smeared Gonan's nose across his right cheek in a burst of blood and mucous. Reflexively the Guard officer stabbed his bayonet into his opponent's kidney, steel puncturing through the ancient jade. If the Khan felt anything, he did not show it. The next punch fractured Gonan's sternum and slammed him against the roll cage of his AM-10.

Gonan had no doubt that in a straight melee, the secessionist would dismantle him piece by piece. The martial sects of Sirene embraced close combat as an art form. He understood now, why the Sirenese culture, so reverent of art and literature, would consider these fighters the greatest artists of all. From glaive dancing to the way of the mauling hand, these men were brutally beautiful to watch. It was suicide to fight them.

Instead the Guard officer drew the laspistol from his chest holster and emptied half a clip to his front. Gonan didn't know what happened next. He may have blacked out temporarily, but for how long he did not know. When the fog of concussion ebbed away, Gonan found himself on the mesh flatbed of his vehicle with a dead secessionist sprawled over him. He felt as if someone had just run a battle tank over his skull and for a moment was content to slip into the velvet black of unconsciousness.

But the sounds of hacking and stabbing soon roused his pain-hazed mind. All around was the killing. Loud and brutal. Gonan heaved the corpse off before pulling himself up behind the mounted heavy stubber. Legs still teetering, he collapsed to his knees before pulling himself upright again and racking the weapon.

'Firing now!' Gonan screamed, voice hoarse.

It was as if a secessionist chose that very moment to rival Gonan's warning with the thick avalanche of his own war cry. Thundering over the AM-10's windshield, the secessionist brandished his spine sabre. Tracking to meet his approach, Gonan thumbed the firing stud on the stubber's butterfly trigger. The stream of high velocity rounds hit his target so hard that the warrior snapped backwards and his sabre spun the other way.

Without pause, Gonan re-sighted the heavy stubber down the column of his convoy and fired again. A long enfilade burst this time. Mosaic armour exploded into chips and splinters as Gonan hosed lambent tracer into a dense maul of Khan-Scholars not more than ten metres to his vehicle's rear.

Despite the devastation wrought by a heavy weapon at point blank range, it was too late to turn the assault. Eight of the AM-10 Hammer Goats were wrecks, their occupants dragged out and butchered by the roadside. By his estimate, Gonan didn't have more than six men left, too few to mount any meaningful resistance. So he did what any Imperial officer should have done, he juiced out the last rounds of his pintle weapon, drew his laspistol and staggered off his vehicle toward the killing.

BY THE TIME Imperial patrols came across Gonan's waylaid convoy, it was well into midnight. They found the body of Captain Saul Gonan horribly desecrated and staked upright on a lance, his men laid out in a neat row before him. They had been stripped of their boots and rifles, yet Captain Gonan still gripped an emptied laspistol in his fist. His eyes were still open.

It was a scene all too common across the wounded landscape of Selene Primal. Imperial and Secessionist forces alike were guilty of inflicting an almost theatrical barbarity towards one another. Entire Guard battalions were crucified while villages and refugee camps would be shelled in reprisal, fuelling a cycle of bitter conflict. Despite this, Imperial historians later argued that events which unfolded toward the latter stages of the war would render the atrocities of the Secessionist Campaign utterly inconsequential.

THE MOUNTAINS WERE treacherous at this time of year.

The polar equinox was at an end, and the ice caps were melting, sluicing great sheets of water and ice down the mountain paths. Thousands of people were migrating that day. The narrow defiles were swollen with caravans, baggage mules and the crush of toiling bodies. Hordes of refugees, the remnants of haemorrhaged villages and cities, and bands of weary secessionists were toiling over the icy spines of those mountains.

It was here that Inquisitor Obodiah Roth found himself, well into the fourth year of the guerrilla war. He had come here on dispatch from the Ordo Hereticus. The case itself was no matter of significance. The original briefing from the Ordo had read – *mild psychic disturbances emanating from*

Sirene Primal, priority – minor. It had never seemed like much to begin with.

Initial disturbances had first occurred eight months ago. Sanctioned psykers of the Imperial war fleet had sensed a strong psychic flux from the planet itself. Then reports from the neighbouring Omei Subsector began to surface. Astropaths of a missionary outpost on the tundras of Alipsia Secundus had slashed their throats, writing the name of the planet in blood, and silently mouthing *Sirene Primal* until death claimed them.

The phenomena had initially been dismissed as the psychic backlash of Sirene Primal's war. It was uncommon but not unheard of, for the anguish of billions in suffering to cause to coalesce into psychic disturbance. Scholars had named it a *planetary swansong*. Regardless, senior members of the Ordo had deemed the matter worthy of further investigation, an open and shut affair perfect for wetting the noses of virgin inquisitors. Or so it had seemed.

Sirene Primal had not always been like this. Set adrift on the Eastern Fringes of the Imperium, it floated like a muted pearl within the oceanic darkness of the universe. The last of the ancients had died aeons ago, their ossified remains forming mountains of colossal spines and plates. Upon them, Sirenese architects had raised the colonnades and flower-draped monoliths of their ziggurat-gardens.

It was a very different world now. Standing on a jagged tusk of rock, Roth watched the menacing shapes of Vulture gunships, prowling across the Sephardi Peaks as they hunted for targets. Higher up amongst the cloud vaults, Imperial Marauder destroyers hurtled like knife points through the sky.

Beneath him, the mountainous slopes swept into a rocky spur. Among the scree and rubble could be seen the glint of shell casings, and even the odd helmet. Further down the pass, the rusted carcass of a battle tank could be seen, submerged in a glacial melt. The cold air was cut with the smell of fuel.

Despite the icy chill, Roth had suited up in Spathean fighting plate. The form-fitting chrome was coated with a hoar of frost that bled vaporous curls into the air. Over this he framed a tabard of tessellating obsidian. The tiny panes of psi-reactive glass, although a potent psi-dampener, did little to insulate him against the temperature. He was cold and thoroughly miserable.

Yet his shivering condition was just another irritation on his long list of simmering anxieties. He had been on-world for close to a month now and no amount of investigation, research or cross-referencing had yielded any clue as to the cause of the psychic disturbances. While millions suffered, he was mousing about with the nuisances of some psychic irregularity that no one in the Ordo really cared about. He felt tired, drained and hopeless. It was, he thought with dry rumination, not a good start to his career.

'They're at it again, sire.' A voice, stern and patrician, jostled Roth out of his brooding.

The man who had spoken was Bastiel Silverstein. One of Roth's best, a xenos game-hunter from the arboreous forests of Veskepine, Silverstein was

right of course. A huntsman with augmented bioscope lenses was seldom wrong about such things.
Already the target reticles oscillating on the pupils
of his eyes had locked on the Marauder destroyers
swooping in the distance.

Beneath the banking aircraft, spherical eruptions of
fire and ash were accompanied by the unmistakeable
rumble of explosives, deep and distant. Even without
Silverstein's optic enhancements, he could see that
the Imperial Navy was bombing south-west of them.

Roth swore terribly.

There would be more killing today. Not the flattening of Chaos Legions, or the epic banishment of
daemon princes that Roth had read about in the
Scholam-Libraries of the Progenium. No. It would be
the killing of more desperate, scared and malnourished refugees. The bombs would fall, people would
die, and by sunset, the war would be no closer to finishing and Roth would be no closer to clearing his
damn case.

As if to emphasis his thoughts, the keening hum of
distant engines began to build sonic pressure. Looking up Roth spotted a Vulture gunship roaring down
from a bar of clouds, two kilometres up and diving
steeply. Roth's blood ran colder. He could almost
anticipate what was about to occur.

From the surge of panic amongst the refugees
down slope, they did too. No more than one hundred paces away from him the mountain defile was
congested with a sea of malnourished faces looking
skyward in mute fear. Most of the native Sirenese did
not know what a Vulture gunship was, but they knew
that the ominous shape in the distance was shrieking
towards them.

His man Silverstein however, scoped it clearly, complete with a statistical read-out that scrolled down in the upper left corner of his vision.

+++ *Obex-Pattern Vulture gunship, VTOL sub-atmospheric combat aircraft. Organic weapon systems: Nose-mounted heavy bolter – Optional wing-mounted autocannons – Pod-racked double missile systems.* +++

Silverstein looked to Roth, clearly concerned.

The inquisitor turned to his companion and mouthed the word 'wait'.

The gunship blurred past their jutting fist of rock, snorting jet exhaust. It sharply arrested its descent forty metres above the exodus, pivoting on the fulcrum of its tail. There it hovered on the monstrous turbines of vector thrust engines.

From his vantage point up the slope, Roth was almost at eye-level with the gunship. He watched with growing trepidation as half a dozen tendrils of rope uncoiled from the belly of its hold, reaching out like the tentacles of a waiting beast. Troops, bulky with combat gear, began to rappel down the steel cables.

Roth recognized them immediately as men of the 45th Montaigh Assault Pioneers. Great shaggy men, broad and bearded, descending with shoulder-slung lascarbines. Their insulated winter fatigues lined with mantine fur and coloured in the distinctive grey and green jigsaw pattern were unmistakeable.

He had been impressed, years before, when he had first studied the elite mountain troops in the Schola Progenium. Their engineering of trenches, field fortifications and bridges was renowned.

Amongst the death marshes of Cetshwayo in M609.M41, Assault Pioneers had spearheaded their advance through supposedly impenetrable terrain with a system of drainage dams and mobile pontoons. Their ingenuity resulted in a single division of Assault Pioneers overwhelming an estimated eighty thousand orks. Where all battles are won by manoeuvre, the men of Montaigh paved the way.

Roth was not so impressed now, as he watched nine Assault Pioneers hit the ground and immediately form supporting fire positions. Fanning out into a loose arrowhead, they took a knee on the steep slope overlooking the refugees, lascarbines sitting firmly against the shoulder. By his side, Silverstein placed a gloved hand to his mouth in disbelief. Surely they wouldn't. But they did.

When they first opened fire, it was aimed above the heads of the people. Warning shots. Hemmed in between the ledge of the defile and the firers, people began to hurl themselves down the almost vertical slope in desperation. White-hot beams lacerated the air, fizzing and snapping.

'Do something!' Silverstein yelled.

In his shock, it took Roth a moment to realize the huntsman was talking to him. He was caught up watching the catastrophe unfold before him. The panic was total. A caravan was almost scuttled off the edge; a pack mule went over tumbling. The press of frightened refugees was pushing their own people down the pass, gathering momentum like a rolling landslide.

'I know! I know! Just let me consider my options–' he began.

'There aren't any options! Just do something!'

Silverstein was right. He would have to improvise. Of course, making it up on the run was one of the rudimentary lessons taught to all Inquisitorial acolytes. His masters had called it *aptitudinal adroitness*, but it amounted to much of the same thing.

Brandishing his Inquisitorial signet in an upthrust hand, Roth broke into a run. The mountain sediment slipped and slid beneath him, pitching his run into a violent descent. He slid half of the distance and slammed his knees and elbows into the shale several times for good measure. Roth ended his skittering plummet with a flying leap over the scree bank, flailing briefly in the air before landing with a shuddering impact. He was right in the thick of it now.

'Cease fire! Cease fire!' he roared.

To the credit of the Guardsmen, their well-drilled fire discipline showed through. The whickering fusillade died out, but they didn't lower their steaming muzzles. Roth was suddenly very aware of nine lascarbines trained on him.

'Lower your weapons, I am Obodiah Roth of the *Inquisition*.' Roth stressed the significance of his last word, thrusting his badge of office towards the troops.

As all soldiers would have done, they looked to their sergeant, a grizzly beast with the well-nourished build of a lumberjack. The sergeant, levelling his gaze on Roth, didn't move.

'Don't listen to him lads,' snarled Grizzly.

Roth breathed deeply. The still air was now heavy with the smell of burnt ozone. The gaping maws of nine las-weapons filled his vision. He didn't realise when exactly the Sirenese behind him had stopped screaming, but they didn't utter a sound now. He could tell the sergeant was staring at the stout chrome-plated plasma pistol in his shoulder rig, daring him to make a move.

Roth drew it.

'Lower. Your. Weapons.' Roth repeated.

'Don't be stupid now. We wouldn't want there to be any accidents between us,' replied Grizzly, his tone cold and even.

'I have the authority.'

'And I have my orders, inquisitor. This isn't your war.'

Roth's pulse felt like a war drum. He could tell they were not going to see reason. They were forcing him to play his final hand and Roth had hoped it wouldn't come to this. The inquisitor clenched his jaw and pointed up the mountain slope.

'Sergeant. Up there, three hundred paces behind you, is a huntsman with a Vindicare-class Exitus rifle. Don't bother looking, he's well hidden. What I can tell you, is that he was trained by the lodge-masters of Veskepine and I've seen him shoot the eyes off an aero-raptor in mid flight. Give him four seconds, he'll put down half your squad. It's your call Sergeant.'

'You're bluffing,' said Grizzly, but his voice wasn't so calm. This wasn't his game anymore.

'If you say so.'

There was a pause. Then the sergeant looked to his men and nodded reluctantly. Nine lascarbines were lowered to the ground. Far up the slope, a crop of slate rock and gorse weed juddered then

moved. Bastiel Silverstein, in a fitted coat of dark
green piranhagator hide unfurled himself from
concealment. In his hands was a rifle, long and
lean. Roth flashed his man the hand signal for *stay
alert* and turned his attention back on the sergeant.

'Sergeant…'

'Sergeant Clais Jedda, 2nd battalion Airborne
Sappers of the 45th Montaigh Assault Pioneers.'

'Sergeant Jedda.' Roth repeated, letting the name
hang heavily in the air before continuing. 'What
the hell are you and your men doing?'

'Clearing a path, until you got in the way,' he
replied, still defiant.

'A path to where?'

'Urgent priority mission. On orders from my battalion colonel. It's none of your concern,
inquisitor.'

'You made it my concern, sergeant. If you tell me
nothing, I will charge both you and your colonel
for collusion of criminal activity. He would be very
displeased, don't you think?' Roth had cornered
him. He knew Jedda was the type of soldier who
would rather risk ire from the Inquisition than the
wrath of his commanding officer.

'There's nothing criminal here. These people are
all potential threats. Two days ago we lost a patrol
of Pioneers on their way to an AOI. Gone. Wiped
out. I'm not taking any chances with my boys.'

AOI. Guard terminology for *area of interest*. Roth
raised an eyebrow, 'What area of interest,
sergeant?'

'An off-world landing craft. A four-man patrol
picked up signs of a large metallic object in an ice
cavern two kilometres west of here. Their last

transmission confirmed it was a lander, frozen
solid with snow. Must have been right under our
noses since before the winter months.'

Roth was definitely interested now. The snow
entombment meant it must have slipped past the
planetary blockade at least six or seven months
ago. Perhaps it was linked to the psychic disturbances, perhaps not, either way he would need to
know more.

'Sergeant Jedda. You will cease terrorising these
people immediately. Furthermore, you will not fire
at all, unless permission is granted.'

'Permission...'. he was really caught off guard
now.

'Yes sergeant. Permission from me. I'm coming
with you.'

THE SHIP WAS a merchant runner, entombed under a
tongue of glacial ice. The burnt sepia of its painted
hull appeared incandescent under the striated ice,
almost aglow with lambent energy. A cavern formed
its cradle, where it slumbered in the throat of a frosty
maw, framed by fangs of icicles.

The ship itself was a blunt-nosed cruiser about two
hundred paces long, the hammerhead of its prow
pockmarked with the scars of asteroid collision. Roth
surmised by its squat boxy frame that it was a blockade runner, similar to the type favoured by illicit
smugglers and errant rogue traders.

Roth and his team approached the ice cave down
a narrow gorge, advancing slowly down the rock
seam. The inquisitor led the way, auspex purring in
his grip. Behind him, Silverstein and the Montaigh
Guardsmen formed a staggered file with weapons

covering every angle of approach. They reached no further than the shadow of the cave entrance when the auspex chimed three warning tones. A solitary target flashed on the display, half a kilometre from their position, almost right on top of the beached cruiser.

Roth signalled for a halt and lower. Sinking to a wary crouch, he squinted into the cavern with his plasma pistol primed. He took in the vastness of the cave, its immensity dwarfing the colossal docking hangars of Imperial battleships. Before him, towering colonnades of ice buttressed a vault ceiling of shimmering white-blue. Arroyos of melt water reached like veins across the cavern floor and forked through the grooves of snow dunes. Roth couldn't see a damn thing.

'Bastiel,' he hissed, almost at a whisper. The huntsman hurried to him, keeping low to the ground.

'Sire, what did you find?'

'Nothing. That's the problem. See what you can make of this.' Roth showed the huntsman his chiming auspex.

Silverstein lowered his Exitus rifle and scanned the cave, optiscopic eyes whirring and feeding data. He achieved a lock-on almost instantly.

+++*Solitary target, stationary. Height 1.5 metres. Mass density approx. 40–50kg. Target identification: Female, human 98% – Female, xenos 57% – Humanoid, other 36%. Target distance: 298.33 metres. Status temperature – ALIVE*+++

'Sire, I'm reading what appears to be a lady sitting on a snow dune, about three hundred metres to our front. What would you like me to do?' Silverstein asked.

'Nothing yet. Good job Bastiel.' Roth then turned around to face Sergeant Clais Jedda and clicked once for his attention. 'Sergeant, were there any women in the patrol which was lost here?'

The sergeant shook his head. 'There aren't any women in the Assault Pioneers, sah.'

Roth chewed his lip, a nervous habit he had never quite shaken off. Finally, he stood up and gave the hand signal for his team to do likewise. 'Bastiel, we're going to press on as before, but I want you to cover that target with your rifle. Make sure it never leaves your sights and tell me what you see. Clear?'

'Clear, sire.'

With that, the team resumed its cautious advance, prodding through the snow. The ship's ice mesa loomed closer and so did the lone figure at its base.

'Sire, it's definitely a woman. She's seen us too and she has stood up.' They were less than two hundred and fifty metres away now.

'What do you see Bastiel? Tell me what you see.'

'She's young; I'd say no more than thirty standard. She has a weapon too. Some sort of polearm. Could be a secessionist, sire.'

Two hundred metres and closing. Roth's eyes darted across the icescape, seeing a possible ambush behind every crest, every ridge. Despite the relentless cold, Roth was suddenly very glad for the frictionless trauma-plates that hugged his body.

'She's looking straight at me sire,' reported Silverstein.

They were within one hundred metres now and Roth no longer needed Silverstein's relay to see the young woman on the snow dune. He could tell she was slim, made slimmer by the brocaded sapphire silks that cascaded down her frame. Where the broad painted sleeves ended, her forearms were tattooed with verse after verse of war-litanies. She was unmistakably a Blade Artisan.

'Kill her!' urged Sergeant Jedda.

'No! Stand down!' Roth turned and snapped ferociously at the Guard squad.

Ahead, on the crest of the dune, the Blade Artisan had anchored her weapon in the snow: if not a sign of peace, then at least a gesture of armistice. The weapon was as exactly long as she was tall. It was a thin glaive, half of it leather-bound staff, half of it straight blade.

'Come forth and announce yourself,' she commanded firmly.

Roth was wary but recognized diplomacy as the greatest faculty at his disposal. He emulated her gesture by inserting his plasma pistol back onto its shoulder rig.

'I am Inquisitor Obodiah Roth of the Ordo Hereticus, and these–,' he said, gesturing to the men behind him, '–are servants of the God-Emperor.'

'Tread lightly, inquisitor. I am Bekaela of the Blade and this ship is mine to guard.'

'Was it you who slew the soldiers, who came here two days past?'

'Nül. The ship killed them.'

At this reply, Roth heard the thrum of lascarbines as the Guardsmen racked their weapons off safety.

Their blood was up and unless Roth could extract some straight answers soon, the situation would be out of his hands.

'Blade Artisan, these men will shoot you soon, unless you tell us what happened.'

Bekaela did not seem at all daunted by his warning. 'Shoot then, if you wish. But I have foresworn my oath to the Sirene Monarch. I have no quarrel with your soldiers.'

'Very well then. What lies in that ship?'

'Nothing. Everything. Sixteen moons ago, they came here to Sirene and claimed to be the Monarch's children – his scions.'

It was not an answer he had been expecting. The Sirene Monarch, Roth knew, had been a cultural figurehead of Sirene, a tradition that harked back to the pre-Imperial history of the planet. It had been the Sirene Monarch who had renounced Imperial dominion and ousted Lord Planetary Governor Vandt. Pre-war records had shown that when the isolated Imperial outposts and missions had been overrun, the natives certainly had no access to interplanetary travel and there had never been mention of the Monarch's offspring.

'Scions?' Roth asked.

Bekaela nodded. 'Yes, his children came in this ship, sixteen moons ago. The Monarch embraced his children and welcomed them home. It had been a grand ceremony; many clan-fighters had feasted there. I know because I was there too.'

'The Sirene Monarch has been in hiding ever since the war began, if not dead,' Roth countered. He could sense something poisonous was at work on this planet and part of him did not want to believe it.

'He is not dead. I know where he hides,' Bekaela said.

That was almost too much information to digest at once. Since the beginning of the campaign, Imperial forces had been driven in relentless pursuit of the fugitive Monarch, slated as the spiritual leadership of the guerrilla insurgency. Hundreds of aerial bombing runs, thousands of infantry patrols had all amounted to nothing. But now this.

'Why would you give us this information?' Roth pressed.

'Because, I've seen what lies in that ship and if they are the Monarch's bloodline, then he is no Monarch of mine!' she proclaimed.

It only dawned on Roth then, that Bekaela was not guarding the ship from intruders. She was guarding against whatever lay within from getting out.

Sergeant Jedda, however, was not one to be convinced. 'It's a trap. That witch probably gave my boys the same speech before they got off'd,' he growled. His men chorused in assent.

Roth was not so quick to make his conclusion. The significance of her story, if true, was far too monumental to dismiss. His duty as an inquisitor compelled him to investigate deeper. Stepping forward, slightly away from his team, Roth summoned a subtle wisp of mind force and gently probed her mind. Bekaela tensed visibly from the intrusion.

'What did you just do?!' she hissed.

'I was testing your intentions.'

'Don't do that again, or I'll kill you and make it painful.'

Roth nodded sincerely. He would not. Besides, he already knew all that he needed to know. She was telling the truth, on both accounts.

'My team and I, we must explore this ship.'

'Then I will come with you,' she said. Her tone brokered no argument.

'So you are willing to aid us?' Roth mused. 'As an ally?'

'No. I hate you. But I will help my people. They do not know what I know. I've been in that ship.'

'What's in there?' Roth asked.

'You will see,' was the answer.

THE SHIP WAS alive.

Or at least that was what Roth first thought. Wet ropes of muscle and pulsing arteries groped and twisted along the walls and mesh decking of the dormant ship. The air was nauseatingly warm and humid. It was as if something infinitely virulent and shapeless was incubating within the cruiser's metal chassis.

Roth's team had entered via a breach in the ship's hull and found themselves in a disused maintenance bay. Banks of workbenches lined the walls where raw tendrils of flesh had begun to creep over them. In the upper-left corner of the ceiling, an enormous balloon of puffy flesh expanded and contracted rhythmically like a monstrous lung.

Further exploration of the ship's corridors, deck and compartment revealed only more of its pulsating innards. The deeper into the heart of the cruiser they progressed, the thicker the infestation. The walkway that led to the ship's bridge funnelled into an orifice of ridged cartilage. They could see no further, as a pink membrane of tissue expanded over the entrance.

'Do you know where we are?' Roth asked Bekaela.

'Nül. I have never been beyond the first compartment. This place is cursed, it's all bad following.'

Roth was not sure the Blade Artisan's prognosis was the correct one, but it was apt enough. He moved toward the membrane, careful not to step in the pools of semi-viscous liquid that collected on the deck plating. He holstered his pistol and was in the act of gingerly reaching out to touch the organic membrane when all three auspexes in his team chimed simultaneously. Roth froze.

'What's the reading?' he asked.

'I'm getting multiple rapid movements converging on this corridor intersection,' one of the assault pioneers reported.

'Yes sir, I'm getting the same readings,' another trooper echoed.

Roth about turned, drew his pistol and trained it on the inflamed flesh cavity that was once a t-junction.

'Readings are too fast. I suspect we're just picking up latent electrical currents from the ship's circuitry,' a third trooper added. They waited in tense silence.

'Trooper Wessel, double time ten paces back and get me a new reading. We could be standing under an electrical hub,' Sergeant Jedda barked.

With his eyes on the auspex and carbine hard against the shoulder, Trooper Wessel approached the intersection. He peered into the gloom, sweeping his auspex about to get a better reading.

The thing slashed out of the darkness so fast it severed Wessel's spine and bounded off his corpse. Streaking through the air in a shower of blood, it landed on another trooper crouched within the corridor and eviscerated him too. An eruption of wild las-fire crazed the spot where the thing had been, but it was moving again.

'What the hell is that?' Roth shouted at Silverstein as his plasma pistol unleashed a mini-nova of energy down the corridor.

The huntsman tried to get a lock on the creature as it slammed into its third victim. He barely registered the profile of its blurring outline.

+++*Target analysis: Xenos, Hormagaunt. Subspecies: Unknown. Origin: Unknown. Hivefleet: Unknown – Data Source: Ultramar (745.M41)*+++

'Tyranid,' Silverstein replied. With a spectacular shot that anticipated the creature's next running leap, he blew out its skull carapace with an Exitus round.

Another two shapes shrieked into the corridor, straight into the storm of fire laid down by Roth's team. The inquisitor aimed his pistol, ready to fire when it seemed like the world exploded behind him. The membrane plugging the ship's command bridge burst, and from the darkness surged a monster so tall it was almost bent double in the corridor. From its segmented torso, four bone scythes connected to hawser cables of muscle slashed like threshing sickles. As an inquisitor, Roth was privy to knowledge otherwise deemed heretical for others. Yet knowing the enemy and its power sometimes replaced ignorance with fear. Roth recognised the thorny frame of sinew and plate hurtling towards him and froze in shocked awe.

It was a genestealer broodlord and it was on him so fast he had no time to react. The only thing that saved him was Bekaela's glaive singing through the air to intercept the beast. The Blade Artisan pirouetted with a twirling downward stroke that severed one of the monstrosity's upper limbs. In reply, the tyranid speared her into the wall with a battering ram of psychic force.

Roth wasted no time in engaging the broodlord. He activated his Tang-War pattern power gauntlet and moved inside the broodlord's guard with a thunderous right-hook. The creature snaked back its torso with serpentine grace, evading the blow and swept in with its three remaining hook-scythes. Roth ducked, feeling an organic blade skip against the frictionless shoulder plate of his armour.

They fought on two separate planes. While their bodies raged, so too were their minds locked in a psychic duel. The tyranid was much stronger, its mind a tidal wave of raw, seething force. Roth was not a potent psyker, but what ability he had, he utilised well, sharpening and tightening his will into a poignard of deliverance. Although the broodlord's mind was like the staggering force of a blind avalanche, Roth's was the clean mind-spikes and mental ripostes of a Progenium-trained psychic duellist. It was like a death struggle between the kraken and the swordfish.

On the physical plane, Bekaela struck again. She was barely conscious and fought purely from muscle memory. Spinning her glaive like a lariat she hoped she was aiming for the right target. The paper-thin blade sliced deep into the broodlord's flank, snapping through the corded muscle. The creature shrieked at a decibel so high, the ship quavered in empathy.

It was exactly the distraction Roth needed. Sensing the sudden gap in the genestealer's mental defences, Roth tightened his will into an atom of focus and surged through the slip in its psychic barrier. Once through, he exploded into a billion slivered needles, expanding infinitesimally outwards.

The broodlord died quickly. With it, the last of the hormagaunts in the corridor lost all synaptic control and were literally disassembled by gunfire. Yet as it expired, the broodlord's mental shell collapsed, plunging Roth into its mind, like a spearman breaking through a shield wall headlong through the other side. Roth was utterly unprepared for what happened next.

He saw a hive fleet, at the furthest edges of his mind's eye. He saw it looming larger, so ravenous and hungry. He felt, no, heard the psychic song that was drawing it closer, like a pulse, like droplets of blood rippling outwards in the ocean. The song was coming from Sirene Primal, a poisonous ugly sound that drove spikes into his psyker mind. A swansong. All at once, it fell into place like a crystal fragmenting in rewind. He saw the ship, and its genestealer brood, the children of the Sirene Monarch. He saw their minds pulsing in unison, calling to their hive, calling for salvation. The psychic vacuum shut down his nervous system and Roth's heart stopped beating.

'Sire! Can you hear me?!'

The voice wrenched Roth back into consciousness, wrenching him to the surface like a drowning man. The first thing he saw was Silverstein, the yellow pupils of his bioscope implants wide with concern. Had it not been for the huntsman's voice, he would have died standing up.

'Sire? You look bloodless,' said the huntsman reaching forward to steady Roth. The inquisitor, in a daze, brushed Silverstein off and fell against the cartilage tunnel, sliding down to his knees.

'Kill it... kill him. Find him. Kill him,' he murmured weakly.

'Kill who?'

'Kill the Monarch,' Roth called, a little louder as he pulled himself up.

'The Monarch. Father of the brood.'

BEYOND THE SEPHARDI ranges, Imperial artillery was pounding the mountains to rubble and the rubble to dust. The steady *krang krang krang* of the batteries sounded like thousand tonne slabs of rockrete in collision. In the tomb-vaults below the mountains, deep within the arterial labyrinth, billions of ancestral caskets tremored under the brutal bombardment. Finally, down amongst their dead, the Sirene Monarch's hidden legions would make ready for their last battle.

The assault on the Sirene tomb-vaults had started before dawn. To their credit, Imperial high command had been quick to react, with Lord Marshal Cambria personally overseeing the mobilization of a quick reaction force within six hours. Inquisitor Roth's discovery had hammered a shockwave through the campaign's war-planners and they were eager to seize the initiative. The stalemate, it seemed, was about to be broken.

By the time the Sirenese sunrise had tinged the night sky a bruised orange, Assault Pioneers of the Montaigh 45th had breached the tomb underworld. Combined elements of the Kurassian Lance-Commandoes and five squadrons of the 8th Amartine Scout Cavalry, alongside three full battalions of Assault Pioneers had been committed to the operation.

It was all a decoy. The decisive strike of the assault had been the insertion of a kill-team directly into the Sirene Monarch's last refuge, once secessionist forces were pre-engaged. Led by Inquisitor Roth and guided by Bekaela of the Blade, a platoon of Montaigh 45th and a squad of bull-necked Kurassian Lance-Commandoes had penetrated the cerebral core of the tomb complex. Precision breach charges rigged up by airborne sappers had seen to that.

The kill team now prowled beneath a monolithic vault of basalt. According to Bekaela's hand-sketched schematics, which Roth had committed to memory, it was the Monarch's atrium. The walls were so thick and black with age they seemed to absorb sound and light. Of the distant sounds of combat, Roth heard nothing. Even their long-range vox-sets were dead.

It was the oceanic silence that unsettled him most.

The atrium was so very still, dark and quiet. A white bar of sun lanced from the soaring heights of the ceiling, laying down a smeared ghostly light. But it wasn't just the silence that was unsettling, there were those damned pools of water too, Inquisitor Roth seethed to himself. There was water everywhere.

From enormous bowls to dishes, troughs and ponds, basins and urns, everywhere Roth looked he saw stagnant bodies of water stretching into the deepest shadows of that chamber. Most of the pools had developed a slick surface of green algae, and others were scattered with pale lotus blossoms; all of them sat stagnant and silent.

'When the Sirene Monarch meets the boys of the Montaigh 45th, I want it to be the most traumatic experience of his life!' Sergeant Jedda's call clapped through the still air. The Guardsmen all roared in unison.

Despite his failings, Jedda was a natural troop leader. As an inquisitor, Roth was glad the Imperium had men like Sergeant Clais Jedda to unleash upon its enemies. The kill-team broke into a run now, cutting for the throne chamber that lay beyond.

Falling in step behind Roth was Bastiel Silverstein. He toggled the target lock of his hunting crossbow to active and loaded a prey-seeker missile. The light polymer sleekness of a Veskepine *arcuballista* was ideal for tunnel assault. Running point was Bekaela, who was now dressed in the Sirenese regalia of vengeance. Her face was painted a leering mask of white and crimson, symbolising the witch-ghosts who claimed the dead. Her sapphire robes were cinched tight by a waist belt, woven from the hair of slain enemies and a flak-musket was slung over her shoulder.

Racing down the thousand-metre walkway, Roth's retinue finally emerged into the Sirene throne chamber. The room was vast, humbling even the impressive scale of the antechamber. Basalt walls and pillars of thickly veined marble soared up into the heavens, the ceiling completely lost from sight. A path of jade flowed down the centre of the throne room, flanked on either side by legions of water-bearing vessels. Once again, Roth noted there was water everywhere. He didn't have time to ask Bekaela why.

'The patient court of the Sirene Monarch bids you welcome,' a smooth androgynous voice announced. The source of the voice came from powerful vox-casters set into the arms of the Monarch's jade throne. Upon that throne sat the Monarch himself.

He wore a high-collared gown of ruby red silk, the hem and sleeves spilling out for several metres from his throne. His hands, folded demurely upon his lap, were capped with long needles of silver. None could look upon his face for a veil of pearls shimmered down his onion-domed crown. The Monarch's ten dozen scions were arrayed below his throne in seated tiers, a chilling calm instilled by their impassive stares.

The aura of ethereal dignity was so great, Roth noticed, that some of the troops lowered their guns and gazes involuntarily. Roth, on the other hand, raised his chin and stared deep into the pearl veil.

'The Ordo Hereticus is here to bury you,' he shouted in reply.

The choir of sons arrayed below the Monarch rippled with shrill chortling. They were exactly as Bekaela had described in the pre-op briefing.

Eunuchs, all of them. Slim and effete, all were clad in ankle-length gowns of pastel silk, pinks and purples and creamy jades. They appeared human enough, but even at a distance Roth could see their coral pink skin, semi-opaque and laced with delicate red veins.

Curiously, all of their left hands had been amputated. The gold-capped stumps of their forearms were attached to thick tendrils of silk cord. The long braids forming a muscular rope of fabric over a metre long. Like some bizarre pendulum, at the end of each length interwoven knots formed a fist-sized sphere of silk.

Roth could not gauge the symbolic significance of these amputations. Dimly, he remembered archival files regarding the Tyrant of Quan, on the fringes of the Tuvalii Subsector. Such was his fear of assassination, the Tyrant had ordered all who entered his court to don fluted gauntlets of glass. The flutes of those fragile gloves had been chased with acid and shattered under the slightest force. So great was his paranoia the Tyrant had even forced his three thousand wives to wear them in his bedchambers. Alas, Roth remembered with a glimmer of dark humour, those gloves did not save him from the mouth dart of a Callidus assassin.

However, if the Monarch was offended by his brazen threat, his veiled visage offered no sign. Instead his soft sexless voice emitted through his throne-casters, emotionless and measured.

'I cannot allow that,' he stated, rising from his throne.

The air immediately grew brittle and cold. To Roth's right, Bekaela's glaive went slack in her grip and her eyes glazed over. To his left, Bastiel Silverstein moaned softly.

'Witchery!' Roth raised his plasma pistol a millisecond too late. A psychic bolt exploded from the Monarch, warping the air around it into an oscillating cone. It tore through Inquisitor Roth and threw him thirty feet down the ivory path in a spray of blood and black glass. The psychic aftershock rippled through the room like a stone in a pond, coating every surface in a thick rime of frost.

The mind blow would have liquefied any normal man. But Obodiah Roth had a trump card. The glinting hauberk of psi-reactive crystal had absorbed the brunt of the psyker's power. As shards of black glass scattered in a blizzard around him, Roth realised the armour would not survive another psychic attack. And neither would he. Blood and bile oozed from his mouth and nose in thick strings. His head swam and he could barely see.

Dimly, he could hear the chatter of gunfire, as if very far away in the distance. He could hear Silverstein yelling but he couldn't make out the words. The only coherent thought in his mind was that the Monarch psyker must be temporarily weakened from his tremendous mind blast. That gave Roth a few seconds to nullify him before he gathered the strength to finish them all off.

He looked up, fighting down the urge to vomit. The world appeared at a slant. The Monarch's scions had formed a phalanx around him. As one, they dipped their long silk pendulums into the many water vessels in the chamber, letting the water soak into the fabric. The innocuous silk spheres instantly become heavy flails.

'Sly bastards,' Roth hissed through a mouthful of broken teeth. To his flanks, the Guardsmen continued to rake a steady stream of las-rounds at the Monarch's scions. 'I'll bet my balls that they're wearing armour under those gowns too,' Roth laughed darkly to himself. Some of the scions were slammed off their feet by the kinetic force of the shots, only to get back up and continue charging the inquisitor's team.

'Fix bayonets!' someone, somewhere, shouted. The voice was washed with distortion to Roth's trauma-shocked ears.

Assault Pioneers did as commanded, forming a staggered rank of fighting blades. The Kurassian Lance-Commandoes drew their serrated short-swords, howling and clashing the weapons to armoured chests. Together they met the charge of the scions.

Roth staggered to his feet, fighting to regain his balance as a eunuch stormed down the ivory path toward him. Bastiel Silverstein's polished boots suddenly filled Roth's vision, as the old retainer stood over the dazed inquisitor. The xenos game hunter aimed his crossbow. He had swapped to a rapid-fire cartridge, designed to bring down swift moving game. On automatic, Silverstein could empty all twelve bolts into his assailant in three seconds. He needed only one. A salvo of bolts tore out the eunuch's face, the neural toxins causing the assailant to spasm so hard his spine broke. He dropped to the floor, his one hand locked into a flexing claw.

'Are you good? Are you good?' Silverstein screamed at the inquisitor.

Roth finally found his footing and nodded vaguely.

'Stop fussing over me and snipe that psyker bastard already,' Roth managed to gasp.

'Can't draw a bead. He's got some sort of force generator. The kill-team almost bled their ammunition dry trying to crack him open. We'll have to get in close,' said Silverstein.

Roth grimaced and ran a hand over his bloodied face. 'Well he's thought of everything then, hasn't he? Cover me.' The inquisitor shook his head once more to clear it. There was a dark spot in his left field of vision and he hoped his brain wasn't haemorrhaging. Casting all doubt aside, he lifted his right hand. The one clad in a slim-fitting gauntlet of blue steel. A Tang War-pattern power gauntlet. The weapon hummed with a deep magnetic throb, the disruption field sparking like a blue halo.

Breaking into a run, he made straight for the throne. Assailants appeared in the corners of his vision but Silverstein's covering fire was lethally efficient. The streaks of grey slashed over his shoulder and head, one passing so close to his face he could feel its passing and hear its viper-like hiss. The bolts intercepted the scions as Roth ran their deadly gauntlet, down the ivory path towards the throne.

The inquisitor kept a mental count of each bolt as they flew past until finally, he counted the full twelve. Silverstein would need to reload. He was only a scant ten paces away from the throne; the Monarch still slumped in his seat recovering when a eunuch threw himself at him.

Roth turned, his reflexes still sluggish from his mind thrashing. Howling, the eunuch whipped the silk flail into his lower ribs and Roth exhaled a painful jet of air. He tried to bring his plasma pistol to bear but the flail lashed in again, this time snapping into his hand. My hand's broken, Roth thought numbly, adding it to his long list of injuries as the pistol slipped from broken fingers.

Eager for the kill, the eunuch pressed his advantage. The silk flail's trajectory arced toward Roth's head. With more luck than timing, the inquisitor slipped under the blow and drove his power fist into the eunuch's chest. The gauntlet's disruption field flared into a bright corona of light as he drove his hand clean through the Eunuch's chest. His assailant simply dropped onto his rear and slumped over backwards.

Knowing he had no time to spare, Roth spun on his heels and turned on the Monarch. The psyker was almost at full strength. Already he had forced himself onto his feet, his eyes turning into milky orbs as he gathered his will for another psychic bolt. The temperature was dropping like a countdown timer. Roth had all of one second to react before he was dead.

'Now!' cried Inquisitor Roth as he launched himself at the psyker. Extending his power fist, he rammed the weapon into the Monarch's invisible force bubble. As disruption field met force field there was a static shriek and a blossoming wall of blinding light. Then the jade throne's force generator blew a fuse. The force field shattered, air filling its void with a low thunderclap. Roth flew himself flat before the throne.

Bastiel Silverstein emptied all twelve bolts into the Monarch in three seconds flat. At fifty paces, every bolt found its mark and pinned the psyker to his throne like a broken marionette. Almost as an afterthought, Bekaela's flak-musket spat a cone of flechette at the corpse, stitching it with smoking holes.

Then it was over, as quickly as it had begun. Except for the cordite hiss of gun smoke, and the baying of the Kurassian Lance-Commandoes as they took the eunuchs apart, the battle was over. The metallic scent of blood and gunfire filled the chamber.

Inquisitor Obodiah Roth picked himself up and brushed himself off. He coughed and spat a bloody tooth at what was left of the Monarch. Bending down, he slapped the Monarch's veiled crown with a backhand.

A face of sharp alien angles stared back at him with dead eyes. Dead dark xenos eyes. The ridged forehead was streaked with blood and his slack mouth was a nest of teeth, like translucent needles.

'Genestealers,' said the inquisitor.

Wearily, he turned to his team and the carnage before him. During his tenure as an interrogator, Roth had survived a clutch of firefights. His mentor, Liszt Vandevern, had been a prolific field inquisitor who believed a raid would always reap more answers than clinical investigation. Before his thirtieth year, Roth had skirmished with half a dozen heretic cults, and even besieged the compound of a narco-baron on the death world of Sans Gaviria. But none of that could compare to the brutality of a close-quarter firearms assault.

The throne room was a butcher's hall. Most of the bodies were dressed in gossamer silks, thrown in disarray like crushed butterflies. Dozens of immense water vessels had been upturned or shot through, flooding the chamber with a pane of rosy, blood-tinted water. Other bodies scattered about were in either Montaigh or Kurassian battledress. Nearest to Roth, a Kurassian commando had died sitting up, the fingers of his gauntlet locked around the throat of an enemy. The Guardsman had been shot over a dozen times, but he had not released the chokehold.

Around Roth, his kill-team moved quickly from body to body. It seemed to him that they were but going through the motions, high-powered weapons at close proximity rarely left survivors.

'Sire – we have a live one sire,' Silverstein said.

Roth snapped out of his post-conflict daze and realised Silverstein had been standing at the base of the throne for some time, calling repeatedly. He followed the huntsman, sloshing through the pink water towards a huddle of Guardsmen with their weapons raised. As the circle parted for the inquisitor, they revealed a scion sitting wounded on the chamber floor.

It was genetically more man than xenos, Roth recognized that immediately. Yet nestled within the brow of its orbed forehead, its eyes were like iridescent pools of black oil devoid of any human quality. Most startling of all was the creature's parody of symbiote weapons. Up close, the silk flail, damp and glistening was not unlike a muscled mace appendage. Its right sleeve was torn, unveiling a hand fused to an obsolete machine pistol, brown with well-worked grease. The flesh and fingers were smeared like wax into the heavy calibre pistol, whether by coincidence or design to resemble some organic biomorph.

'It can talk, sire,' said Silverstein, nodding towards the creature.

The scion had taken the stray round of a Kurassian shotgun. Its left leg was peppered with bleeding perforations and pockmarked with powder burns. It looked up, met Roth's gaze and smiled mockingly, revealing clusters of quill-like teeth.

Perhaps if Roth had been older, wiser and more patient he could have dealt with the matter by more tactful means. But as it was, Roth was none of those things. The inquisitor simply pounded forward and snagged the scion's collar in his fist.

'How long has this planet been infected?!' Roth screamed into the creature's face.

'Why does it matter?' the scion replied, his vocal cords cut with a coarse alien inflection.

'Because I asked you!' shouted Roth. He hauled down on the scion's embroidered collar, slamming its head into the marble floor. The creature came up snorting water out of its nostril slits and started to laugh, a thrilled harmonic peal that bounced around the chamber walls.

Bekaela appeared by Roth's side and laid a hand on his shoulder. 'Kill him. Just kill him and be done,' she said.

'Not until it answers me!' hissed Roth. Still tight in his clinch, he manhandled the creature, jerking the scion from its seated position and forcing it down on its wounded side. The action elicited a shuddering exhalation of agony. Satisfied, Roth repeated the question again. 'How did it start?'

'Three generations ago,' the scion snarled through its teeth. 'Our fathers came to Sirene as missionaries to spread the seed of the great family and his blessed children.'

In truth, the admission did not surprise Roth. It was almost elementary. Sirene was a frontier world and missionaries had been the only true Imperial outposts on the planet. Incidentally, those clerics and ecclesiarches were also the only ones to access warp-capable vessels.

'It was perfect,' crooned the scion. 'By seven winters of equinox, Sirene's firstborn prince was of blessed blood. He was the father of fathers. When He ascended the throne, this world was ours for the taking.'

'When did the taint spread to the rest of Sirene?' Roth asked through gritted teeth.

'Patience, patience. I'm getting to that,' chortled the creature. It was clearly enjoying the narrative, drawing itself up theatrically. 'We did not need to, you see. The martial sects had always chafed under Imperial occupation and when our Monarch declared rebellion, they were our herd and we their shepherd. With the sect warriors under our banner, the rest of the Sirenese followed quietly enough.

'We set about purging all Imperial influence from this realm. Sect-Chieftains who were resistant quickly became silent when their wives were poisoned and denounced as conspirators. There were a thousand public executions of Imperial loyalists each day for many years. The Sirene renaissance was endemic.

'The PDF did not even try to fight but we cleansed them anyway. Soft and idle, they were civic militia drawn from the ranks of poets, sculptors and merchants, for no sect fighter would ever debase himself by devotion to the Imperium. Any Sirenese in the PDF uniform of tan brocades and gilded tallhelm was a traitor. When the executions started, they barely knew how to operate their autorifles. Most of their weapons were still wrapped in the soft plastic covers they were delivered in.

'They died so quickly. On the Isles of Khyber the blessed children killed an entire division of them in one day. Can you believe it? Twelve thousand loyalists lined up and buried alive. Oh, it was a golden age.'

At this Bekeala interjected, her eyes red and watery with rage, 'Enough! We do not need to hear this. Let me kill him!'

'One more thing,' growled Roth as he pulled the scion's grinning visage close to his face. 'The psychic backlash, the planetary swansong. Your brood is responsible...'

'I am surprised you belittle yourself by asking,' it said smugly.

Roth released the scion and took a step back. He let the answer settle heavily on his chest and sink into the pit of his stomach. Like the final stroke of an oiled brush, the painting was complete. He had resolved the matter for the ordo, but it would be a pyrrhic victory. It was already too late for Sirene Primal.

'Absolutely correct psyker. It is far too late. Our choir has been singing to the family, calling out to the warp and the family answered our call.'

Looking down, Roth drew his sidearm in anger. He had slackened his guard and the xenos breed had gleaned his surface thoughts. 'How long do we have?' asked Roth, reasserting his question with an octave of psychic amplification.

The scion simply rolled back his head and laughed. His laughter came in great shrieking bursts, resonating with the thunderous acoustics of a cyclopean hall. It was all too much. Roth took aim with his pistol. His finger slipped inside the trigger. Yet before he applied pressure, the scion's face threw out a great crest of blood.

Roth lowered his weapon, breathing heavily. Bekaela was by his side, her silver glaive streaked with strings of crimson gore. She was terrifying. The paint on her face smeared with sweat and fury, a daemonic visage melting down her cheeks. At her feet the scion lay, a cloud of bright red hazing the water and forming a halo around its skull.

But the laughter did not abate. Long after the scion was dead, the laughter continued to toll through the chamber.

THE ANNALS OF Imperial history would not be kind to Sirene Primal. It was recorded in M866.M41 that a xenos armada known collectively as a hivefleet entered the Orco-Pelica Subsector. On the most urgent warning of an Inquisitor Obodiah Roth, all senior officers and dignitaries were evacuated. The Imperial Navy was ordered to withdraw, regroup and re-engage. Sporadic reports from retreating naval forces described the incursion as a *seething wave of oblivion*.

On Sirene Primal, seventy thousand Guardsmen of Montaigh, Kurass and Amartine dug in on the rugged

Sephardi ranges to stall the xenos advance. It is said, that within three months the mountains had been transformed into a sprawling network of artillery palisades, tunnelled barbicans and interlocking firing nests. Once the xenos made landfall, the Guardsmen were expected to hold out for eight weeks. They lasted less than five hours.

The ensuing campaign to reclaim the subsector is itself a historic epic worthy of narrative, but of Sirene Primal there was no more. In the end, the lonely jewel on the Eastern Fringes became little more than a smudged ink record in the forgotten archives of Terra.

MORTAL FUEL

Richard Williams

THE PATRIARCH WATCHED as the young man named
Asphar was brought in. He paused for a moment at
the threshold; the patriarch could see him quickly
assess his surroundings. This one was not careless.
Good, good, the patriarch thought, they had chosen
well with this one. He motioned for the youth to sit
by the furnace. Asphar did so, head lowered in
respect. The patriarch smiled, this one did not lack
faith either. When Asphar finally glanced up, the
light from the furnace burned in his eyes. Yes, the
patriarch concluded, this one would do. But first,
before he could be ready, he had to understand
why.

'When our ancestors were first brought here,' the
patriarch began, 'they saw this world from space
and they named it Bahani, meaning "Blue". For
when they came here the deserts were oceans, the

winds were soft and the land swelled with fruit and grain. Our people thought this was the great reward from the Emperor, and so they helped the masters, the Imperial men, to build their towers and their factories. We served them willingly, never knowing that they would cloud the skies, boil away the seas and turn the air to smoke.'

'Now, all we eat is brought in crates from other worlds. All we make is taken away. Our world has been stolen from us, shipment by shipment, and we helped them destroy us at every step. That is our sin, the sin for which you must be our absolution. So that the Emperor may turn to us once more and grant our people life, even after this world has died.'

'Will you do so? Will you be one of the swords of our absolution?'

'On my life. On my soul,' Asphar swore.

'Then here is your path…'

MIDSHIPMAN MARCHER SQUINTED into the wind. It had blown up quickly, quicker than anyone in the landing party from the *Relentless* had expected. It had only taken a few minutes after the transport landed to open the airlock, but in that time the wind had swept up from a bluster to a full force gale. They had landed at the very edge of one of the cities on Bahani's western continent, on top of a range of cliffs overlooking ranks of structures on the plain below. If he should fall off the cliff, it would be a premature end to his career. He took another step towards the control spire ahead of him and stumbled, blown back several paces by the wind.

'Emperor's arse!' he cursed, and then spluttered as the grit in the air blew into his mouth.

The vox crackled in his ear, but he couldn't make out the transmission. Probably Lieutenant Roche, sitting safe back on the transport. Marcher knew he was supposed to respect his superiors, but that one never put himself in the least risk if he could avoid it. That was not the behaviour Marcher expected from an officer. Marcher sat up and peered into the storm. He had gotten himself turned around. The shadows of buildings loomed all around him, giant, long buildings, channelling the dust so that it buffeted him from every side. In one direction though there was movement. It was a man, his cloak wrapped around him tight, coming to his aid. He pulled Marcher to his feet and guided him steadily into the lee of one of the buildings. Marcher shook the worst of the dust off his uniform. The man rolled down the cloth across his face. He was a Bahani, but he bore Imperial rank-tattoos. A foreman, most likely, probably promised a seat on the departing convoy in return for his loyalty.

Tensions were high between the hundreds of Administratum officials in the process of decommissioning the Imperium's assets and the millions of indentured workers that they were to leave behind. It meant an end to the tithes; no longer would they have to labour within the mega-processing plants or on the vapour-ships evaporating seawater to extract the minerals it held. They would be free, or at least as free as any man could be in this dark galaxy. But, more than anything else, theirs would also be the freedom to starve, to fight and to die. Every industry on Bahani was devoted to the extraction of raw materials that other worlds craved and the Administratum and their indentured workers had systematically boiled the seas and eviscerated the land over the millennia of their occupation. Now, the Imperium had taken all it could and was moving on; the workers had only just realised that the Imperium's plans, though, did not include them. There had been protests, fighting, even assassinations.

'The storms here along the coast, they whip up quick, but they never last long,' the foreman said. 'Listen, they already dropping.'

'Coast?' Marcher asked, surprised. 'Are we on the coast? I didn't see the ocean when we were landing.'

'Coast is just our name. No ocean here for long time now. Look now, there, you can see.'

The storm had nearly died away completely. Marcher looked out over the cliffs at the city below, except that it wasn't a city. Not of buildings and people at least. The structures he had seen when they landed, they were ships. Huge factory ships, old and gutted, their hulls pock-marked with rust. There was rank upon rank of these hulks, settled, immovable, upon the salty plain.

'My grandfather,' the worker continued, 'he said that this used to be the deepest part of the Great Western Sea. That is why all the vapour-ships, they ended up here. To finish off the last of it.'

These cliffs, these hills, were once islands, and before that mountains, but hidden deep within the sea. It barely seemed possible.

Another crackle of the vox shocked Marcher from the sight. The foreman led him into the control spire. Marcher stepped inside and was hit by a wall of noise. The interior floor rose up in a great spiral to the top. People were everywhere, workers mainly. Administratum and Munitorum officials, distinctive in their uniform, were dotted around: directing, shouting, ordering, entreating the workers to fetch and carry, load and push. No sooner had a controller moved away from a piece of equipment then it was grabbed, dismantled, boxed and loaded onto the cargo trolleys rolling down around the far edge.

The foreman pointed Marcher in the direction of the ranking official, Governor-Adept Kaizen, who was pacing down around the inner curve of the spiral dragging a train of human servitors in his wake.

'Take that. That's done.' Kaizen fired orders like an autocannon. 'No, no delay for this schedule. I've approved this already. No to this. No to this. This is acceptable. This one, there is an error in the contingencies, rework it–'

'Governor Kaizen!' Marcher shouted, striding as quickly as he could to keep pace with the governor and his retinue.

'This one is fine. Halve the schedule for this, he always pads his estimates. Get it done. Get it done. Who are you?'

'I am Midshipman Mar–'

'You're here for your cargo. Follow me. Keep up. Keep up.'

Governor Kaizen increased his pace as he headed down the spiral further. Marcher decided to let propriety go hang and broke into a trot to keep up.

'My lieutenant sends his comp–' Marcher began.

'I know you Navy men like your formalities, but I am in the midst of the final disentanglement of our presence on this entire planet. An operation of which I am the centre, the core, the nexus, the overmind. So do excuse me the formalities, for I have no time, no time.'

'Yes, governor.'

'Here,' Kaizen said, drawing up to the side of a pit. 'Here is your cargo.'

Marcher looked down. A sea of human faces looked back up.

'Sign this.' Kaizen slapped a data-slate into Marcher's hand.

'I think the lieutenant should be–'

'No time. No time. Sign it.' Marcher did so. Kaizen took the data-slate, tore off the top sheet and handed it back to Marcher.

'That's yours. Take it. Keep it.'

Marcher read what he had signed. It was a recruitment order. The men in the pit below had just been freed from their service to the Administratum and instantly bonded once more, this time to the Navy. They were to serve out their time in the work-crews on the lowest decks of the *Relentless*. Conditions were poor, mortality rates were high, these men were to be the mortal fuel the *Relentless* consumed. And they were volunteering. Better the bowels of a Battlefleet warship than what remained for them on Bahani after the Imperium left.

'Three hundred men, Governor?'

'Three hundred, fifty-seven. More than we expected. Men, women, somewhere in between, your captain's request did not specify.'

'It was from our first officer, Commander Ward. Our captain died several months ago.'

'Still no replacement? Sloppy man management in the Battlefleet, always said so. Wouldn't be acceptable in logistics. No, not at all.'

One of the servitors, a vox-unit built into its head, chirped. Its eyes unfocused and rolled back into its head as it opened its mouth to relay a message.

'Governor, this is a security alert. We are under attack. Locals are massing at the main gate. A vehicle has breached the southern perimeter and is heading straight for the control spire. '

'The control spire?' Kaizen said, his voice rising. 'I'm in the control spire! Call out the reserve squads; I want every one of them guarding this entrance…'

Marcher watched as Kaizen continued barking orders at the passive servitor who was faithfully relaying them to the security detail. Marcher noticed, however, what Kaizen hadn't, that all the workers around them had started to run. They weren't running from the main entrance, though, they were running directly away from the Governor. Marcher heard a noise from outside, an engine, roaring closer and closer. They weren't going for the entrance, the midshipman realised, they were coming straight through the–

The vehicle, a heavy loader weighed down with metal plates welded on as armour, crashed through the spire's wall. Marcher had already taken a hold on the Governor and yanked him out of the way as the loader ground to a halt, buried under the debris.

Brilliant sunlight streamed into the gloomy spire, as Bahani gunmen clambered through the breach in the wall. One of them clambered onto the loader's cabin and levelled an autorifle at the Governor's servitors still milling around in confusion.

'I will not have this,' Kaizen complained beneath Marcher. 'I will not have this operation disrupt–'

The shots interrupted Kaizen in mid-flow. A servitor fell beside them, its head a mess of blood and bone. Marcher's navy pistol was in his hand and he shot back. The head of the gunman snapped to the side and he fell. There were shouts from above as the guards at the entrance realised what had happened and redeployed. The Bahani gunmen pouring in found themselves being shot at from the levels above and began to duck behind cover to return fire. Marcher dragged Kaizen further from the firefight behind the lip of the pit. The crowd of people inside had heard the shots and wailed and screamed for their own lives.

One of the Bahanis saw them move and crouched up, a grenade in his hand, ready to throw. A shot somewhere above caught him. Too late. Marcher watched as the grenade sailed up into the air straight towards him. There was no time to run; his mind froze, but his body moved. He snatched the data-slate from Kaizen's unresisting hand and took a mighty swing and felt the solid contact as the data-slate smacked the grenade away. It flew back out through the breach and exploded with a heavy *krump*. It was then that Marcher's mind clicked in and he realised what a stupendously stupid thing that had been to do. The mere impact alone might have set the grenade off in his face.

'Well done, midshipman.' Kaizen pulled Marcher back down into cover. 'Good job protecting your cargo.'

Kaizen took the data-slate back from Marcher's unresisting hand and peered at it. 'I'd check them anyway if I were you, as I believe you've invalidated your receipt.'

THE YOUNG BAHANI named Asphar gritted his teeth as the lifter rocket struggled against the planet's gravity and the pressure piled upon his body. Though he could feel himself being crushed, he was not scared. They had told him that this would happen. Had told him to expect it. He had not been scared when they had closed the cargo container lid upon him; not even when they had taken him to see the patriarch who had explained the mission he was to undertake. One of the Bahani's young starwarriors, the patriarch had called him; one who would cleanse the sins of all the Bahani people in the eyes of the Emperor by punishing His false servants. That was the Imperial men, Asphar knew, who had come to Bahani using the Emperor's name but then had despoiled His gift to them.

The Bahani people had been blind to it, the patriarch had explained, but their eyes had been opened in time. This last shipment was to be the vehicle of the Emperor's wrath upon them and Asphar was to be His herald. Then, when their mission was complete, the Emperor would guide them home as heroes.

They had chosen only the best, the patriarch had told him that. Asphar was the best of his class, the smartest, the fittest, the most faithful. It was no immodesty to say so; he rejoiced in the gifts that the Emperor had given him. And so, even as the lifter rocket threatened to shake itself apart, he forced

himself to unclench his teeth and begin to pray. He
would not be scared.

THE RELENTLESS, A Lunar-class cruiser, warship of
the most-revered Emperor's Navy, hung in silent
orbit as the Imperial departure from Bahani continued apace. From the tip of its heavy prow, with
armour metres thick, to the mighty engines at its
stern it measured more than eight kilometres long
and over a mile high. Every crenelation, every
tower that festooned its hull was unique, having
been repaired or replaced countless times over its
centuries of service. Every cannon and launcher
that made up the batteries along its flanks had its
name and a gun-crew whose sole purpose was its
service.

The man who now commanded those guns, First
Officer Ward, sat quietly in his study, secreted
within the suite of rooms that were his personal
quarters. It was not a large chamber, and it felt all
the more crowded because of the trophies that hung
from every wall. Rich, thick furs covered the dull
battleship walls; a set of razor-sharp antlers crested
the doorway, the heads of dead animals and xenos
species were crowded on every surface. Each of
them, at one time or another, had crossed paths
with the *Relentless*.

He had not garnered them all himself, of course. No,
they were a tradition, one that each second-in-command
had continued and built upon for generations now. He
had added his own choice pieces, though: the skull of a
stegadon, the chair made from a dragon turtle shell,
and the arm of an insectoid xenos species (the head was
too hideous to display). The collection had become

most imposing and it gave him a great sense of continuity: in its way it kept alive all those great men who had come before him.

It had been just that comfort that he had sought today. He had brought the shift reports back with him to read, but they were still untouched in a pile upon the desk. Instead, he stared at a harqeagle, posed with wings spread and considered the ambitions of his second, Lieutenant Commander Guir.

After the old captain had died in such an unfortunate manner, the two of them had agreed that it would have been unwise to expedite word back to the admirals of Battlefleet Bethesba back at Emcor. The old captain had been so well-loved by both officers and crew, and his death so sudden, they reasoned, that to replace him quickly with a newcomer, a captain unversed in the ways and traditions of the *Relentless*, could damage ship morale irrevocably. So they had delayed sending the communiqué as long as possible and Ward had quietly assumed the responsibilities of the captaincy.

Last shift, however, Guir had asked out of the blue whether an acknowledgement had been received from Battlefleet. Ward had said that it had not and Guir, after a moment, had let the matter drop. That moment's pause had been telling. He had checked with his informants on the upper decks and they had confirmed his suspicions. His authority was being questioned; the occasional joke, an inflection in a comment, nothing more, but he knew how quickly such talk could turn serious. Perhaps once, in the glory years of Battlefleet Bethesba, the officer corps of the *Relentless* had served selflessly, out of pride and loyalty to the Emperor, but now all that seemed to motivate them was personal profit and advancement. Much of his time as first officer had been spent ensuring the officers stayed in line, but since taking over the onus of the captaincy he had had to delegate that to Guir. Perhaps he should not have trusted him so.

Ward regretted now the decision to delay the news of the old captain's death. He had realised that they would not foist an outsider upon them; they would offer him the post. Though promotion to the captaincy of a cruiser of the line such as the *Relentless* would be quite a jump in rank, who better than he to take on the role? And once he was confirmed as captain his officers would instinctively buckle down again.

In the meantime, though, they had grown slack, complacent and they were taking liberties with his authority. They didn't see him as a proper captain. They needed to be reminded of their place and the power he had over each of them. An example needed to be made. One which would bring his officers back to him and not solidify the opposition. Someone who was easily replaced.

Ward picked up the sheaf of reports again and started to flick through them. One of them had caught his eye before. There. The report of the incident on the surface by one Midshipman Marcher.

'AND SO FOR the heroism in the face of the enemy displayed by Midshipman Dal Henrik Marcher and attested to by Governor Kaizen, he shall at this time be accorded the rank of sub-lieutenant with all the duties and privileges thereof...'

Those words still rang proudly within Marcher's head as he stood at his new post on the command deck. He had been attached to the Imperia Ordinatus and was only a short distance away from where the imposing master of ordnance sat surrounded by servitors, each one linked into a battery of consoles feeding them data regarding the ready condition of the ship's torpedoes and smaller craft. In battle, this position would resound with a cacophony of noises; for the moment, however, it was quiet. More so than usual even. A solemn ceremony was about to begin.

Marcher looked up at the bridge which formed an arch across the width of the command deck. Up there he could see the first officer standing calmly upon the central dais and beside him, Governor Kaizen, unaccompanied for once by his retinue. The two of them were about to kill a world.

The quiet in the Ordnance station was broken by the crackle of the master's vox. He turned his head slightly to hear it better and then beckoned Marcher over.

'Commander Ward requested this,' the master grunted, handing him a data-slate. 'Take it up to him.'

Marcher froze 'Now, sir?' he managed. Disturb him just as the ceremony was starting?

'Of course now. Get to it.' The master turned back to his screens.

Marcher strode as quickly as formality allowed up the side of the bridge to the central dais. His heart pounded as he approached the first officer, who was engaged in conversation by the Governor. For a moment Marcher held back, unsure whether he was to interrupt them, but then the first officer turned and acknowledged him.

'Thank you, sub-lieutenant,' he said, taking the pad. 'Governor, I believe you're already acquainted with our newest commissioned officer.'

'Yes, of course.' Kaizen said, concealing his annoyance at the interruption.

'Congratulations,' he said, struggling for something else to say. 'I'm sure you'll do the Battlefleet proud.'

'Yes, sir,' Marcher replied unbidden. 'I most certainly intend to, Governor, sir.'

Kaizen glanced back and Marcher realised that he had spoken out of turn. He could feel the eyes of everyone on the dais looking at him: Commissar Bedrossian sitting back beside the captain's chair, Senior Armsman Vickers standing coolly at ease, the bridge officers at their consoles to the front. Lieutenant Roche was one of them, he had half-turned to watch. Marcher felt the blood rush to his face but forced it back with an effort of will. He was not a child midshipman any longer, he was an officer and he would hold steady in the face of any consequences.

'Well said, Sub-Lieutenant Marcher,' the first officer announced. 'Now, Governor, shall we begin?'

The Governor nodded and Marcher, relieved, began to edge away.

'Sub-Lieutenant,' the first officer continued, handing the pad back to him. 'I shall attend to this once we are done here. You may as well wait and observe the proceedings. It is, after all, an historic occasion. Don't you agree, Governor?'

The Governor nodded again and the two of them took up their positions at the front of the dais.

'I, Governor Horsl Kaizen, speak for the Adeptus Terra. For this world before us designated 129 Tai D, known as Bahani, I hereby declare all tithe-treaties void and debts extant cancelled and declare this world as *orbis cassi* – of no further worth.'

'I, Commander Tomias Ward, first officer of the Emperor's warship *Relentless*, speak for Battlefleet Bethesba. For this world before us designated 129 Tai D, I hereby declare this world as *orbis non contegnum*. We entrust the defence of this world back to its people. May they stand strong and faithful in their new age of His service.'

Marcher watched as Commander Ward stepped down to the bridge vox-officer, who glanced up, waiting for him to confirm the order.

'Do it.'

The vox-officer tapped a single key. In an instant the communiqué flashed from his screen to the command deck data-nexus and from there flew through space to strike its intended target: one of Bahani's orbital beacons. Within the same second, the beacon digested its contents and had taken the necessary action and passed the same message onto its fellows. The message itself was complex, it had taken days to prepare with the necessary encryptions, authorisations and passwords, but its essence was simple:

You are no longer a part of the Imperium.

The planet would be excised from the Administratum's great volumes of the Emperor's worlds; if it were attacked, the Imperium would not listen to its cries for help. Trade and transport routes would be redefined, no longer would the merchant fleets that Bahani relied upon for its food venture there.

The twelve million inhabitants of Bahani, the indentured workers insufficiently valuable to take away, did not know it, but their doom had come. Their machinery would break down and they would freeze in the nights and bake in the day. Food stores would be exhausted and they would inevitably fight amongst themselves and kill to hold those few areas where something could still be grown. Their numbers would be devastated, the civilisation they had built would be extinguished and the few who survived would fall prey to marauding xenos raiders and the monsters that lurked in the dark.

On the bridge of the *Relentless* the vox-officer signalled to Commander Ward that the communiqué had been sent and received.

'Well,' Ward said, turning to Kaizen, 'Now that's done, Governor, would you dine with us before you return to your ship? I find I have quite an appetite.'

TWELVE HOURS LATER, the Imperial convoy broke orbit and left Bahani behind. At its centre travelled the *Gloriana Vance*, the Barbican-class liner carrying the Administratum officials and those valuable goods and machinery deemed worthy of removal in the evacuation. In formation around it were the *Spur*, *Illys* and *Onyx*, Sword-class frigates assigned as escort. Behind these trailed three dozen cargo scows carrying the last shipment of processed ore that the factories of Bahani would produce. At the fore, dwarfing the smaller ships, the cruiser *Relentless* majestically swung into the lead position.

Marcher watched the planet recede into the distance from his post on the command deck. How different he felt from when they had arrived. He had risen fast, he thought with no small sense of self-satisfaction, and now that his abilities had caught the first officer's eye that rise would continue.

Asphar, hidden within a cargo container in the dark hold of the scow designated Terminus Three, felt the change in direction, but thought nothing of it. He had faith that he would see his home soon enough.

Far away, hidden in the darkness of space, other eyes watched the laden convoy depart. The souls they had abandoned on the planet would keep, but here was a prize that they could not let slip away. A command was given in an alien tongue and a portion of the darkness shifted to follow the human fleet.

THE FIRST JUMP of the journey back passed without incident, though for the Navigators of the *Relentless* it was grindingly slow. On each occasion they chanced across a favourable warp current that would normally speed their progress they had to cross-tack and delay to allow the cargo scows to keep pace. Thanks to their exhausting labour, however, all ships were undamaged and in formation when the fleet emerged back into realspace.

After allowing time for the warp engines to recharge, Commander Ward formally handed over defence of the convoy to Lieutenant Zeath, commanding the *Spur*. The convoy jumped out; the *Relentless* was finally free.

ASPHAR'S HEART RACED and his blood pounded in his ears. Now, he was scared. He clutched the sides of the container to ensure they were still solid. He could have sworn he saw them ripple and flow during that last jump. He had heard of warp jumps; they had allowed the brightest of his class the privilege to talk to one of the traders who journeyed between the stars. He had discounted much of what the trader had said of the jump into the maelstrom as fiction told to impress children, but all of it was true. The sounds and sights were bad enough, but he had been rattled and shaken within his little cell as though he were a die within a gaming pot. He checked his suit and helmet again, and praised the Emperor when he found no tears or cracks in either. The cargo scows did not bother keeping much atmosphere within their holds. Without his suit and air canisters he would never have survived.

His current canister was running low, no doubt he was breathing far too hard. He had to make it last longer or he would suffocate in here. He took up another and made to connect it when he noticed the gauge. It read empty. It hadn't been used already, he was sure of that, he had been very careful to keep those he had used separate. He turned the canister over; maybe it was the gauge that was broken. No, there it was, an imperfection in one of the welds. All the air inside had slowly leaked away. Asphar's heart started to beat harder again. He could not stay hidden within his container. He would have to venture out into the ship.

EVEN THOUGH MARCHER'S commission would remain unconfirmed until Battlefleet could give their approval, he was entitled to every privilege his new rank conferred. The latest was an appointment with the Gastromo of the junior officers' mess to transfer his tab and dining rights there. Marcher had felt a warm thrill as he stepped inside the mess. He had been there before, but only running messages or errands. Never with the chance to appreciate it. Never as an equal. Now he was free to take his ease there off-shift, sit in the deep, brass-studded chairs or spend an evening at the bar talking with his fellow officers. It was all so different to eating amongst the, sometimes frankly puerile, midshipmen.

It was mid-shift so the mess was mostly empty. He recognised Lieutenant Roche in a chair, engrossed in something he was reading, and a few of the acting sub-lieutenants. Strange, Marcher thought, not long ago, they would have chased him out of here unless he were on official business. Today, they had to address him as 'Sir'.

The Gastromo greeted him formally and brought out the necessary dockets for him to sign. He, at least, was not fazed by their change of circumstances. And so it should be with me, Marcher considered. It was the proper way for an officer to behave. The necessary slips signed, the Gastromo offered to serve him his first drink, which he happily accepted. Inspired with a sense of fellow-feeling, Marcher paid for a glass to be sent to Lieutenant Roche as well. A server took it over and discreetly interrupted Roche from his reading. Roche glanced up to listen, his eyes flicked over to Marcher.

Marcher raised his glass slightly in salute and turned back, satisfied, to the bar. The server reappeared and whispered hurriedly to the Gastromo, the glass was untouched.

'I am afraid the gentleman declined your offer, sir.'

'What's that?' Marcher turned back but Roche was already leaving. The acting sub-lieutenants saw him go and, recognising Marcher, walked out as well.

'Would you care for it yourself?' the Gastromo asked with such courtesy as to be condescending.

'No,' Marcher grimaced, trying to contain the mixture of anger and embarrassment welling up inside him. 'No, thank you.'

'I'll take it,' a figure spoke behind him. It was Senior Armsman Vickers. Marcher nodded and Vickers scooped the glass up easily in his large hand and took a sip.

'My compliments, Mister Marcher.'

'Thank you, Mister Vickers.' Marcher did not know if the senior armsman was even allowed in the junior officers' mess. Technically he held no commission, indeed the midshipmen scuttlebutt was that he had come aboard as a conscript in the work gangs who toiled below decks. How he had risen out of that pit to the post he now held had been the topic of much speculation amongst them, and a good few tall tales. Whatever his status, Marcher said to himself, eyeing the tapestry of scars the senior armsman wore; he was not going to be the one to ask him to leave.

'A decent bottle for once,' Vickers said, indicating the glass.

'Yes.' The word 'sir' hung on Marcher's tongue.

'Not as good as in the officers' mess. But this isn't bad. When you make it there, Mister Marcher, I'll show you their selection.'

'Yes…' Marcher rallied. 'That would be very good of you, Mister Vickers.'

The senior armsman swirled the drink thoughtfully for a moment.

'Mister Marcher, let me give you some advice. Your new fellows, you will never win them over with kindness. Don't even bother with them. They're relics; washed-up officers who have less than half your ability and none of your promise. They are not there for you to befriend; they're there for you to outshine. Be exceptional, and those who matter will not ignore you.'

'Thank you, Mister Vickers,' Marcher replied, surprised and flattered at the attention.

Vickers nodded, swallowed the rest of the drink and left. Everyone knew the senior armsman was close to the first officer. Another rush went through Marcher; his future was bright indeed with Commander Ward smiling down upon him.

'Confirm the origin of that message,' Ward bit, unable to hide the irritation in his voice. 'If the astropath has made any mistake then I'll have his head!'

'The Telepathica sanctuary confirms, sir,' the vox-officer replied. 'Message coding is correct – Optimus level.'

Ward swore under his breath. He could not possibly ignore an Optimus level distress call; even the slightest delay might be questioned.

'Contact the Navis dome, give them the coordinates.'

'Already done, sir.'

This vox-officer was keen to the point of presumption, Ward reflected.

'Tell them this, then, Lieutenant. Flank speed and nothing less.'

THE TABLE SHOOK again and Governor Kaizen grabbed at the teetering stacks of data-slates to prevent them from falling.

'Call up to the bridge,' he snapped. 'Find out what in the devil's name is going on.'

One of his assistants ran to obey his command while the others shrank back, as much as from their Governor's wrath as from the sounds of the attack. He had commandeered the top-level grand suite of the *Gloriana Vance*, rather than be on the bridge, specifically so he could escape the mundane interruptions of the trip and get on with the real work: the plans the industrialisation of Reeza. And now this!

The ship lurched and this time the data-slates practically flew from his hands.

'This is contemptible,' he exclaimed. 'I want to talk to the bridge. Is a squadron of the Battlefleet's frigates not sufficient to keep us safe from one pathetic raider attack? I do not expect to have to be disturbed for every little thing.'

He stormed over to one of the portholes, but nothing could be seen apart from the starfield whirling as the *Gloriana Vance* banked and turned. Then there was a flash. It was too close to be another ship; it was the flash of a point-defence turret. Costs and quotas, Kaizen realised, they must be right on top of them!

'Get out,' Kaizen bellowed at his assistants. 'We've got to get back to–'

The impact threw Kaizen from his feet. An ear-splitting whine drilled into his head. He glanced back at the porthole. The starfield had gone; in its place he looked straight down the maw of the evil machinery that was cutting through the hull.

'They're boarding!'

THE RELENTLESS BURST from warp and the command deck was immediately overwhelmed by a tumult of new data. Ward restrained his impatience and remained still within the captain's chair. Nothing he could do would hurry the initial reports. They had made excellent time. Ward knew there was no love lost between him and the Navis dome, but whatever else he thought of them he could never claim they had shown less than exemplary talent in the role for which they were born. Thanks to them, he may just have a chance to save his neck.

'Situation analysis compiling, sir,' the auspex officer reported.

'Let's have it then, Mister Aden.'

The battle appeared upon the main view-portal. The convoy was in disarray. The dozens of cargo scows were scattered, the *Gloriana Vance* was bucking like a bull trying to throw an unwelcome rider, the frigates...

'Where are the escorts?' Ward demanded. 'Where are the enemy? Find them, Mister Aden.'

'They were dispersed after their last jump, sir. The *Spur* and the *Illys* are reporting bomber attacks, minimal damage. The *Onyx* is out of position but on a heading back to the *Spur*. The–'

The auspex officer paused as a light winked out on his display.

'The *Illys* has been destroyed.'

'How?'

'It's... it's not clear, commander.'

'Incoming transmission from the *Gloriana Vance*, sir,' the vox-officer reported.

'Put it through, but get me the *Spur*. Show me the *Gloriana*.'

The view-portal swivelled to close on the liner. Its pale hull was pock-marked with dark spots, assault boats biting into its skin like tiny parasites. It looked diseased, being eaten from the inside out. Governor Kaizen's voice cut straight through the chatter of the command deck.

'Commander Ward. I demand that you immediately–'

'What is the tactical situation, Governor?' Ward cut him off.

'–you must attack them at once. They're taking my men. They're taking my men! You must get them back. They're priceless–'

'Ordnance! Assault crews to the transports. Reinforce the *Gloriana*.'

Below on the command deck, the master of ordnance ordered his officers down to the launch bays. Ward noted that his protégé, Mister Marcher, was amongst them, trying to conceal his eagerness with a mask of professionalism. Senior Armsman Vickers, in his usual place beside the command dais, shifted and Ward gave him the nod. The first officer never allowed anyone but him to lead his boarding parties.

Ward turned back to the bridge officers. 'As soon as they're away move us over to the *Illys*'s last position and order the *Spur* to fall into formation. Bombers, assault boats, they didn't get here on their own. We're going to find that carrier.'

* * *

ENEMY FIRE RIPPED along the top of the cargo-loader which sheltered Marcher and his men. Their entry into the *Gloriana Vance* was not going to be as uncontested as they had hoped. No sooner had their transport burned into the Gloriana's docking bay than Marcher had heard the shots bouncing off their hull. It had been too late to find an alternative boarding point; they were already committed. The transport had landed, its exit ramp had dropped and Marcher and his men had scrambled for what cover they could find as the transport's multilasers ran red-hot, providing covering fire.

Marcher's chest felt tight; this was not the same as the fight back on Bahani. This time he was responsible for the life of every single man with him. He could not afford just to think about himself, he had to lead. He had not even had a clear glimpse of the raiders yet. He had to get control of the situation. He had to know what was going on, and then he could give proper orders.

He peered over his cover and tried to get a sense of the battlefield. There, on the upper level, he could make out the shapes. The raiders had a fire-team up there, maybe an officer too; he would have to take their firing lines into account. He inched a little higher to get a view on their ground level positions. Maybe if they could circle around to the left...

Marcher felt something hit him hard in the side and knock him down, as a barrage of shots tore through the space he had just been occupying.

'I'd keep down if I were you.' It was Petty Officer Buller, one of Vickers's veterans who had made it plain that he obeyed Marcher only at the behest of the senior armsman. 'Sir,' Buller added as a grudging afterthought.

'What are your orders, sir?'

'Well, we need to take down that fire-team on the upper level, then I was thinking if we could flank–'

'Advance on all sides. Very good, sir.' Buller cut him off. 'Armsmen! In your pairs, cover and advance! Ram your shotguns down their throats!' Buller glanced back at Marcher. 'Gibbs! See that fire position up there? Keep their heads down!'

All around them the armsmen advanced, half of the party firing, while the other half scrambled for the next position. Marcher picked himself up. Those were the orders he should have given. Right now, he was not commanding this party, Buller was. But he did not blame the petty officer, he had asked for orders and Marcher had given him suggestions.

'Forward!' he cried as he dived for cover, then rose, found a target and fired. The shot went wide as the target ducked back, lightning fast. Inhumanly fast, even. The raiders were retreating in the face of the armsmen's determined attack. Marcher, for a brief second, caught sight of a silhouette. The same shape as a man but tall, too tall, its limbs spindly and elongated like a spider's. Then it was gone. It was an alien, a xenos.

ELDAR, WARD BROODED on the bridge of the *Relentless*, almost certainly one of the piratical sects of that abominable species. Despite its long history, the *Relentless* had rarely encountered them, but they had had several engagements with other ships of Battlefleet Bethesba down through the millennia, and some of the Battlefleet ships had even survived to report back. The eldar were dangerous, he knew, their motives often unfathomable but at their core they were decadent cowards, liable to hide or run as often as stand and fight. Even now their carrier was hiding somewhere out there instead of giving proper battle. Well, he would smoke them out.

'GET OUT THE way!' 'Let us through!' 'Clear a path! Clear a path!' Marcher and his men forced their way through the crowds of the panicking Administratum officials who were blocking the main concourse. The tall, narrow street was choked with people, pushing and shoving to get to safety. Nowhere was safe; small bands of raiders were all over the ship, refugees were coming from every direction with tales of attacks and slaughter which merely added to the hysteria and confusion. Beside him, Marcher saw that Buller was as much out of his depth as he was, and all he could do was shout himself hoarse and shove the officials away. Marcher's orders were to get to the bow end of the concourse; with teams from the *Relentless* at every critical junction maybe they could clip these cursed aliens' wings.

Suddenly, a scream rose up, though not one that could be made by a human voice. One scream and then more. A half dozen of the raiders burst from the top level, soaring and screeching on armoured sky-boards. The human crush below looked up at the sound and panicked, their shoving turned to clawing in their desperation to escape, they pushed their colleagues aside and trampled the fallen underfoot. Marcher caught sight of one of the sky-boarders as it swooped low, buzzing the crowds and blowing men aside in its wash. More of the raiders dived, but this time it was not for show; they struck out at the backs of the crowd with their heavy halberds as they scorched overhead, lopping off limbs and heads with insolent ease. One, heavier than the rest, had an ugly cannon slung underneath which spat splinter-shot, stitching a bloody line along the deck, slicing apart the bodies of those trying to flee.

'Armsmen!' Marcher and Buller shouted at the same time. Those armsmen who could see brought up their shotguns and fired. It was a difficult shot, but Marcher saw one of the raiders knocked back. For a moment, it looked as though he might fall but then he bent his body impossibly and caught himself back on his board. The raiders had clearly not expected such resistance, but they reacted instantly: sweeping back up to the higher levels and then disappearing from sight.

'They're gone.' Marcher breathed, trying to keep his voice from trembling.

'Wait,' Buller said and at that moment the sky-boarders blew back onto the concourse. They had returned and, worse, they had brought others. Three times more than their original number. They stayed high, spiralling effortlessly in between each other, tracing intricate patterns in the air. Marcher reached for his vox.

'Mister Vickers,' Marcher reported. 'We have contact with a large concentration of enemy sky-boarders, bow-end of the main concourse. Please–'

'They're coming down!' an armsman shouted, cutting him off. Four of them had peeled away from their aerial display and were bombing down the narrow aisle towards the armsmen crouched on the deck. Buller had seen them and was already issuing orders.

'Keep to the sides, men, keep to the sides. Close as you can, don't let them get too close.' Marcher saw the men obey him instantly, flattening themselves against the walls on each side of the concourse, forcing the raiders to keep their distance for fear of crashing into the sides themselves. The raiders saw it too and a second wave dropped down, this time led by the heavy sky-board with the cannon.

'Buller, no!' Marcher yelled at the armsman. 'Get them away from the wall. Disperse!'

Buller glanced across angrily at Marcher. 'What?'

It was too late. The first wave had pulled up early, blossoming apart in each direction and wheeling back, and the second wave dove through their trails: it was a clean run at targets who had so conveniently lined themselves up with nowhere to run. The cannon spat again, a clean line of explosions bit along the wall at waist-height, catching those crouching in the shoulders and face and cutting the armsmen standing in two. The blood and the dust billowed up and obscured the carnage beneath for a moment before it was blown clear by the sky-boards sweeping past. The scream of their engines faded to be replaced by the screams of the armsmen left with arms and legs hanging from their perforated torsos.

Marcher froze for a moment, but only for a moment. He looked to Buller, but he was down, his head nearly severed by a flashing halberd. A voice on the vox was telling him to pull back, but he ignored it. He was not afraid. He was angry. So very angry.

A couple of the surviving armsmen had gone to their fallen comrades. Marcher snapped at them to come back, his voice clear, even through the sounds of the wounded and dying.

'Keep scattered. Keep moving,' he shouted at them all. He glanced up; another wave was coming, and another behind that. 'Fire only on my order! Target the leader!'

Marcher brought up his own shotgun as the armsmen shifted around him. Now, now they were obeying him. No, that wasn't the difference; the difference was that now he was leading them.

The four raiders swooping down were sliding this way and that trying to follow the armsmen scurrying below them. The humans' officer though stood stock still in the centre of his men and so they instinctively drew together, focusing on him. They liked to take the officers first, the humans ran so much quicker once their officers were dead. Closer, closer, so close they could taste the kill.

'Fire!' Marcher commanded. The shot flew in a swarm straight at the lead sky-boarder. The sky-boarder tried to jink but he could not dodge such a volley. His body was torn apart, his board spun and the other fliers screeched as they realised their formation was too tight for safety. Two of them managed to wheel away, the other over-steered and fell. He twisted through the air and landed rolling onto the deck. He sprang to his feet, pulling at a pistol and was blown back by a single shot, half his face missing.

Marcher ejected the spent cartridge. The next wave was coming. 'Move! Move!' he ordered, but the armsmen were already moving, weapons ready and tracking the sky-boarder in the lead.

'Fire!' They fired in unison. This time the raider was already turning, flipping his board, thinking to use it as a shield. Useless thought. The heavy shot punctured the board's engine and it spiralled out of control and exploded. The other raiders however had kept well separated and swept down amongst the armsmen.

'Duck and roll!' Marcher shouted before diving aside himself. There was a scream behind him from an armsman too slow to react.

The next wave's leader had seen what had gone before and throttled back. The armsmen smoothly shifted their aim to the new frontrunner, blew him from the sky and then ducked and rolled. In his eagerness for the kill, another of the raiders misjudged the distance and caught an armsman with his halberd but then slammed at full speed into the deck. He tumbled from his board and the barrage of shot from the armsman's fellows kept him twitching long after he was dead.

Then, Marcher saw something strange happen. The next wave should have been barrelling down upon them, but all the fliers stayed circling near the ceiling. They had lost nearly a third of their number and the humans, instead of fleeing, were knocking them from the sky. A few of the fliers started to drop but as one took the lead he throttled back and then so did the rest and they rose back up to rejoin their fellows.

Marcher could see the eldar commander on the cannon-board, circling faster and faster, berating the others, dragging them back into another attack. The cannon-board led the way, sights set firmly on Marcher.

'Men of the *Relentless*!' Marcher called. 'With me!' And he ran at the diving attackers.

The raider saw his run and steepened his dive to compensate. Marcher sprinted all the harder and the raider pushed the cannon-board's nose down even further. Further and further, until he was nearly pitched straight down. His fellows were unable to hold on and pulled out, but he wanted the head of this human who dared defy him. He triggered the board's cannon and saw the deadly fire intersect the runner's path. The human fell and the raider desperately gunned back on his board, clawing its nose up away from the deck racing towards him. The bottom of the board screeched along the floor and the raider felt something strike him in the back and then the board's nose jerked up and climbed again. The raider found himself starting to slip and tried to readjust his stance. His legs wouldn't move. He could feel nothing below his waist. He reached round to his back and there he could feel the shot buried into his flesh, buried into his spine. He brought his bloody hand back before his eyes and then fell neatly head-first from the climbing board.

Marcher saw the fall, heard the neck snap as the raider hit the deck and then slowly released the breath he had been holding and loosened his grip on the still-smoking shotgun. Two armsmen were at his side, helping him to his feet. He bit his cheek at the pain from the splinter-shot that had creased his thigh as he had jumped aside. He looked up at the circling fliers. Although there were still a dozen of them left, not one of them was prepared to lead another attack. Their circles strayed wider as they began to look for an escape route.

'Fire!' the order came, not from Marcher, but from far above. Shots rang out from the upper levels and three of the fliers dropped, corkscrewing down to a fatal impact on the deck. The armsmen helping him clutched for their weapons and Marcher fell painfully to one knee.

'Fire!' it came again, the voice sounding more familiar. Two more raiders fell and now the rest split and fled through any hatch they could find.

'Mister Marcher.' Marcher peered up and Vickers emerged on the ledge, his armsmen flanking him on either side. 'The bridge has been secured. When you are finished with your rest, perhaps you and your men will join us there.' His words were hard, but his tone was light.

Marcher shouted his acknowledgement and struggled back to his feet. He called his men back to order, but they could not just move on. They had wounded who must be cared for and dead who needed words spoken over them before their spirits could find the Emperor's Peace. A few of the armsmen were crouched over the dead of the enemy also, taking trophies. Marcher's eyes drifted to the pistol of the first raider he had downed himself. A trophy piece? Why not? It was certainly no less than he deserved.

COMMANDER WARD STOOD at the shoulder of the auspex bridge officer. The young lieutenant was working feverishly with the main station down on the command deck trying to locate any sign of the main eldar ship. Obviously with no result yet, Ward noticed, as the lieutenant was starting to sweat. Ward had had enough of this incompetence.

'Report, Mister Aden.'

'Nothing yet, sir,' the auspex officer replied too quickly. 'We're still trying to localise–'

'Contact the *Spur*,' Ward cut him off. 'Get the exit vector for those bombers and trace it back, look for anything, anything that could be hiding that damn ship!'

Ward stepped away and sat back in the captain's chair. His underlings could follow his commands, while he monitored the results of their work on his personal screen. He could barely believe that these, these children, had had the temerity to start whispering against him. They were soft, too used to easy patrols and easier 'battles' that were little more than the intimidation of merchant navy ships suspected of smuggling. They thought Guir was the answer for them; that he would give them a bigger cut of the spoils and maybe he would be that stupid. But, the first officer wondered, how would Guir fare out here in the dark when they had a ghost on their scanners and an alien knife at their throat?

'Commander, I have something!'

'I see it, Mister Aden.'

There was something out there; nothing that could be detected unless one was staring straight at it. It was a shadow against the stars; ten times larger than any ship could be, but Ward could tell that there was nothing natural about it. The eldar had to be in there.

'Set a heading towards that location, load the–'

An alarm trilled from the command deck below.

'Enemy torpedoes detected!'

'What's their target?'

'It's the *Onyx*, sir.'

'Warn the ship. Tell them to brace for impact.' Ward held his calm, with a few minutes' warning the *Onyx* could lock itself down tight enough to weather the strike. 'Time to impact?'

'Impacting now!'

The view-portal flicked to a view of the Sword frigate behind them. Its point-defence turrets flashed for a second, valiantly trying to track the missiles detected too late. One, two and then a third explosion rocked the frigate, blowing away the dorsal control towers and chunks of the engine. The frigate held firm for a moment and then a series of secondary blasts ripped through its interior.

The bridge officers were silent, they had heard the reports of the destruction of the *Illys* as they jumped in, but most of them had never seen a warship die so close. Ward, though, felt the chill run down his spine for a different reason: the *Relentless* was in-between the shadow and the *Onyx*. Those torpedoes had sailed right past his ship without any warning at all.

'The *Onyx* is launching sanctuary pods, sir. They're abandoning ship.'

'Ordnance!' Ward shouted over the head of Lieutenant Roche, the weapons officer, down across the command deck to the Imperia Ordinatus. 'Ready our torpedoes to launch!'

'Target, sir?' Roche tried to interject, that order should have been relayed through him.

Ward was in no mood to pander to junior officers who needed to be told the obvious.

'That, Mister Roche!' he said, pointing at the shadow. 'Angle a wide arc across its centre. Maintain a link with the torpedoes; be ready to detonate them at my instruction.'

The *Relentless*'s manoeuvring rockets fired and the mighty ship began to turn. Amongst the lists and gantry cranes of the prow torpedo bays, artificers chanted their final blessings over their charges. They had had them ready as soon as the distress call had been received.

The fearsome plasma engines of the torpedoes ignited in strict order, launching as the *Relentless* turned across that cursed shadow. Ward stared intently at their scopes, judging their speed, the distance.

'Mister Aden,' he said without so much as a glance at the auspex officer, 'watch your readings. If you so much as blink then I will cut off your eyelids.'

The torpedoes entered the shadow thousands of miles apart from each other. Far too distant from each other to be effective as a combat strike, but their purpose was not to damage the enemy, just to find him.

'Detonate!' Ward snapped.

Explosions flared in the space before them, tiny against the vast shadow, but the streams of data flowing back into the auspex arrays spiked.

'Well?' Ward demanded.

Lieutenant Aden opened his mouth and it hung there for a second. 'Yes... a distortion in one explosion.'

'Feed those coordinates through,' Ward crowed. 'Mister Crichell, take us in, bring our broadside to bear. Mister Roche, ready the port gun batteries. No excuses!'

'What range, sir?' Crichell asked.

Ward knew what his order should be; they should close as much as they could. Yet such a move would expose the *Relentless* as well. Only the Emperor knew what lurked within that shadow and Ward would be damned before he allowed those xenos attack craft to leech the life from the *Relentless* as they had done the *Gloriana Vance*.

'Battery effective range will suffice, lieutenant.' The *Relentless* wheeled and Ward heard the reassuring sound of its decks of gun batteries firing in turn, saturating their target area. He just needed a glimpse, a single glimpse of his foe and then he could destroy him.

The alarm shrilled across the command deck. 'Enemy torpedoes!'

Ward barely dared ask. 'Target?'

'Right at us!'

Ward was instantly back on his feet.

'Turrets, lock-on and fire!' he grabbed his vox and hit the ship-wide sigil. 'All hands, this is the first officer, brace for impact! Brace for impact!'

The force of the explosions knocked Ward back into the chair and he held on for dear life as the bridge rocked and threatened to pitch them all onto the command deck below. One of the logistician pods broke off from the wall and tumbled down onto the deck. The servitors caught beneath trilled distress at the damage they took. The Scutatum Cluster and Curatium Pit flared into life as they struggled to maintain the shields and structural integrity of the impacted sections. Damage reports poured through onto Ward's screen, but the information he wanted to know wasn't there.

'Auspex. Auspex!' he shouted. 'Do we still have them?'

Lieutenant Aden looked around, ready to report, but Ward could already see the answer written across his face.

The shadow was gone.

'WE MADE IT to the liner's bridge, by then most of the raiders were on the run dragging whatever sorry souls they had taken with them. Their main force though had the remains of the *Gloriana*'s crew bottled up near the atmospheric recyclers. If the bastard xenos took that then they could force us to abandon ship!'

Marcher banged the table for emphasis and sent the crowd of drinks rattling. He leaned in and the dozen junior officers listening avidly to the tale leaned in closer as well.

'We went down there at once. The senior arms-man had all of the parties converging on the raiders. They were going to be caught like rats in a trap! As soon as they saw us, they scattered, tried to escape, but we had cut them off. So they ran straight at us, straight at our lines. I tell you all nothing human could ever move so quickly. And their war-cries, their evil faces, it was like every single nightmare racing towards you.

'My men and I held firm, though there were some I tell you that didn't, and we fired and fired until our shotgun-barrels grew so hot they burned our hands. Our shot plucked their front-most ranks from their feet, but still the rest came for us, not a glance at their fellows, and sliced through our lines. One of them, his armour covered in blades, stuck the man next to me with a bayonet and would have done for me next if I had not smashed him in the side of his head with the butt of my gun. He looked fearsome but, trust me, his skull broke easier than any man's and I saw examples enough!'

The young officers clustered around the table laughed at that. They were fascinated by Marcher's exploits; he who had actually met the enemy face-to-face and not merely watched them on scopes a thousand miles distant.

Not every patron in the junior officers' mess, however, shared their enthusiasm for the boastful sub-lieutenant who had attracted so much attention in such a short time. Those who did not sat quietly, though, waiting patiently for their moment. The evening progressed and Marcher retold his story over and over. Marcher was being stood his drinks by his listeners and grew steadily merrier, and more flamboyant, with each retelling, grabbing bottles and mugs for props and leaping upon tables and chairs, to the delight of his audience. This, he felt, this was the taste of glory that he had craved. This was the life for which he was destined.

It grew late. Many of Marcher's earlier listeners had retired for the night and he finally rose from the table to turn in. It was then that three older officers appeared before him.

'Mister Marcher,' one of them said. Marcher focused on the speaker.

'Lieutenant Roche,' he replied unsteadily. 'Sir.'

'Not leaving already, are you? My friends and I were so hoping to hear your story ourselves.'

They urged him back to his seat and Marcher, seeing no harm in it, launched into it one last time.

ASPHAR HID UNDERNEATH the gantry within the hold of his cargo scow. He did not bother to get back inside his container anymore. The first few times he had sneaked out, he had conscientiously returned to it and bolted it back up from the inside, but now there seemed little point. None of the few crew aboard bothered to come back into the hold. Asphar could see the suits they would have worn in the intersection airlock and they had been untouched. Out here he was closer at least to their emergency air canisters, which he was now dependent upon. Even if his canister hadn't broken he would have been out of air nearly a day ago.

Asphar wondered if the patriarch had known how long it would take the Imperial men to get back to their stronghold. He wondered also if the patriarch knew that the igniters they had been given were calibrated to too short a time period. He had scouted out what he could of the ship, there was no way he could be clear of it within the time assumed. He had reprogrammed them, but the questions still hung in his mind. He had asked himself whether he should warn the star warriors in the other ships, but then the patriarch had told him nothing about them. Even if he knew which ships they were in, if they even existed, then he had no means to communicate with them. It had seemed so straightforward to him back on Bahani, but here, on his own, it wasn't so clear. Even if the air had been enough, even if he had escaped, how would he get back home? The

Imperium was leaving Bahani for good. Even if he could stow away again, no ship would take him home. How would the patriarch know if the star warriors had succeeded if no one ever visited the planet again?

The answer was that he wouldn't. And therefore, it must be that it did not matter to him whether they succeeded or failed.

'WAKE UP, MISTER Marcher.' Senior Armsman Vickers drummed his baton across the cell's bars. The young man splayed across the bunk inside began to stir. Vickers watched as Marcher struggled back to consciousness.

Commander Ward had ordered Vickers to keep an eye on the boy; make sure that he did not fall foul of the predations of his colleagues. In plain words, Commander Ward had said; give him the liberty to be as loud and obnoxious as he could be. Vickers, of course, had no choice but to accept, though he had no enthusiasm in playing babysitter to a troublemaker. Now in contrast, Vickers felt quite amiably disposed to the sub-lieutenant; though he doubted it was a sentiment that many other of the command officers shared.

He had been in the junior officers' mess the night before. He had seen Roche, Crichell and Aster go over to Marcher determined to provoke him into a fight. Marcher, full of himself as much as the drink, did not need much encouragement to say something from which the command officers could infer insult. After some pushing and shoving the desired brawl broke out and Crichell and Aster grabbed Marcher and tried to hold him still as Roche drew back his fist to give the arrogant upstart something to remember him by. Vickers had almost intervened then, but he delayed a moment to glance at the other officers in the mess and fix them to their chairs. By the time he looked around again: Aster's nose was running with his own blood, Crichell was clutching his belly and Marcher was grappling for Roche's throat.

Roche had thought that Marcher, tired and drunk, would be easily bested. Roche, Vickers reflected, was an idiot. He and his aging cronies were out-of-shape, overweight from long hours seated in front of their consoles on the bridge; Marcher was young, in his physical prime, and all the drink did for him was to stop him holding back. Roche tried to play by the rules, those unspoken boundaries of one officer settling his differences with another. Marcher's fighting instincts, meanwhile, still burned from the dreadful combat before where it was kill or be killed. Every part of his body was a weapon; anywhere he could hit was a target. Roche tripped back and hit the ground hard, Crichell took a glass to the face, Aster tried to grab Marcher and had his arm broken for his trouble. It was only when Marcher took Roche's head in his hands and started to smash it repeatedly against the deck that Vickers finally needed to pull him away; the boy swearing and cursing the command officers as he went.

It had been a job very well done; now that the command officers had been humiliated in their own attempts at 'below deck' justice they would turn to Guir and Guir would have to beg favour from Ward. Marcher could have had quite a career aboard ship, Vickers reflected as the young officer rolled from the bunk and struggled to his feet. But not aboard the *Relentless*, no. There was nowhere on the *Relentless* for officers like him any more.

'SIR,' LIEUTENANT COMMANDER Guir began, 'before we finish, there is one other matter I would like to raise with you.'

'What is it, Mister Guir?' Ward replied. He had decided to call Guir into his study for the shift hand-over for a change. The staring eyes of the dead animals always put the man on edge, Ward had noticed. Perhaps he feared having his own head up there one day.

'It relates to the conduct of one of the junior officers, a Sub-Lieutenant Marcher, sir.'

'Marcher, I've heard of him. The young man who distinguished himself in the action on the *Gloriana Vance*. Yes, there may be great things in that man's future.'

'Ah, yes, sir.' Guir paused for a moment, weighting his tone carefully. 'It's that young man's future that I would like to discuss.'

'Go on.'

'Though he undoubtedly... excelled himself in that action, more recent events cast a new pall over his conduct. At this very moment he's in the brig after having assaulted and severely injured three of my officers in the junior officers' mess last night.'

'My' officers, Ward noted Guir's slip.

'He was drunk and abusive,' Guir carried on. 'He and his friends set about them when one of them asked him to behave as an officer. The three are all currently still under the care of the medicae. It's a very serious matter, sir.'

'Of course it is, Mister Guir. Very serious. Let us make a full investigation of it. Have it all out in the open. Get all the facts.'

'Not advisable, sir. Making a dispute amongst officers too public. Would set a bad example for the ordinary crewmen. But I have had more general reports from officers of Marcher's poor conduct: dereliction of duty, insubordination, a failure to carry out orders–'

'A few subjective assessments from older officers touched by envy, perhaps? Afraid of being outstripped by a more able man?'

'I think not, sir. Why even upon the *Gloriana* he disobeyed direct orders to fall back when he was first attacked.'

'With commendable results, though, wouldn't you say?'

Guir hesitated. Ward toyed with the idea of letting him twist in the wind, the officers who had given Guir their backing were demanding he get rid of this arrogant young nuisance who had shaken their own vaunted self-image, and he had promised he would. To go back empty-handed would make him look weak. Shake their support. But not enough, Ward decided. It might push Guir to something desperate and, Ward knew, Guir and his officers were more valuable to him than one lucky sub-lieutenant. He would stick to his plan.

'But then, perhaps you are right.' Ward continued. 'Perhaps Mister Marcher is a little too young. A little too cocksure. Perhaps he has... ruffled a few too many feathers aboard. Perhaps his career would benefit from an alternate posting. Perhaps there are arguments both ways. I feel it very much depends?'

'Depends on what?'

'Are you still curious as to when, if at all, our vacant captaincy may be filled?'

'Ah… no, of course not.'

'And are there any… concerns that you have about my command that you might consider raising to a higher authority sometime in the future?'

'The officers and I have complete confidence in you, sir.'

'Good.'

Commander Ward turned back to his desk leaving silence between them. After a moment, Guir spoke.

'And about the other matter, sir?'

'That matter?' Ward looked up. 'Upon reflection, I feel the arguments on one side weigh heavier than the other. Don't you agree?'

'Yes, sir.'

'Dismissed.' Guir nodded and made to leave. 'Oh, and Lieutenant Commander, do tell "your" officers to watch what happens to Marcher with a keen eye. What happens to him is just a fraction of what I could do to each one of them. If they should venture any doubt about my command in the future.'

Guir left then. Ward contacted Vickers and told him to put the endgame into effect. Sub-Lieutenant Marcher had served his purpose and now was merely a liability. His actions had brought the officers back to their first officer, more even, for they would be grateful to him for the young man's removal. Now, his fate must serve as a cautionary example to the rest.

Ward did intend thereafter to turn in, however he found himself standing in the middle of the room, staring into the eyes of the head of a white-crested lolx. Did he feel any qualms of conscience about what was about to happen to young Mister Marcher? No, he decided, Marcher had been his creation and so was his to deconstruct when he had been used for his purpose.

In any case, there was too much of the hero about Marcher; the *Relentless* was not the place for heroes any more. The *Relentless* had a glorious history, but that is just what it was: history. Ward wanted only obedience; it was more reliable than heroism.

COMMANDER WARD WAS still at his desk when Senior Armsman Vickers reported back to him.

'Is it done?' Ward demanded, without looking up.

Vickers did not reply instantly. Ward looked him in the eye and saw the spark there.

'Do not catch the idea of defiance from young Mister Marcher, senior armsman,' Ward said carefully. 'You know what it would cost you.'

'Yes, sir.'

'Is it done?'

'There was no need, sir. He had some hidden already.'

'Did he really?' Ward smiled at that, his first honest smile in days. Now there was irony. Absolute irony.

BETRAYAL, ASPHAR RAGED, that was the only word for it. The patriarch had used him. He did not care whether he lived or died, whether he succeeded or not. Asphar could imagine the chaos after the Imperium's departure. The Bahani would fight over what little was left, tearing themselves apart because the real enemy was no longer within their grasp. It

would be then that the patriarch would emerge
from his sanctuary, his mouth full of lies. He would
tell the weary people the story of his star warriors,
the brave youths taken from every corner of Bahani
who had struck a blow against the detested
Imperium. A blow in the name of the Bahani people, all of them united. He would have the families
present as proof, who would speak with tears of
their pride for their sons, lost to them but chosen by
the Emperor, while those same sons floated long-
dead in the cargo containers that the patriarch had
made their coffins.

Who of the Bahani would not love that story?
Would not praise the patriarch for his wisdom?
Would not chant his name as he so humbly
accepted the leadership of the people and vowed
that the sacrifice of the star warriors would not be in
vain?

Asphar had to return to Bahani; he had to expose
the patriarch for the false priest of the Emperor that
he was. He could not be allowed to profit so from
his lies. But how, Asphar fumed, could he make his
way back?

He could give himself up. He could walk through
to the scow's crew cabin and turn himself over to
them, praying that they would not shoot him out of
hand. Could he not be of use to them? The patriarch
would lead the Bahani people in their hate of the
Imperium; if the Imperium took Asphar back they
could expose the patriarch and break his power.

Yet would the Imperium even care? They had taken
what they wished from Bahani and left the remains.
Forget the patriarch, Asphar reasoned, he owed him
nothing, but still it was the Imperium who had

committed the greater crime here, the devastation of Bahani and its people. The Emperor would want them punished, more so because they had inflicted this wrong under His name. Should he then carry out the mission as he was told as their proper punishment? Then perhaps, if the Emperor willed, somehow return to Bahani and then expose the patriarch for what he was.

Expose the patriarch, perhaps, but what then for Bahani? If the patriarch really could unite them, save them from the fate to which the Imperium had consigned them, could Asphar then allow himself to tear that down? Was the sacrifice of his people the price of his revenge? Asphar thought of his family, his worried mother, his stern father, they would be lost too. But then it had been they who had given him over to the patriarch, had convinced their son that the patriarch did His will. Had they known? Had they suspected that the priest's promise that the star warriors would return had been deceit? Had they been blind to it? Had they betrayed him? If they did... had they been right?

The simplest course, Asphar knew, was to do what they willed: sit and wait, breath by breath, as his air ran down. Maybe then the Emperor would come for him; maybe He could make it clear. But Asphar could not allow himself to end that way. The patriarch and the Imperium were criminals both. They had both used him, consumed his life to benefit themselves. Asphar's head pounded, his soul pulled first one way and then another. What should he do?

IN HIS CELL, Marcher sat devastated scrolling through the charges against him: endangerment of crew, endangerment of ship, smuggling of alien technology. He could barely swallow. His stomach felt like a yawning pit.

'They were trophies, Mister Vickers. That was all. I brought them back as trophies of the victory. Our victory.'

'A pistol, some kind of electro-knife, a half a dozen more items we can't even identify. It's xenotech. Strictly forbidden. You can never tell what they might do, what they might be carrying. In a closed environment such as this ship; can't tell what they might be capable of.'

'I can't deny I brought them onboard, but it was just a few pieces. I had a right!' Marcher flared. 'They were taken in battle!'

'If you admit it, then at least the first officer has some discretion on what might become of you. It will be bad, yes, but if you try to fight it then you leave him no choice. You'll be executed.'

Marcher sagged. 'Death… or disgrace?'

'Mister Marcher,' Vickers said, not unkindly, 'let me give you some advice.'

IN THE DAYS following the battle with the eldar, the convoy, with the *Relentless* alongside, made the rest of the journey to their first destination, the Reeza-class Orbital Station above the planet 42 Mai T. There the machinery and men carried by the *Gloriana Vance* would allow the factories to sprout up across the planet's surface as they had done millennia before upon Bahani. The *Spur* was to continue on with the rest of the convoy, carrying news of the loss of its sister ships back to Battlefleet Command at Emcor.

As the *Relentless* stood guard over the transfer of
material from the *Gloriana Vance* to the station a
small reassignment of personnel took place. A disgraced midshipman had to be ferried to his new
berth on one of the cargo scows.

ASPHAR STOOD ON tip-toe in the hold, peering
through the porthole at the grey and white orbital
station that covered the sky like a web. This was it.
The stronghold that the patriarch had described. He
had survived. He had made his journey, he had
been tested and at his darkest times, he had faced
his doubt, his weakness, but the Emperor had
shown him his path. He had chosen; he would ful-
fil the mission that he had been sent here to
perform.

He set the bomb's timer and ran.

MARCHER SAT QUIETLY at the back of the shuttle as it
made its final docking manoeuvres. The rest of the
passenger compartment was empty aside from a
single crate that contained all his possessions. After
he had entered his plea, the ship's commissar had
sped through the remaining proceedings like a shot.
In light of his previous meritorious conduct and
admission of guilt, the ultimate penalty was not
requested. He was a lucky man, the commissar had
told him.

'Midshipman,' the pilot's voice crackled over the
vox. 'The airlock is sealed. Transfer now.'

Marcher floated to the airlock and went through.
Through the shuttle window he had seen the ugly,
snub-nosed profile of the cargo scow that was to be
his new assignment. He'd been told he was lucky.

After that moment, though, he could no longer believe it.

THE TIMER STRUCK zero. The igniter fired. For a millisecond the cargo hold contained the blast and then it ruptured and flew apart. Each fragment of the mineral the scow held was instantly superheated and shattered. The scow designated Terminus Three flared like a new star and then was extinguished. The small, deadly shards of rock blossomed out like shrapnel, puncturing hull and flesh alike. The final blow of the abandoned people of Bahani had been struck.

Asphar did not see the explosion he had created. He had already leapt from the scow towards the station. He had leapt and left his old life behind. He was Bahani, born and raised. He had given his life to cleanse them of their sins. Should the explosion catch him, should he smash into the station hull, should he be blown off into space, then he owed them no less. Should the Emperor decide, though, that He might grant Asphar another life, and he was saved, then the Bahani would have no claim on that.

THE INITIAL EXPLOSION within the cargo scow Terminus Three, and the following chain-reaction detonation of the mineral it carried, rocked both the station and the rest of the convoy. The scows closest to it, Terminus Two and Four, both took critical damage, though their crews were able to make it to the sanctuary pods and survive. The same was not true of the six merchant crew of Terminus Three who were killed instantly. All of them, as many of the rest of the convoy crew, were Bahani born.

The damage to the polar terminal of the station was significant. Debris from the explosion impacted and compromised over a dozen sections within the terminal causing significant loss of life in each. Nearly ten per cent of casualties were Imperial officials, the highest ranking of whom was Governor Andersen. The remainder of casualties were indentured labourers or conscripts either attached to the station or awaiting transfer to the planet below.

The Battlefleet warships, *Relentless* and *Spur*, were sufficiently distant from the explosion to be unaffected. Both ships deployed their transports to help rescue what survivors they could, who included one Bahani merchant crewman who had been caught outside the scow and had leapt clear.

The *Relentless* however did suffer the loss of a single junior officer. His name was Lieutenant Roche, who had been reassigned from bridge duty under a cloud to aid in the transfers from the *Gloriana Vance* to the station. He had been on a scouting inspection on the station when that section was breached. His colleagues considered him doubly unfortunate as he was a replacement for that duty. The original officer assigned was one sub-lieutenant (now Midshipman) Marcher, who due to other circumstances had been transferred off the *Relentless*. At the time of the explosion, Midshipman Marcher was in the process of taking command of Terminus Seven and was unharmed.

Governor Kaizen, taking command of the station, swore that, explosion or no explosion, he would brook no delay in the full installation of extraction and processing infrastructure onto the surface of the verdant planet 42 Mai T, known as Msuti to the workers who had recently been transported there. Initial surveys had suggested that Msuti could sustain full mining operations for at least three thousand years before it would become exhausted and uninhabitable. Not long in galactic terms, but it would do until the Imperium found the next one.

THE HERACLITUS
EFFECT

Graham McNeill

THE MONSTER WITH the patchwork face was right behind him. He could hear it crashing through the overgrown forest with bludgeoning force, trampling the fruits of their invention with every giant stride. He kept running. Running was all he could do. He couldn't fight such a terrible thing, it was too much.

Magos Third Class Evlame fled through the forest in panicked flight, a forest that had once been a place of wonder and miracles, a place that had literally blossomed as a result of their labours. Every day spent here had been a day spent with the thrill of discovery and pride in their achievements, but now it was a place of horror, a blood-drenched nightmare of dismembered bodies and death.

Evlame's breath came in sharp spikes in his chest, his overlarge frame unused to such exertion and his heartbeat pounding in his ears as he ran. Massively wide leaves and sharp branches whipped past him, cutting his face and hands as he pushed through the forest. The ripe smell of new growth filled his nostrils and ruptured fruits, larger than his head, hung dripping from branches shredded with gunfire.

The sweet smell of pulped vegetation was almost overpowering, catching in the back of his throat as his lungs heaved in panicked breath after panicked breath. Breathless, Evlame paused to get his bearings, seeking something familiar in the landscape around him.

Swollen trees with trunks thicker than a Titan's leg surrounded him, their tops lost in the claws of mist that hung in the stagnant, moist atmosphere. Drooping branches laden with vivid growths in a rainbow of colours hung almost to the ground and gleaming chemical atomisers stood amongst the trees like the silver sculptures he'd seen in shrine parks, their waving, articulated limbs dispensing microscopic amounts of the Heraclitus strain into the atmosphere in controlled puffs of vapour.

A bright yellow generator hummed at the base of a towering, copper-barked tree laden with thick golden orbs that were wonderfully sweet and nutritious. The generator was stencilled with the number seventeen, which told him he was to the north of the Adeptus Mechanicus compound and home.

He heard the crunch of a heavy footfall beyond the limit of sight and froze in place as he tried to pinpoint the source. The reek of spoiled meat drifted on the wind, a rank, unpleasant odour after the fragrances he was used to in the forest. His eyes scanned left and right.

And then he saw it…

A glint of sunlight on armour, a reflection on dulled steel and a glimpse of his hunter's grey, nightmare face. Though he had only the briefest flicker of the features, he wished for no more complete a view, for the dead face was the horror of a badly maimed mannequin, the bloody remnants of a bomb blast victim.

Evlame turned and ran, knowing the genhanced vegetation underfoot and rampant growth of the forest would make stealthy movement impossible. He fled south, following the route of ribbed copper cables as they snaked through the humid forest like indigenous serpents. Pungent mulch carpeted the forest floor and Evlame felt like he was running in some terrible nightmare, where the monster is forever at your shoulder and your feet move as though through the most viscous glue.

Tears and snot covered his face as he blundered onwards, praying to the God-Emperor and every saint he could think of to deliver him from this terrible killer. He risked a glance over his shoulder, but could see nothing behind him. His foot connected with something solid and his world cartwheeled as he tumbled to the ground.

Evlame hit hard, the breath driven from his lungs by the impact and bright light exploded before his eyes. The cloying texture of fruit mash filled his mouth, as well as a pungent smell of opened meat. He spat seeds and fruit flesh, shaking his head as he pushed himself upright.

He knelt in an open clearing of enormous, ovoid fruit, most reaching to his chest in height and at least as wide – their enhanced growth rendering them swollen and ripe.

A headless body lay beside him, the ragged stump of neck still enthusiastically pumping blood onto the dark, almost black, soil. Another corpse lay amid the dripping carcass of an exploded fruit, its chest cavity ripped open as though an explosive charge had detonated within. Other bodies lay in similar states of terrible ruin – heads crushed, limbs removed or torsos ripped apart.

Evlame's mouth dropped open in mute horror, unable to take in such brutal, visceral evidence of murder. He pushed himself upright and set off towards the habitat domes, following the twisting cables like a lifeline. Rasping breath, like that of a consumptive, hissed behind him and he whimpered in terror, awaiting the blow that would split him open as surely as the ripened, overlarge fruits that surrounded him.

Such a blow never landed and he pushed his burning legs onwards, trampling through the soft mulch of pulped fruit and bloody earth. He sobbed with every step, his limbs flailing and his eyes streaming with tears of raw, unmanning fear.

Through his tears he saw the gleam of the silverskinned habitat domes between the thick trunks of the towering forest and aimed his flight towards salvation. Surely Magos Szalin would know what to do? An entire company of cybernetically enhanced Tech-Guard were stationed at the Golbasto Facility and he began to laugh uncontrollably at the thought of reaching safety, his hysteria bubbling up like a geyser.

Evlame emerged into the open and stumbled across the automated firebreaks and pesticide barriers that protected the facility from the rampant growth of the genhanced forest. After the gloomy, spectral twilight of the undergrowth, the glare of the planet's warm yellow sun was dazzlingly bright and he shielded his eyes as he staggered and swayed like a drunk towards the Adeptus Mechanicus experimentation facility, the domes blurred through his lens of tears.

He saw movement and heard voices. He wiped his sodden face with the sleeve of his robe and wept in joy as he saw scores of massively broad warriors in burnished battle plate, their bulk unmistakable as anything other than Adeptus Astartes.

The Space Marines had come!

Relief lent his battered limbs new strength and he ran towards the facility with fresh vigour, anxious to have these brave protectors of mankind between him and the monster that pursued him. Evlame ran like a man possessed, smelling an acrid chemical stink from the smashed domes and seeing flame-shot smoke as it billowed into the clear sky.

Bodies littered the ground and the skins of the domes were pocked with bullet holes.

Clearly the monster had not come alone...

But now the Adeptus Astartes were here, there was surely nothing to fear, for what could stand against such perfect warriors – their flesh enhanced by the artifice of the Emperor and fragments of His greatness encoded into their very bones. Such holy vision had served as the model for their work on Golbasto and Evlame longed to speak to these warriors of legend to tell them of the achievements wrought here.

'Over here!' he yelled, his voice hoarse and rasping after his lung-searing run through the forest. 'Help! It's coming after me. There's another one in the forest!'

The armoured giants turned at the sound of his voice, their massive, oversized weapons trained on him in an instant. He saw a confusing mix of armour marks and colours and laughed as he shook his head at their mistake.

'No, no! It's Magos Third Class Evlame!' he shouted, the brief vigour lent to his limbs fading and his steps becoming more uneven. He laughed and waved his arms like a madman, simultaneously amused and terrified at the irony of nearly being gunned down by his rescuers. 'I work here, I minister to the atomiser machines of the forest! I...'

His words trailed off as he dropped to his knees, his strength spent. He sank onto his rump, head tilted to the sun and his chest heaving as he sucked in shuddering breaths.

Evlame heard crunching footfalls and a chill fell across him as he was enveloped in the broad shadows of the towering warriors. He squinted into the glare of the sky and wiped the back of his hand across his tear-swollen eyes.

A trio of cruel faces cut from cold steel stared down at him, scarred and battle worn. One warrior's face was that of a killer, hostile and unforgiving. His skull was partly shaven and a ragged mohawk ran across its centre. Another warrior in dark plate wore his long black hair in a tight scalp lock, hooded eyes deep set in angular, pale features.

Half the final warrior's face was a ruined, knotted fist of crude augmetics, a glowing blue gem where his left eye ought to have been. His other eye glittered with cruel amusement and his close-cropped dark hair was smeared with blood spatters.

The one with the killer's face itched to do him harm and Evlame felt a burgeoning horror swell within him as the truth of the matter began to dawn on him.

No Astartes these, but...

'You work here?' said the warrior with the ravaged face, squatting down on his haunches before him. Evlame nodded, his jaw slack with terror and he felt himself lose control of his bodily functions. The warrior reached out and took hold of his chin. Even in his fear-demented state, Evlame was Mechanicus enough to notice that the arm was fashioned from shimmering silver, a prosthetic quite unlike anything he had seen before. The digits were cold and smooth and articulated without recourse to any joints he could see.

The icy grip turned his head left and right, as though he were being regarded like a specimen in a jar.

'Ardaric,' said the warrior with the strange arm, 'has Cycerin got everything we need?'

'He's almost done extracting the information from the senior magos,' answered the warrior in the black armour with jagged red crosses painted across his shoulder guards. 'The cogitators were smashed before we got to him, but the fool didn't think to wipe his own cranial memory coils.'

'And the canisters we came for?'

'Servitors are loading them onto the Stormbird as we speak.'

The killer with the mohawk said, 'Kill this last one, Honsou, and let's be on our way.'

The warrior named Honsou lifted his gaze to something behind Evlame. 'Not yet, Grendel. I think I'll let my new champion finish what he started.'

The warrior released Evlame and pushed himself to his feet. It took an effort of will for Evlame to tear his eyes from Honsou's incredible silver arm.

He heard the whine of automatic targeting servos behind him and turned to see the incinerator units that had been used to contain the forest's expansion aiming at a singular figure that marched across the scorched borders of the Mechanicus facility.

Evlame whimpered in terror as the patchwork-faced monster that had killed the rest of his colleagues walked towards him. Its pace was leisurely, though he could see a fire of agony in its storm-cloud eyes, as though its every step was painful.

Like most of the others in this terrible group, it wore Astartes battle plate the colour of bare metal with chevron trims of yellow and black. The closer it came, the more he could see its aquiline features were drawn in a mask of anguish.

Its skin clung to its skull but loosely, as though ill-fitting and not intended to clothe the skull beneath it. Wire stitching criss-crossed its ashen face and Evlame felt he was looking into the eyes of a madman staring through a mask of stolen flesh.

'No...' he whispered. 'Please don't... I never did anything to hurt you...'

The leathery-faced monster leaned down and said, 'I live in pain. Why should you not?'

TRAVELLING THROUGH THE empyrean was something Honsou of the Iron Warriors never enjoyed, for the placing his fate in the hands of others and the lack of influence he could bring to bear should something go wrong was anathema to him.

The strategium of the *Warbreed* thrummed with noise, the pounding beat of distant hammers and far-off machines vibrating the deck plates with industrious motion.

The ship had belonged to Honsou's former master and had been moored above Medrengard for a timeless age. Honsou and his few hundred warriors had travelled from the wrecked fortress of Khalan-Ghol to the impossible landmark of the Crooked Tower in order to claim the vessel as their own.

A twisted spire of jagged black rock, the numberless steps of the Crooked Tower spiralled downwards into the bowels of Perturabo's deepest forges and soared to the lost stars that orbited the dead world of the Iron Warriors.

They had climbed for an age, each footfall a lifetime and a heartbeat in the same breath, and the blasted earth of Medrengard had fallen away until they climbed to the stars themselves. Blackness enveloped them and a host of starships surrounded them, drifting in the utter dark and still of space.

The sheer impossibility of their physical surroundings had not fazed Honsou, and he had not been surprised when the steep stairs had led straight to the open hatches of the *Warbreed*.

The mighty ship had once taken the fire of the warmaster to the followers of the false Emperor in days now ancient to those who had once defied them. Its guns had bombarded the last vestiges of life from Isstvan V and its orbital strikes had helped tear open the walls of the Imperial palace on Terra.

Its pedigree was mighty and its history proud, and Honsou could think of no finer vessel to take from the silent fleet berthed around the tower's summit.

Hissing vapours billowed and mighty pistons wheezed and ground up and down at the edges of the vaulted chamber, its walls arched with great girders of brazen metal and hung with ragged war banners of gold and black.

Cabals of hardwired crew submerged in vats of oxygen-rich oils regulated the workings of the ship and hissing mechanical creatures with multi-jointed legs drifted over the glistening pools with crackling cables trailing into the fluid.

The strategium tapered towards its front, the deck crew stationed here and plugged into the ship's vitals more like ordinary humans, tending to the ship's needs as it negotiated a passage between the stars through the swirling maelstrom of the immaterium. At the apex of the strategium stood the hulking, purple-robed form of Adept Cycerin, his mecha-organic flesh and kinship with the raw matter of the warp making him the perfect steersman.

'How much longer?' asked Honsou, his voice easily carrying the length of the strategium.

Cycerin turned his massive, machine-bulk to face Honsou, his swollen head buzzing with living circuitry and organic techno-viral strains. Slithering, blackened arms writhed like snakes from the tattered sleeves of his robes, the flesh and machine parts running like waxen mercury to form withered digits like mechanised quills.

Cycerin's green and yellow eyes brightened with a pulse of irritation as his hands described a series of complex motions in the suddenly misty air before him. Honsou stared at the plotting table before him as the adept's angular script appeared on the hololithic slate.

As it was every time he asked, the answer was frustratingly vague, but then what had he expected? Travel through the warp was unpredictable, even aboard a ship with a pilot uniquely qualified to ply its treacherous depths and who possessed a sense for the currents of the immaterium keener than the most aberrant patriarch of the Navis Nobilite.

Once, Cycerin had been Adeptus Mechanicus, but following his capture on the far distant world of Hydra Cordatus, he had been elevated from his paltry hybridised form of man and machine to something infinitely greater. Strands of the Obliterator virus had been merged with his augmetics and his fundamental gene structure, rendering him into something post-human and far beyond simple cybernetics.

The techno-virus had made him superior, but it had also made him arrogant.

Honsou's memories of the Hydra Cordatus campaign felt as though they belonged to a previous life. Much had changed since then and his remembrance of the bloody siege had blurred into one unending hurricane of battle that had fanned the smouldering coal of his resentment into a roaring inferno of ambition.

Schemes of murder circled like carrion birds in his mind, threads woven from fragments of his new champion's fractured memories and the libraries worth of knowledge in Cycerin's cybernetic brain coming together to set them on their current course of revenge…

Many aboard the Warbreed thought him mad to pursue such a plan so soon after the bloody battle against Berossus and Toramino, but Honsou knew he would not be satisfied until he had inflicted the most wretched humiliations on the one enemy to escape him.

'If you want to hurt the fox, first strike at its cubs…' he whispered.

He resumed his pacing of the deck, his bearing that of a caged predator, his face a mask of irritation and anticipation. It chafed him to have set such grand designs in motion, but then be forced to wait while such mundane concerns such as warp travel forced delays upon them.

'Pacing won't make us travel faster,' said Cadaras Grendel, who stood behind him, his gleaming bolter held lightly in one scarred hand, an oiled cleaning rag in the other.

'I know,' said Honsou, 'but it gives me something to do instead of just waiting.'

'You mean instead of training with your new champion.'

Honsou stopped in his pacing and said, 'I tasked Ardaric Vaanes with his training.'

'And that's the only reason you're not down there in the battle deck?'

'Of course, what of it?'

'It's not him,' said Grendel at last. 'It's not Ventris. It has his likeness, but it's not him.'

'I know that,' snapped Honsou. 'I'm not stupid, Grendel.'

'I don't blame you for not wanting to look at him,' said Grendel, wiping the cloth along the hard edges of the gun. 'After all, he's the spit of the only warrior to ever beat you.'

'Ventris did not beat me!' shouted Honsou, rounding on his captain of arms, a warrior who had formerly served his enemy, Lord Berossus. Honsou's axe leapt to his hands, its edge lethal and hungry.

Cadaras Grendel didn't flinch as the axe came up to his neck.

'Whatever you say, Warsmith,' said the warrior, pushing the blade of the axe away with the barrel of his bolter. The muzzle passed before Honsou's face and he saw a smile crease Grendel's face as he stared into it. 'He didn't beat you, but then... you didn't beat him either. And it's your fortress that's a pile of rubble, eh?'

Honsou turned away from the confrontation, irritated that Grendel had managed to rile him with such ease. Ever since the destruction of Khalan-Ghol on Medrengard, Honsou's temper had been on a short fuse. The merest slight against his victory over the combined armies of Berossus and Toramino filled his blood with a surge of killing rage.

In any case, Grendel was right.

Each time he looked upon the face of his new champion (the newborn as it insisted on being called) he could see the features of the warrior who'd defied him and then thrown his offer to join him back in his face.

Uriel Ventris and his companion were of the Ultramarines Chapter, but what crime they had committed to be banished to a daemon world in the Eye of Terror he didn't know. However they had come to Medrengard, they had proved to be resourceful enemies.

They had survived the Halls of the Savage Morticians and freed the Heart of Blood, the mighty daemon imprisoned within the heart of Khalan-Ghol.

Honsou took a deep breath and said, 'By all the twelve sigils of the Rapturous Ruin, you almost make me wish Forrix and Kroeger weren't dead.'

'Who?'

'Former captains who also commanded elements of the Warsmith's grand company back on Hydra Cordatus,' said Honsou, before adding pointedly. 'They're long dead now.'

'Did you kill them?'

Honsou shook his head. 'No, though I would have if they hadn't managed it themselves.'

'What happened to them?'

'Forrix went up against a Titan. He lost,' laughed Honsou, his good humour restored at the memory of his rival's obliteration by the great war-machine's guns.

'And Kroeger? What did he take on?'

'I don't know,' admitted Honsou. 'Forrix told me he vanished through some kind of warp rift, but when we broke down the siege works, we found a body in his dugout.'

'Was it Kroeger?'

Honsou shrugged. 'Maybe, I didn't bother to find out. Kroeger was gone, what did I care where? With them both dead, the Warsmith's army and his fortress were mine.'

'Until Toramino blasted it from under you,' reminded Grendel with a viperous smile.

Honsou smiled grimly. 'Aye, he did, but he hadn't reckoned with the Heart of Blood.'

'No one did. Not even you,' said Grendel, his normally gruff voice hushed at the mention of the ancient daemon. Honsou could well understand Grendel's tone, shuddering as he remembered rousing the daemon by kicking its head in rage at Ventris's escape.

'No,' he said, 'not even me.'

Fortunately, the creature had sensed that his flesh had once briefly hosted a creature of the warp and ignored him, instead wreaking its bloodlust on Toramino's army beyond the walls.

The slaughter and destruction the daemon had unleashed was unlike anything Honsou had ever seen before, its ancient fury deeper than the darkest chasm in Perturabo's lair. It had reduced everything before it utterly to ruin and Medrengard's blazing black sun had gorged on the souls released into the dead sky.

'Let's hope you haven't overlooked anything this time, eh?' said Grendel.

'I haven't,' promised Honsou.

'We'll see.'

'One day I'll kill you for your presumption,' said Honsou. 'You know that, don't you?'

'You'll try,' replied Grendel. 'Whether you succeed... well, that'll be an interesting day.'

Honsou ignored Grendel's challenge and asked, 'The newborn? You said it's with Vaanes?'

Grendel nodded. 'Aye, he and his misfits are training it on the battle deck below.'

'Good.'

'No,' chuckled Grendel. 'There's nothing good about that thing at all.'

THREE WARRIORS SURROUNDED the crouching figure in the centre of the chamber, their weapons raised before them. If their victim felt threatened, he gave no sign, his posture relaxed and his mien unconcerned at the potential violence to be unleashed against him. The three attackers were clad in armour, though no one suit resembled another in colour or repair.

One suit was a battered grey, another a faded white and the last a gleaming black. All that bound the three in any visible form of confraternity were the red crosses painted on their shoulder guards, but even those unifying marks had largely disappeared as paint flaked or was scraped away by battle damage.

Though there were no visible signs of rank, it was clear that the leader of the three was the tall warrior in black armour: Ardaric Vaanes, formerly of the Raven Guard. Vaanes was tall and slender, his bulk massive compared to a mortal, but slight for a Space Marine. Possessed of the strength to shatter bones and bend steel, his speed and poise marked him as more than a simple weapon of brute force.

The warrior to his left, Jeffar San, had once been of the White Consuls, though he now reserved his most bitter hatred for his former battle brothers. Vainglorious masters had stripped his honour from him, yet fierce warrior pride had kept him alive through their attempts to destroy him. Proud and haughty, Jeffar San was a warrior who embodied what it was to be cast from superior clay, his elegant, rapier-like sword held in the guard position.

To his right, Svoljard of the Wolf Brothers – an ill-fated Chapter from the beginning – bounced impatiently from foot to foot, his axe gripped tightly in his meaty fists. Where Vaanes exemplified the swift and sure strike, Svoljard was the wild blow that cut a man in two with a flurry of wild slashes.

All three were killers of men and xenos, warriors whose craft had been honed on a thousand battle-fields under a thousand suns and who had faced the darkest horrors of the galaxy.

Yet none could quell the loathing each felt for the crouching figure between them.

The newborn squatted on one knee, his head bowed as though in some meditative trance and his grey flesh reeking of spoiled food. Unlike the war-riors around him, the newborn was unarmoured, clad only in the flesh sutured to his muscle and bone.

His fists were clenched at his side and his every breath fought for existence.

'Begin,' said Vaanes, twin lightning claws unsheath-ing from his gauntlets.

Svoljard moved first, howling with an ululating war cry and slashing his axe towards the newborn. His target moved without warning, the newborn leaping from his crouched position to somersault backwards over the blow. Vaanes moved to the side, his claws raised as the newborn landed. Svoljard was exposed, his reckless attack overbalancing him, but the newborn spun away from him and batted away Jeffar San's swinging blade with the flat of his palm.

Vaanes saw his opening and thrust with his claws, the crackling energy that normally sheathed his blades deactivated for this training session. The newborn swayed aside from the blow and pistoned the flat of his palm towards Vaanes. The former Raven Guard threw himself back to avoid the blow, but was too slow, the spoiled-meat smell of the newborn's flesh nauseatingly strong as it hammered into his chin.

Even as he reeled from the blow, he knew it had been pulled at the last moment. He shook his head clear of the newborn's stink, wondering briefly what Svoljard's preternaturally sharp senses must be enduring. Perhaps that was why he was fighting with such reckless abandon, the better to end this session quickly...

The Wolf Brother howled as he attacked, his axe slashing in complex arcs as it sought to find a home in the newborn's body. Vaanes cursed as he saw that Svoljard's wild blows had allowed the newborn to break from being surrounded. Jeffar San fought with precise skill, but his thrusts were being hampered by Svoljard's frenzy.

The newborn ducked a decapitating sweep of the Wolf Brother's axe and hammered his elbow into his attacker's side. Had any normal enemy struck such a blow, it would have barely registered on Svoljard, but ceramite plate cracked under the force of it and sent the Wolf Brother crashing to the floor.

Jeffar San had pulled back to marshal his next attack and Svoljard was completely exposed, his throat there to be ripped out.

But the newborn ignored his fallen enemy and spun to face Vaanes as the lightning claws descended to slash him open. Too slow, the newborn threw up his forearm to block the blow, and Vaanes's claws tore down his chest, opening his sheath of flesh and laying bare his glistening musculature.

The newborn howled in agony and dropped to his knees as Jeffar San lunged and thrust his blade between his ribs from behind. The tip of the weapon punched through the newborn's chest and a froth of stinking blood washed down his opened chest.

Svoljard rolled to his feet with a roar of anger and swept his axe high to cleave the newborn from top to bottom, but Vaanes retracted his claws and thundered his fist into the charging warrior's face. Svoljard crashed to the deck, his face a mask of anger and blood where Vaanes had broken his nose.

'Enough!' shouted Vaanes. 'It's over.'

'I'll kill you!' snarled Svoljard, spitting a wad of coagulated blood from between his fanged teeth. 'You shame me in front of his... pet.'

'You shame yourself with your anger,' spat Vaanes. 'Now clean yourself up before we go again.'

Svoljard spat more blood on the deck, but turned and stalked off to the benches at the side of the deck. Vaanes let out a relieved breath as he watched Svoljard's retreating back. Without the discipline he had been used to in his time with his Chapter, the Wolf Brother was becoming more feral and uncontrolled, his anger making him more of a liability than an ally.

'Be careful, Vaanes,' warned Jeffar San, appearing at his side and running a hand through his long blond hair. 'One day he will not hold his rage in check.'

'I know,' replied Vaanes sourly, 'but I have you to watch my back, don't I?'

The White Consul nodded stiffly and sheathed his sword in one smooth motion. 'I swore an oath to do so on that dead world, did I not?'

Vaanes gave a short bark of bitter laughter and said, 'We all swore oaths a long time ago, my friend and look where it's got us.'

Jeffar San did not reply, but bowed stiffly before turning on his heel and marching towards his weapon rack. Vaanes sighed and hung his head as the last of his surviving warriors took his leave.

'You antagonise the warriors who follow you,' said a thick voice behind him. 'I do not think that will foster their loyalty, or is there something I am missing?'

'No,' said Vaanes, turning to see the newborn standing behind him. A raw, sucking sound rippled from his flesh as the dead skin that clothed the newborn reknit itself whole once more.

A crawling yellow glow, like the last light of a wounded sun, seeped from the wounds he and Jeffar San had caused, the warp-born energies that had fuelled this... creature's unnatural growth, keeping him alive despite injuries that would have killed a normal man thrice over.

Such grievous wounds would have put down even one of the Adeptus Astartes, but the newborn barely registered them now.

The newborn followed his gaze and said, 'We travel through the realm of my masters. Here I heal quicker.'

'And you already heal fast,' said Vaanes.

'The power of Chaos is everywhere and grows stronger every day.'

'Spoken like a true pupil.'

'What do you mean?' asked the newborn, his curiosity genuine.

'I mean that sounds like something someone told you rather than something you know.'

'Is there a difference?'

'Of course there is,' said Vaanes, his patience wearing thin at the newborn's insatiable curiosity. He had joined Honsou to train the newborn to fight, not to be his teacher of ethics and knowledge.

'Tell me the difference.'

'It means that you are being told a lot of things, but are learning very little,' said Vaanes.

The newborn considered this for a moment, cocking his head to one side and chewing its bottom lip like a child thinking hard. Vaanes let his eyes drift away from the creature... he still couldn't think of him as a person, not when he had been a child mere months ago.

The fact that he so closely resembled a man he hated didn't help much either.

The last he had seen of Uriel Ventris had been in the mountains of Medrengard as the fool had been about to attack Honsou's fortress with a pack of rabid, cannibalistic monsters at his heel. Though Vaanes had been sure Ventris would perish within the fortress, it appeared that the resourceful captain had prevailed and helped bring down Khalan-Ghol.

'Do you hate me?' asked the newborn suddenly.

'What?' he asked.

'Do you hate me?' repeated the newborn. 'I think you do.'

'Hate you? I don't even know what you really are or what to call you.'

'I don't have a name,' said the newborn. 'I have not earned one yet.'

'You don't earn names, they're given to you when you're born.'

'I remember my birth,' said the newborn.

'You do?'

'Yes.'

'What... what was it like?' asked Vaanes, curious despite himself.

'Painful.'

Vaanes knew little about how creatures such as the newborn were created, save what Ventris had told him when he had sold the lie of honour to his warrior band at the Sanctuary. But he had learned enough to know that the newborn had been little more than a child when the transformation of his entire flesh had begun.

Biological hot-housing, daemonic magic and debased techniques of genetic theft had accelerated his growth with strands of geneseed ripped from the meat and bone of Uriel Ventris. Diabolical suckling within the womb of a daemonic host creature had nourished it and sagging skin carved from the bodies of slaves had clothed him.

Though he had the flesh and physique of a Space Marine, he had the mind of a neophyte.

'Painful…' said Vaanes. 'I imagine it was.'

'Was?' said the newborn, shaking his head. 'It still is. My every waking moment is pain.'

'I know what you mean,' said Vaanes.

'No,' said the newborn, stepping close to him with its teeth bared. 'You don't. I am the broken shards of a human being, Ardaric Vaanes. My every breath is pain. Every beat of my heart is pain. Everything is pain. Why should I be the only one to suffer like this? I want everyone to hurt like I do.'

'And you do a good job of that,' said Vaanes, meeting the angry stare of the newborn, and remembering the horrific, mutilating death of the magos on Golbasto.

'It is all I have,' spat the newborn. 'You have your name and a lifetime of memory, all I have are nightmares and the stolen memories of another.'

'You have Ventris's memories? I didn't know that.'

'Not memories really,' said the newborn, his anger diminishing. 'More like fragments of half-remembered dreams. The world we travel to is one I see in those fragments.'

'Do you know this world's name?' asked Vaanes, intrigued.

'No,' said the newborn, 'but I know it is precious to him. An army of great and terrible hunger came here, but it was defeated.'

'Is that all you know?'

'I think so... I... I... know things of him and I feel the soul of his flesh within me, but...'

'But what?' asked Vaanes.

'But everything I am taught by my masters of the power of Chaos tells me to reject such feelings. I am an instrument of the will of gods that were and ever shall be, a weapon to be used in their service and nothing more.'

'Aren't we all...' said Vaanes, beckoning Svoljard and Jeffar San back to the centre of the battle deck. 'But it does explain something.'

'What?'

'Why we keep beating you,' said Vaanes. 'It's Ventris. Everything about him is part of you. The things that make him who he is are imprinted in your very flesh and as much as Honsou and Grendel try to beat that out of you, it's always going to be there.'

'Are you saying I am imperfect?'

Vaanes laughed. 'That goes without saying, but Ventris's childish sense of right and wrong, good and evil... they're pulling you apart from the inside. You fight fair and that's not how we do things around here.'

Svoljard and Jeffar San rejoined Vaanes and he jabbed his finger into the newborn's chest as he said, 'We fight again and this time no pulling of punches. You had Svoljard at your mercy and you didn't finish him. Don't make that mistake again. Understood?'

'Understood,' growled the newborn, casting a hostile glance at the Wolf Brother.

Once again, the three warriors surrounded the newborn and made ready to fight.

'Now–' began Vaanes.

Before he could finish, the newborn was in motion, his fist smashing into Svoljard's jaw and tearing it off in a shower of blood and splintered bone. The stricken warrior dropped his axe and clutched at his ruined face. Blood jetted from the wound and a horrific, wet scream gurgled from Svoljard's throat.

The axe fell and the newborn swept it up, spinning on his heel to smash it into Jeffar San's breastplate. The blade clove through ceramite plate and ossified bone to lodge deep within the White Consul's chest cavity. Jeffar San's legs buckled and he collapsed to his knees, an awful mask of shock and pain twisting his proud features in horror.

Even as Vaanes registered the speed with which the newborn had moved, he leapt upon him, his bloody fists reaching for his neck.

Vaanes moved in tune with the newborn's attack, swaying backwards and buying himself precious moments of life. He twisted his body along the direction of its lunge.

Razor claws snapped from his gauntlets.

He punched up into the newborn's belly and heaved.

The impaled newborn sailed over him, landing in a crumpled heap on the deck.

Vaanes rolled to his feet as the newborn wailed in pain and Jeffar San fell forwards onto the deck with a solid thump.

Had the fight taken so short a time?

Vaanes drew back his lightning claws into a fighting posture and activated the crackling energy sheath with a thought. The newborn was in killing mood and Vaanes could afford to take no chances.

But it seemed the fight had gone out of the newborn as he pushed himself painfully to his knees. Blood and the familiar oily, yellow glow oozed from the mortal wound at his belly as it closed, but he seemed not to care.

'Was that better?' hissed the newborn, grinning at the suffering he had caused.

'Much better,' said Vaanes.

THE IMPERIAL BATTLESHIP sailed away from the *War-breed*, its enormous bulk a slab of bristling, ancient metal as it plied its stately course through the stars, oblivious to the enemy that passed beneath it. Its name was a mystery, but the threat it represented should any of its surveyors, auspex or escorts discover them was very real indeed.

Ever since Cycerin had brought the ship through the gates of the empyrean, they had followed a stuttering course towards their target, avoiding patrol flotillas, system monitors and listening posts scattered throughout the system.

Now the image of the planet filled the viewing bay, a frigid white orb with ugly blotches of unnatural colour spread over its surface like liver spots on the skull of a withered old man. Honsou neither knew nor cared for its name. That it was known and valued by Ventris was all that mattered.

Honsou smiled as he watched the image of the battleship recede on the plotting table, his fear that the ship would discover them diminishing along with its engine signature. The strategium of the *Warbreed* was subdued, as though their Imperial enemies might somehow hear them from so far away.

'They've missed us!' breathed Cadaras Grendel, gripping the edge of the plotting table with white knuckled hands. 'I don't believe it...'

Honsou nodded and said, 'That was the last one. We're inside their patrol ring now.'

Grendel smiled a predator's grin and shook his head in disbelieving amusement. 'Now all we have to do is worry about the planetary monitor ships. All it'll take is one of them to get so much as a sniff of us and we're dead.'

'That's why we have our guide,' said Honsou, nodding towards the strategium's prow.

Adept Cycerin stood before his iron lectern as always, his hands clasped either side of the newborn's head, who knelt with his back to the monstrously transformed magos. Ardaric Vaanes stood a little to one side of the lectern, grimacing in disgust at the sight of the organic plugs Cycerin's hands had become as they slithered within the back of the newborn's skull.

The newborn's skin rippled with a grotesque undulant motion as the bio-dendrites rooted around in his brain for the information they needed to survive this journey. His eyes fluttered behind tightly squeezed lids and his lips moved in a soundless mantra.

'Does that hurt it?' wondered Grendel.

'Does it matter?' countered Honsou. 'Ventris was here and he knows the deployment protocols of the ships and that means the newborn knows them. Maybe not consciously, but the deployments, the Veritas codes, everything. They're all in there. We need that if we're to get close enough to do what we planned.'

'True enough,' agreed Grendel. 'I'm all for whatever gets us out of here in one piece.'

'Likewise,' said Honsou. 'Though a little risk is never a bad thing, eh?'

'Sometimes I think you like risk too much.'

Honsou nodded and said, 'You might be right. I remember Obax Zakayo said the same thing when we attacked the artillery battery in Berossus's camp.'

'Sensible man,' said Grendel.

'Not really, he betrayed me.'

'He's dead then?'

'Yes, very dead,' agreed Honsou. 'You could learn from him.'

'I learn quick,' said Grendel, 'but you'll bite off more than you can chew one day.'

'Maybe,' shrugged Honsou with a grin. 'But not today.'

Ardaric Vaanes marched towards them along the central nave of the strategium, his attention switching between the image on the viewing bay to the pain of the newborn.

Honsou and Grendel looked up as he approached.

'Well?' asked Honsou.

'Cycerin says that one will do,' he said, pointing to a flicker of light above a point on the planet's equator. 'It's furthest from the ships and is above the largest concentration of xeno vegetation.'

Honsou nodded and fixed his attention on the light, knowing it meant the first step to wreaking a great and terrible vengeance upon Ventris. What he did here would be a blatant challenge, a call to arms that a stickler like Ventris would not be able to resist answering.

The three warriors watched the pinpoint of light grow from a speck in the darkness to something more angular and blocky. As the distance lessened, the shape resolved into a gently spinning orbital defence platform, though the majority of its launch bays were angled towards the planet's surface.

The defence platform hung in geostationary orbit above the planet's equator above a loathsome stretch of purple that spread across a wide, ochre landmass.

'Tell me something,' said Vaanes, turning from the image of the orbital station. 'Once you'd defeated Berossus and Toramino, why did you not stay on Medrengard?'

'Khalan-Ghol was ruined, there was nothing left of it.'

'You could have built another fortress. Isn't that what you Iron Warriors do?'

'I could have,' agreed Honsou. 'But fortresses are static and when everyone on the planet has armies geared for siege, it's only a matter of time until some-one attacks you. I made a mistake going back to Medrengard. I should have stayed out in the galaxy and carried on the Long War.'

'That war was ten thousand years ago,' said Vaanes.

'To you maybe, but to the Iron Warriors it was yes-terday, the blink of an eye. You think the passage of years matters to something as powerful as vengeance? When you dwell in a place where time itself is a meaningless concept, the defeats and glo-ries of the past are only a heartbeat away. I fought alongside warriors who once bestrode the surface of Terra and marched with the primarchs at their head, and it galls me to see the pale shadows the great Astartes have become. You are weaklings compared to what those warriors achieved.'

Honsou felt his anger threaten to overcome his composure and forced himself to calm down as he pondered the strength of his fervour. Before the battles on Medrengard, he had no such high notions of the warriors who had fought in Horus's war, openly mocking Forrix and Kroeger for their misty-eyed reminiscences of a campaign he had not taken part in.

He took a deep breath and looked back to the glinting form of the orbital platform.

'Cycerin!' he shouted. 'Give them something to worry about.'

The magos withdrew his crawling plugs from the back of the newborn's head and turned to face him. The newborn slumped forward, supporting himself on his forearms as his breath came in ragged, wheezing gulps.

Without answering Honsou, the magos slid his morphing limbs into the lectern and a pulsing hum travelled the length of the strategium. The lights dimmed as the magos became one with the *Warbreed* and bent his unknown powers to the misdirection of their enemies.

'What's he doing?' asked Ardaric Vaanes.

'Watch and see,' said Honsou.

The image on the viewing bay remained much as before, the station gently spinning before them as the *Warbreed* drifted closer, unseen and unknown. Then, slowly, the station's guns and surveyor arrays came to life, swivelling in their mounts to train on a distant portion of space.

Honsou glanced down at the plotting table as a flickering icon appeared, representing the location the nameless Imperial servants had just targetted.

As they watched, the platform came alive with vox-chatter, the words of its occupants crackling the length and breadth of the strategium as they barked from a freshly formed amplifier unit on Cycerin's chest.

The words were scratchy and overlaid with static, but the panic in them was unmistakable.

'...tress one, three omega! Contact in grid delta-epsilon-omega! Auger signatures indicate hostile xenos life form! Request intercept. On present course, contact will be in range in two hours. Any ships capable of rendering assistance please respond!'

Vaanes watched as the phantom icon drifted slowly across the plotting table towards the platform and said, 'That's nowhere near us.'

'Exactly,' said Honsou. 'And thanks to Cycerin's deceptions, that's where the planetary monitors will head. By the time they realise there's nothing there, we'll be long gone.'

Honsou turned from the image of the orbital platform and lifted his bolter.

'They're looking for help,' he laughed. 'So let's go give them some.'

ALARM BELLS ECHOED along the bare metal corridors of Defence Platform Ultra Nine, ear-splittingly loud as First Officer Alevov raced towards the embarkation deck. Calling it a deck gave it a sense of scale it did not possess, the pressurised chamber where crew transferred onto docked ships simply a vaulted chamber with bare bronze walls and numerous pipes and locking wheels that led to the various umbilicals.

Imperial Guardsmen raced to prearranged choke points, ready to defend the orbital platform against boarders, though Alevov knew such precautions were likely unnecessary. Given the heightened state of alert the fleet had maintained since the initial invasion, it was unlikely that the lone enemy contact would reach the platform intact.

Even so, it had been a stroke of luck to have the nearby monitor on station. They hadn't detected it, but as it was engine-on to the sun's corona that wasn't surprising. The Veritas codes were old ones, but were still genuine and permission had been granted for it to dock.

The captain's offer of assistance had been gratefully accepted, for, as much as the soldiers on the platform seemed to know what they were doing, more bodies wouldn't hurt in case something unexpected happened.

Alevov passed the turn in the defensive architecture leading to the embarkation deck and pushed past two blue-jacketed soldiers fixing a gun with a long, perforated barrel to a bipod.

He felt his ears pop as he entered the bronze chamber, making a mental note to have the enginseers check the pressure seals. A green light winked into life above a thick blast door and he breathed a sigh of relief.

The clank of metal on metal sounded from beyond the door as he took hold of the locking clamp and turned the wheel. Jets of stale atmosphere gusted from the door seals as air from different worlds mingled.

'Glad to have you aboard,' said Alevov as the door swung open. 'Probably a bit unnecessary, but you can never be too careful, can you?'

'No,' said Honsou, stepping from the airlock, 'but apparently you can be too stupid.'

Honsou raised his bolter and shot First Officer Alevov in the face.

THE HEADLESS BODY slammed against the bronze walls of the airlock and the gun's report echoed deafeningly in the confined chamber. Honsou moved swiftly forward, seeing two open-mouthed soldiers at the chamber's exit with a heavy calibre weapon.

Shock and horror had paralysed them for a moment, but it was all Honsou needed. His bolter roared again and the soldiers were torn in two by a sawing arc of bolter shells.

'With me!' he yelled, slamming his back into the wall at the chamber's door. He ducked his helmeted head through the doorway, seeing more of the blue-jacketed soldiers manning defended positions further around the curving corridor.

Honsou rolled around the door; his bolter raised to his shoulder and pumping out lethally aimed shots directed by his augmetic eye. Three soldiers flopped back, their chests pulped to ruptured craters by three shots.

Iron Warriors moved past him, deploying with grim, wordless efficiency to secure the passages leading to the platform's hub. Honsou was pleased at the accuracy of his shots, for it had taken him a little time to retrain his body to fire the bolter left-handed and sync it to his newly grafted eye, but the results spoke for themselves.

Cadaras Grendel and Ardaric Vaanes moved past him, moving anticlockwise around the rim of the orbital and firing as they went. Grendel's underslung melta gun trailed smoke and Vaanes's lightning claws threw off arcs of blue lightning, making the air taste of ozone.

He smelled the newborn before he saw it, despite the case of armour it wore about its body. Even his own helmet's filters couldn't keep the stench of it from him.

'Stay with me,' ordered Honsou. 'Kill anything that isn't ours.'

The newborn nodded and they set off after the sound of gunfire.

CADARAS GRENDEL GRINNED like a madman as he charged down the curving corridor, his teeth bared and his heart beating wildly in his chest. It had been too long since he had killed something and he itched to fight something worthwhile, though he suspected there would be precious little sport on this grubby little platform.

But Cadaras Grendel wasn't fussy; he'd kill whatever came his way.

He and Vaanes pounded down the corridor, its walls strobed by red warning lights and ringing with blaring klaxons. It was the symphony of battle and needed only the bark of gunfire and the screams of the dying to make it complete.

As if in answer to his thoughts, a ragged squad of soldiers rose from a defensive position before him and opened fire. Their weapons spat bright bolts of energy, daggers to fight a Titan, and Grendel laughed as he opened fire, the vox-unit on his armour broadcasting his demented, psychotic amusement as a howling yell of rebellion.

One soldier crumpled, his shoulder blasted away and his face shredded by exploding fragments of bone. Another ran screaming from the barricade, while the rest stood with grim stoicism in the face of Grendel's onslaught.

Las-fire spat, the impacts against his armour insignificant. His bolter fired again, a bark of shots that cut down a handful of the men in sprays of blood and shattered armour.

Vaanes had eschewed his jump pack for this close and dirty fight, but Grendel had to admit his speed was impressive nonetheless. The former Raven Guard was faster than Grendel and reached the barrier first, leaping forward in an arcing dive that took him over the barricade and into the midst of the soldiers.

Actinic blurs of silver steel flashed and squirts of blood sprayed the walls as Vaanes rolled to his feet, striking left and right with his lightning claws. Arms flopped to the metal decking and torsos sheared from bodies as the energised edges cut through armour, meat and bone with an electric hiss and spit.

Screams of pain and terror echoed from the walls, and in seconds the skirmish was over.

Grendel nodded in approval as he rounded the barricade to see Vaanes standing in a circle of blood, chuckling as he found it impossible to tell how many had died given the profusion of dismembered body parts.

His amusement turned to glee as he saw a pair of soldiers huddled in the shadow of the barricade, clinging to one another and weeping in terror. Their blue uniforms bore the wreckage of their fellow soldiers' deaths and they were little more than mindless sacks of blood and pain now.

Grendel reached down and hoisted one of the soldiers from the ground, letting him dangle above the deck as his wrist was slowly crushed.

'Don't seem like much, do they?' he asked.

Vaanes didn't answer immediately, his helmet fixed on the carnage his deadly claws had wrought. For all the motion Vaanes displayed, he might as well have been a statue.

'Vaanes?'

'I heard you.'

Grendel shrugged and dropped the wailing soldier, who crawled away holding his shattered wrist close to his chest. Grendel let him get a few metres away before turning his weapon on him and unleashing a superheated blast of energy from the underslung melta gun.

The protective senses of his helmet dimmed momentarily as the white-hot blast engulfed the soldier and Grendel laughed as the glow faded and he saw the stumps of feet and charred skull lid that was all that remained.

He turned to Vaanes and said, 'I'll leave the last one for you.'

FIGHTING ALONGSIDE THE newborn was much easier when it wore a helmet, for Honsou was not forced to look upon the face of Ventris in the midst of a battle. The fight for the outer ring of the orbital platform was virtually over, the soldiers defending it no match for the relentless ferocity of an assault of the Iron Warriors.

Few soldiers were.

Honsou watched his champion kill their enemies without mercy, fighting with a skill and familiar style that took him a moment to recognise. The blows it struck were practiced and precise, the very image of those taught to the Adeptus Astartes... exactly how a warrior of the Ultramarines would fight.

The challenge of killing mortals with his bolter had grown stale, and Honsou now fought with his axe, cleaving a screaming path through his enemies. Truth be told, there was little more challenge in fighting them in close quarters, but it had the virtue of being bloody.

Honsou's axe growled as it slew, the monstrous entity within it feeding on the souls of the dead even as it feasted on the blood of their burst bodies. His blade reaped a fearsome tally, the blue-jacketed soldiers fighting on despite the impossibility of their victory. Honsou admired their courage, if not their ability.

He wrenched his axe from the golden breastplate of some kind of officer, the axe protesting with a ripple of dead eyes across the blade's glossy surface. A tremor of rage passed along his arms from the weapon and Honsou snarled as he exerted the force of his will to quiet the daemon within.

The sounds of battle were diminishing throughout the station and Honsou knew the battle was almost won. Even as he relished the victory, he saw a ragged scramble from the end of one of the spoke passageways that led to the central hub. One soldier carried a stubby tube on his shoulder, into which another man stuffed a finned missile.

Honsou wanted to laugh at the desperation of the weapon, before realising that the detonation of such a missile would explosively decompress the entire outer ring and send everyone within hurtling into space.

He tried to move, but his limbs would not obey his commands and he looked down in anger at the axe that shuddered in his grip, its will to dominate pushing back against him.

'Now is really not the time!' he snarled through gritted teeth, fighting to force the essence of the daemon back into the darkly shimmering depths of the blade.

A bloom of noise, light and smoke erupted from the soldiers and, though it was surely impossible to see such a fast moving object, Honsou saw a needle-nosed missile streaking towards him.

Honsou felt the daemon withdraw into the weapon and end the battle for control, but knew it was far too late to avoid the missile. He threw his arm up before him in an instinctive gesture of defence.

The force of the impact hurled him from his feet and he felt a terrible, leeching power within him, as though a loathsome, dark force tapped into his life-force. His head slammed against the wall and he looked down to see the smoking, hissing fins of the missile embedded in the rippling silver of the arm he had taken from the Ultramarines sergeant.

Light pulsed in the depths of the arm, flitting fire-flies of energy that spoke of technology wrought in an age long forgotten and a race of such malice that his own petty evils were insignificant when measured alongside theirs. Even as he watched, a fiery orange line hissed around the circumference of the portion of the missile that protruded from his arm and it fell to the deck with a clatter of metal.

Honsou stared in wonder at the unblemished surface of his arm, looking up as the equally astounded soldiers reloaded the weapon.

He scrambled to his feet, but quickly saw there was no need for haste as the newborn launched himself towards the soldiers and began their butchery. Until now, Honsou had only seen the newborn kill with the mechanical precision of the Adeptus Astartes, albeit employed with a vicious joy no Space Marine would condone, but his champion now fought with brutal savagery, every blow excruciatingly mortal and delivered with fluid economy of force.

No movement was wasted, no blow more powerful than required and no opening left unexploited. Within seconds the soldiers were dead and the battle over.

Honsou joined the newborn at the scene of the slaughter as more Iron Warriors secured the spoke corridor. Specialists with shaped charges moved down its length and prepared to blow the doors to the central hub. Within moments, the orbital platform would be theirs.

Honsou put a hand on the newborn's shoulder, feeling his hostility towards his new champion diminish in the face of the obvious relish taken in causing death.

'Ardaric Vaanes is training you well,' he said.

ARDARIC VAANES INCLINED his head to the last trooper. The man's face was a mask of tears and blood, his eyes glazed as his head shook back and forth in terror. Cadaras Grendel stood with his shoulders squared, the threat and challenge of his body language plain.

'He's dead already,' said Vaanes.

'What?'

'I said he's dead already. He's no threat to us anymore.'

'So? What's that got to do with anything?' said Grendel, moving to stand inches in front of him. 'You not got the stomach for killing a man unless he's got a gun pointed at you?'

'I just don't see the need anymore.'

'The need?' said Grendel. 'Who said anything about need? Kill him. Now.'

Vaanes met Grendel's angry stare, the challenge and hostility evident even through the masks of ceramite that separated them. The sound of battle surrounded them, the fighting pushing ever closer to the hub of the orbital platform, but Grendel was ignoring it, intent on pushing Vaanes and seeing what he was made of.

'I don't think you've got the guts, Vaanes,' said Grendel. 'I think maybe you're still working with the Imperials. Honsou thinks so too, I can tell he doesn't trust you.'

'He doesn't trust you either,' pointed out Vaanes.

'No, but I don't try and pretend like I won't betray him someday. He and I, well, we got ourselves an understanding.'

Grendel turned away from Vaanes and scooped up the last surviving trooper. He held him up before Vaanes and said, 'Go on. Kill him. Kill him or I'll kill you, I swear.'

Vaanes took a breath, wondering if he would have to fight Grendel now. The warrior had been spoiling for it ever since he had joined Honsou's band, but as he tensed his muscles in readiness for action, his eyes caught a glint of silver on the dangling trooper's uniform.

An honour badge pinned to his collar.

Droplets of blood had stained the uniform around it, but not a single drop sullied the badge itself and the image of a stylised silver 'U' upon a rich blue background was unmistakable...

Ultramarines.

Picked out in gold behind the symbol of the Ultramarines was the numeral IV, and Vaanes felt a surge of anger as he realised the meaning of the symbol. It was a campaign badge awarded to those who had fought alongside the Fourth Company of the Ultramarines.

Vaanes leaned down and said, 'How did you get this?'

The soldier didn't answer, his mouth working in a monotone wail of pure terror, his eyes squeezed shut as though he could escape the terror of his situation by keeping it from sight.

'How did you get this?' shouted Vaanes, gripping the soldier's jacket and tearing him from Cadaras Grendel. Hysterical babbling was his only answer and Vaanes screamed his question again, his right fist pulled back and ready to strike, the fizzing crackle of the lightning energy loud in his ears.

'Do it...' hissed Grendel, and the urge to kill this man, to hurt him, to maim him and inflict suffering beyond measure was greater than anything Vaanes had ever known. Vaanes heard a sibilant whisper in his ear as though an unseen speaker's voice was hidden in the rising buzz of his lightning claw, a voice only he could hear.

The sensation was not unpleasant, a silent urging and a silken pressure on his mind that promised new wonders, pleasures undreamed of and the ecstasy of experience. All this and more were encapsulated in the wordless whisper and Ardaric Vaanes knew without understanding that this was the offer and the price of the bargain he had struck with Honsou on Medrengard.

His vision narrowed until all he could see was the Ultramarines honour badge, the winking silver and gold mocking him with their purity and lustre. The face of Uriel Ventris appeared in the forefront of his mind and he cried out in anguished rage.

The lightning claw slammed forward, punching through the trooper's chest and exploding from his back. The blow continued and his fist followed the claws through the man's torso, pulverising bone, heart and lungs on its way through the substance of his body.

Vaanes tore at the body until his hissing claws had reduced it to scraps of torn meat, a ruined gruel of smashed bone and offal. The breath heaved in his lungs and he stepped back from the wreckage of the man's remains and felt a wave of acceptance pour through him, his limbs filled with energy and exhilaration.

He heard Cadaras Grendel laughing and felt the killer's gauntlet slap him on the shoulder guard. Words were spoken, but he didn't hear them, too caught up in the wonder he had just experienced.

Vaanes stared down at what he had done, the bodies around him so torn that their very humanity was obliterated. Finally, he understood the lie he had been living since the shame that had driven him from the Raven Guard.

There was no self-delusional status he could impart to salve his own conscience and no middle ground between loyalist and traitor. In the Long War, such labels were meaningless anyway – there were only victors and defeated.

At last, the truth of what he had become was apparent in this baptism of murder and blood.

Ardaric Vaanes welcomed it.

THE CENTRAL CONTROL room of Defence Platform Ultra Nine reeked of blasting charges and blood. With the doors blown, the men inside had no chance of life and had made the best job they could of disabling the systems and calling for reinforcements, but Honsou knew the nearest Imperial ship was many hours distant.

Adept Cycerin stood before the smashed consoles, a morass of writhing cables snaking from the cavity of his bio-mechanical chest to mesh with the inner workings of the smashed consoles.

The doomed mortals had been thorough in their vandalism, but Cycerin had made swift work in undoing the damage, and his unique talents allowed him to coax the required life from the smashed systems without difficulty.

'Is everything ready?' asked Honsou, impatient to see the results of his labours bear fruit.

Cadaras Grendel shrugged as he ran his eyes over the buckled and las-shot console. Red lights winked on surviving, brass-rimmed dials and sparks fizzed and sputtered.

'Hard to say for sure, but we swapped over the missiles' payload,' said Grendel. 'All but one is loaded up with the stuff we took from Golbasto. It's up to Cycerin now.'

'Why all but one?' asked Ardaric Vaanes and Honsou caught a subtle change in the warrior's voice, a shift in tone of a warrior who has at last come to know himself.

'The last one is a message to Ventris.'

'What does it say?'

'It's not what it says,' said Honsou, 'it's what it represents.'

'And what's that?'

'That you don't walk away from a fight with Honsou without paying a price.'

A SALVO OF sixteen orbital torpedoes surged from the planetside launch bays, followed by another rippling salvo seconds later. Another three salvos launched until all but one of the platform's entire payload of missiles was expended. Each missile dropped away rapidly from the platform, the blue-hot coals of their engines firing for long enough to put them in a ballistic trajectory towards the planet's surface.

They swooped downwards like hunting raptors, their formation breaking up as the spread pattern implanted into each warhead by Adept Cycerin took hold of each one. The missiles diverged until their contrails were spread around the planet like a glittering spiderweb.

Heat shields burned with conical fire as the missiles plunged through the atmosphere, emerging into the crystal skies of the planet. Hurried defences scrambled to lock onto the missiles, but launched from low orbit, they were already travelling too quickly and were too close to be engaged with any hope of success.

As the missiles reached a predetermined altitude over the planet's surface, each one exploded and spread its viral payload into the air. Vast quantities of

the experimental Heraclitus strain were released into
the atmosphere in doses billions of times greater
than had been employed on Golbasto.

All across the planet, a terrible rain fell, the genius
of Magos Szalin of the Ordos Biologis wreaking terrible damage as it went to work on the indigenous
and xenos vegetation.

A few short years ago, this world had suffered the
horror of invasion, monstrous swarms of ferocious
alien killers rampaging across its surface. A great war
had been fought; in space, in the air, on land and
finally in the very bowels of a living spacecraft that
had travelled from another galaxy for uncounted
aeons.

Though the invasion had been defeated, the dreadful legacy of the alien invaders remained to taint the
planet's ecology forever. From pole to pole, horrific
spires of dreadful alien vegetable matter towered over
the landscape, slowly choking the life from the natural landscape.

The alien flora had subsumed entire continents,
a rapacious instinct to devour encoded in every
strand of its genetic structure. Nutrients were
leeched from the soil and used to create hyper-
fertile spore growths that drifted on the heated
currents of the air to seed new regions and pollute
yet more land.

Only rigorous burning policies ensured the
planet's survival – for a world of the Imperium could
not simply be abandoned, not after all the blood that
had been shed in its defence. The shining steel cities,
islands in a sea of alien growth, still produced masses
of munitions and armoured vehicles for Imperial
wars throughout the subsector.

Salvoes of anti-plant missiles, slash and burn pogroms and pesticide overflights were a matter of routine since the defeat of the invasion.

Such things were thankless tasks, but necessary for the planet's continued survival.

But all that was rendered moot in the face of Magos Szalin's creation.

Developed from a partial fragment of ancient research conducted by Magos Heraclitus, the bio-toxins were intended to increase the growth rate of crops on agri-worlds. Magos Szalin had taken the next step and pioneered techniques designed to increase the productivity of such worlds a thousand fold.

Now that work was put to the ultimate test, mixing its monstrous potential for increased growth with an alien organism that was at the apex of its biological efficiency.

Within seconds of the Heraclitus strain being released into the atmosphere, the alien growths reacted to its touch, surging upwards and over the planet's terrain. Slash and burn teams were instantly overwhelmed by mutant growths, poisonous plant life expanding kilometres in seconds as the virulent growth strain sent its metabolism into overdrive.

Huge amounts of nutrients were sucked from the ground and released as enormous quantities of heat, raising the ambient temperature of the world in a matter of moments. Oxygen was sucked greedily from the atmosphere by horrifyingly massive spore chimneys and the planet's protective layers were gradually stripped in unthinking biological genocide.

This was not the rapid death of Exterminatus, but ecological death of worldwide proportions.

Panicked messages were hurled out into the immaterium and only those with the money, influence or cunning escaped on hastily prepped ships that fled the planet's destruction.

But these were few compared to the billions left behind and, weeks later, as the last of the planet's atmosphere was stripped from it by the hyperevolved alien biology, stellar radiation swept the surface, killing every living thing and laying waste to all that remained.

Months after the launch of the missiles, nothing remained alive, the deadly alien vegetation killed by lethal levels of radiation and the frigid cold that gripped the planet without its protective atmosphere.

All that now remained of the planet was a dead, lifeless ball of rock, its surface seared and barren, with only the skeletal remains of its blackened cities left as evidence that human beings had once lived upon it.

THE SILVER-SKINNED drop-ship fell through the airless vacuum of the planet. A host of Marauders and Raptors followed it down, though nothing lived here now. The drop-ship's retros screamed as the pilot brought it in on final approach, the skids deploying just before it landed in the midst of dead plant matter and scorched alien trees.

A drogue arm deployed to test the external environment and once it retracted, the pressure door on the side of the craft opened and a heavy ramp extended to the surface.

Cautiously, for none aboard truly felt safe, a squad of Adeptus Mechanicus Tech-Guard clad in heavy environment suits – similar in function and design to the Terminator armour employed by the Adeptus Astartes – emerged and descended to the planet's surface.

Following the group was a figure whose heavy armour was swathed in vivid red robes emblazoned with the black and white cog symbol of the Adeptus Mechanicus.

His name was Magos Locard and this was not the first time he had come to this world.

With quick, precise gestures, Locard directed the Tech-Guard to collect samples of the dead plants and the underlying strata. Diggers and corers rolled down from the drop-ship and Locard watched them as they gathered information that might offer some clue as to what had caused this catastrophe.

Despite the many augmentations applied to his flesh, Locard was not so far removed from humanity that the fate of this world did not cause him great sadness. Like many others, he had fought to save it and had been instrumental in what he had thought was its salvation.

Now all that was ashes and Locard felt a great anger build within him.

Whoever had done this would pay.

A Tech-Guard soldier approached Locard and said, 'My lord, we've found it.'

Locard followed the man as he waded through thick piles of ashen vegetation to the source of what had led them to this exact place. Though the planet was now bereft of life, a constantly repeating signal had reached into space, its plaintive voice almost lost in the void, but shrill and insistent, demanding attention.

The vegetation thinned and Locard realised he was walking in a deep trench carved by the impact of something that had fallen from the skies.

'Here, my lord,' said the Tech-Guard, backing away from Locard.

Locard saw a battered silver tube, perhaps ten metres in length – an orbital torpedo, though his exo-armour's auspex told him there was no ordnance or explosives loaded in the warhead. This was the source of the signal and Locard knew that someone had wanted them to find this.

He walked along the length of the torpedo towards the payload bay and deployed bolt-clasps from the forearm of his armour. One by one, he removed the bolts of the payload bay and hurled it aside when he unscrewed the last one.

The inside of the bay was dark, but his enhanced ocular implants could easily make out what it contained. He frowned and reached inside the bay to remove its contents.

He turned to the Tech-Guard next to him and handed him a cracked helmet, the paint chipped and one eye lens missing. The helmet was a deep blue and bore a symbol on the forehead that was known to Locard.

The inverted omega of the Ultramarines Chapter of the Adeptus Astartes.

'I don't understand,' said the Tech-Guard, turning the helmet over in his hands.

'Nor I,' said Locard, turning and marching from the missile. 'Not yet.'

As the Tech-Guard followed Locard he said, 'What happened to this place?'

'This place has a name, soldier,' snapped Locard. 'Imperial citizens died here.'

'Apologies, my lord, I meant no disrespect,' said the Tech-Guard. 'What was it called?'

Locard paused, casting his gaze across the blasted wasteland that was all that remained of a once proud Imperial world that had stood defiantly before the horror of a Tyranid invasion.

'It was called Tarsis Ultra.'

THE EMPEROR WEPT

Simon Dyton

PLANET-FALL WAS a long time ago. Adept Biologis Hieronym Rottle could remember marvelling at the enormous barbs and blisters punching through the lower atmosphere like islands in an ocean of curdled milk. Under scalding clouds, continental forges glittered and winked over magma fields and core plunges. He could remember vast tectonic fractures splitting the dim surface of the planet.

It was all such a long time ago.

He could remember the drop-ship swooping over the vast, viscous northern sea, black, stagnant, rolling slowly on rotten tides. He could remember the genetor facility looming out of the mist, towering towards the pale sun like a barbaric totem to the Omnissiah. That was all he could remember of his arrival.

Such a long, long time ago.

After the cortical splicing of his own brain, Rottle couldn't remember why he was transferred from the chemical sinks of Mars. But he didn't need to remember. Reason was logic enough; his transferral was the consequence of cause – all premised upon service to the blessed Machine.

He could remember that the data conduit onboard the drop-ship did not register the research laboratorium's identifying code or the existence of the planet below. It was as if the fortress-like facility hung in cold, lonely space, unknown and utterly knowable but for his presence.

There had been rumours during the long journey from Mars. He had heard in his one remaining organic ear that the planet had no *official* name, which was long ago expunged from Explorator records, Imperial Navy charts and Terran libraria by deletion orders from the highest offices of the Adeptus Terra, from the High Lords of Terra themselves. Even the Inquisition had been persuaded to overlook its existence. The only off-world record of the planet was on Mars, deep within the most ancient datacores, buried beneath the iron-plated flanks of Olympus Mons. The rumours said that the Adeptus Mechanicus were the sole overlords of the genetor facility here – and of the unnamed planet that it called home.

One talkative initiate, his humanity still partially intact before neural enhancement, had told Rottle that the planet was once Umbracogg's World, named after a pilgrim who settled the world after explorator fleet *Majestechnicum* discovered the ball of rock, fire and bile thousands of years ago. But no one knew why the Adeptus Mechanicus reclaimed it. Another initiate, fearfully awaiting cerebral spooling, told Rottle that the name Umbracogg was only intended to remind the planet's handful of inhabitants that they lived in the shadow of the Cog, *in umbra Coga* in low Gothic, where the Omnissiah's most dangerous knowledge might be hidden. Perhaps the initiate was raving, Rottle had thought. Cerebral spooling was a trauma to the flesh. For Rottle, knowing did not need naming; that the Omnissiah's intent was known unto Himself was data-sufficient.

Hieronym Rottle had wanted only to begin his work. There was no higher worship of the Omnissiah than the sanctification of a gene-vat with a binary hymn, the holy mechanistration of a techvigil, or the ignition of a blessed lumosphoid. Rottle sought no learning for himself; he sought only to celebrate the Omnissiah's knowledge, the sanctity of data preserved and cherished.

When the drop-ship landed, he never saw the initiates again. They vanished, taken swiftly into the facility's lower levels. Years later, Archmagos Biologis Vaeyvor would tell Rottle that such initiates became monitoring servitors, vital parts of the research station's security network. Rottle recorded this information in his memarchive. By then, he had long ceased to contemplate the fleshed.

Hieronym Rottle was nothing if not a servant of the Omnissiah.

His work was its own salvation.

For such work it was.

On this anonymous planet, in an unnamed Mechanicus fortress-laboratorium, Hieronym Rottle made the Life-Eater.

The Life-Eater. One of the hallowed munitions of Exterminatus, the *Killer of Worlds*, the direst sentence brought to bear by the Holy Ordos of the Emperor's Inquisition against a planetary population whose crimes against the Throne of Terra deserved annihilation, absolute and entire. Wholesale planetary destruction.

This planet was where servants of the Adeptus Mechanicus made the Life-Eater virus for the great fleets of the Segmentum Obscurus. In an age when Cyclonic and Incineratus torpedoes were widely used for Exterminatus, and when even some members of the Inquisition frowned upon the Life-Eater for reasons the Mechanicus had long forgotten, the magi biologi of the Adeptus Mechanicus still made one of ancient Terra's most prodigious weapons. Flesh was imperfect, as Archmagos Biologis Vaeyvor had said so many times, and the engine of its annihilation was praise indeed to the Omnissiah.

And the Omnissiah was praised with unceasing industry. Tox-flues and convection stacks ran through the towering facility like veins, steering noxious waste into the rotten atmosphere and the curdled sea. In secure laboratoria, some even surrounded by void shields, wizened genetors created what natural biological processes could never devise. Their chemical creations were processed and refined in vacuum-sealed cauldrons, stretching across vast vat-galleries, which looked out over dead oceans. In filtration and infusion chambers, servitors were hard-wired into endless banks of support and monitoring machinery. Their organics were all but eroded by the corrosive toxins and, despite the durability of steel and plasticide tissue, many disintegrated within days of exposure.

Rottle's cortical splicing had not only robbed him of knowing why he left Mars, but why he was part of this magnificent process. He calculated that his service in Martian genetoria had qualified him or perhaps won him preferment. Upon arrival, he was responsible for overseeing the purity-choirs that kept the Life-Eater's toxins dormant during refinement, for calibrating gene-vats, and igniting the lumosphoids to ensure uncorrupted organics – all in the blessed name of the Omnissiah. He could no longer remember the risks involved. Glory unto the Omnissiah was all.

Adept Biologis Hieronym Rottle was one day pro-moted to Magos Biologis. It was his status when he interfaced with the core data-net. He did not remem-ber when this happened.

He did remember that Archmagos Biologis Vaeyvor said that comprehension of risk was directly propor-tional to apprehension of self – and members of the Mechanicus were but the tiniest teeth in the smallest cogs of the Machine God's infinite artifice. So it was during a moment of weakness when Rottle recalled his *self* that his story began. It was a moment of humanity, of which Rottle had little left, that burned the remainder away.

He had long ceased to calculate the passage of time in Standard Imperial increments – years, days, hours, and so on – because time had long ago become a measurement of only viral gestation, germination, and genetic refinement. But Hieronym Rottle did remember that planet-fall was a long, long time ago when he finally left his humanity behind.

THE VAT-GALLERY stretched across the entire spire's width, capped at either end by great bulbous windows of strengthened plexi-glass. Despite the roaring thermals outside, the wind's scream barely filtered into the gallery. At one end, Rottle inspected a gene-vat, checking ignition nodes and the gene-spool assembly. Sickly light yellowed the very air. Further down the gallery, darkness engulfed the endless rows of vats and cauldrons. Here, shadows fell away sharply before the shimmering plexi-glass.

The light suddenly changed. Darkness fell across Rottle's back, swooping across the floor before him. He turned, servos whining with the discomfort of unfamiliar speed. He was reminded of Vaeyvor's admonitions: the Machine God's cogs need only turn the holy P'i-solute, they need not be quick. Rottle was unaccustomed to speed.

Beyond the plexi-glass, drifting towards the facility on boiling thermals, was a leviathan. The leviathans were native to the planet. They were enormous creatures, the size of a cargo lander, with great gas-filled sacs that gave them enough buoyancy to graze the upper atmosphere above the planet's pollution. Vaeyvor said they were harmless, like the extinct whales of Terra. In the high thermals, they grazed upon krillions, microscopic bacteria that synthesized less poisonous pollutants and toxins. This allowed them to survive the vast extinctions that mankind's presence had heralded on the planet, and instead they thrived. No other life existed, yet Rottle would occasionally consider the resilience of such weakling flesh with something akin to surprise – or at least what his remaining emotive centres recognized as the residual synaptic shudder of astonishment.

Yet this leviathan was dying. It had sunk into the bilious toxins of the ocean's convection currents. Its skin was flaking and cracking as it slewed towards the facility. Its gas sacs were swollen and distended, livid and ugly. As Rottle watched, it wheeled round, flexing and gleaming in the sun's pale light. One sac burst. A gout of watery gore fell away, then another, and another. The leviathan lunged at the facility, crashing like an orbital blimp.

There was very little humanity left in Magos Biologis Rottle, but there was enough to feel fear. His mandible-tines fluttered and his plasticide jowls quivered. One augmetic eye opened to unnatural size, telescoping polished lenses towards the oncoming leviathan. He calculated mass, acceleration, torque and trajectory. His throat had long ceased to conduct air through his mouth and his olfactory and nasal filters whined awkwardly. Rottle had lost the ability to scream long ago.

His augmented legs juddered as he determined the optimum direction for flight and the most hopeful place of safety. Strengthened plexi-glass might withstand bolter fire, but not a crashing leviathan. The entire spire could collapse. The servitor overhead continued to murmur its binary catechism, unaware of the imminent impact. Rottle leapt towards the overhang of the nearest gene-vat.

But that tiny part of humanity in Rottle was enough – just enough to cloud the cold certainty of calculation, to blur his tightly angled path of flight. Rottle struck the gene-vat head-on. Though only the size of a modest man, he weighed far more. Durasteel fittings and plasticide and rubbrete tissue all weighed much more than human organics. Rottle's humanity was but a humble fraction of his mass. His momentum was immense.

The gene-vat shook, swayed, and settled – its legs buckled and the suspensor field growled and fizzed. Rottle staggered, almost losing sentient operable function – *consciousness* – and his auditory sensors shrilled with the impact.

In that moment, he never saw the long-dormant spire defences growl into action as gyros swivelled onto the incoming target. Several racks of Hurricane bolters – three linked boltguns – opened up and a furious torrent of hot metal strafed the leviathan. The Hurricanes blew great chunks of rancid meat from the creature, disintegrating it in a blizzard of shells. To the targeting scanners, the target simply evaporated. When Rottle looked, staggering and reeling, he saw nothing. Neither did he see three drops of dormant Life-Eater drop to the floor from the vat's sizzling lip. Outside of the vat's stasis field, the Life-Eater awoke.

'A miracle,' Rottle hissed weakly, marvelling at the leviathan's disappearance. Then he collapsed, which was when the miracle really began.

CANYONS SAT BETWEEN the cog's teeth. They stretched into the distance to join the cog's body, a great plateau made of iron. Across this burnished vastness, great engines and machines reared up against the horizon. The sky was pink, stained and slashed by swathes of coppered cloud. Rottle noticed the towering majesty of Olympus Mons, larger than he would ever have believed and, above it, in a strange orbit – that hardly calculated correctly – was Terra itself, all gleaming steel and chrome. Everything turned slowly, inevitably, reclaiming perfection from a forgotten past. From the greatest pounding of the giant cogs' teeth to the sympathetic vibration of the tiniest gear, a binary hymn thundered into eternity.

It filled Rottle with life – even as what remained of his mortal body disintegrated in the vapours of the Life-Eater.

The great cog boomed its impossible rotation, its teeth grinding like glacial ice across the world before him. Arcane machines rumbled and screeched their praise to the Omnissiah. Bulbous pistons and grand, gargoyled chimney stacks belched forth great clouds of incense. Endless lines of venting spines spat out superheated air that roared into the thin atmosphere. It all echoed against the iron buttresses that towered above him like cliffs and the vast data-stacks that scratched the blooded sky like obsidian claws.

Above it all, the teeth of every cog and gear clicked and hammered their praise to the Omnissiah; endless arrangements of teeth, some sharp, some blunt, some jagged tessellations of impossibly complex angles, all sang their praise – like mouths of the Machine-God made manifest, like the Omnissiah speaking the binary truth of knowledge itself.

Rottle began to listen for meaning.

The binary thunder skipped a beat and lowered its tone. It gained awkward pitch and asymmetric rhythm.

It was then that the Omnissiah spoke to Hieronym Rottle.

'My servant,' the voice emanated. 'You have come to me.'

Rottle's mandible-tines fluttered. His vox failed him.

More words flowed from the endless majesty of Mars's machinery fields. 'I have watched you. I have come to make your destiny. I have come to teach you the weakness of flesh.'

Rottle's vox-piece couldn't compete with the sheer scale of sound that the Omnissiah vocalized. All he managed was a prolonged and pathetic *Yes*.

'I have come to show you the destiny of all flesh, Hieronym Rottle. I have come to turn your Life-Eater into the death of fleshed and living form. I have come to show you *knowledge*.' There was a strange ecstasy in the Omnissiah's words. Rottle recognized it: the adoration of uncorrupted information, perfect data, purest knowing. 'That is, Hieronym Rottle, if you will listen.'

Rottle's neck sheath flexed as he nodded. His beard of trim mechadendrites lapsed into flaccid obeisance as he listened. While his mortal remains liquefied in the vapours of the Life-Eater, the Omnissiah showed Rottle everything.

'A miracle,' said a hushed voice.

'Indeed,' conceded another, his speech falling away into a grating fizzle. 'But permissible?' The intonation turned into an electronic whine like a vox-caster switching channels.

'2.05%, Archmagos Biologis Vaeyvor. His remains constitute the Lex Organicum, He is still human. The chassis cybernetics and servitor systems have not compromised his humanity.'

'*Extraordinary*, adept. The probability of his survival was less than a deciota underpowered to the fifth quarter. A mathematical miracle – something I believed that the Omnissiah spurned.'

'My lord?' Wonder and disbelief mingled in the adept's voice. There was too much humanity there for Vaeyvor's liking.

'The Omnissiah works by knowledge alone,' the archmagos replied severely. 'This is an unprecedented incident, but a numerically permissible one.' It was only unprecedented in so far as the Holy Ordos remained ignorant of Rottle's accident and recovery. Other permissible incidents had occurred in the past – such as the flensing of Reppertrix Straynge on Crux II or the ascension of Enginseer Heliope – but the Ordos would descend upon the Mechanicus and eradicate all records and recollections. Vaeyvor rarely regretted such culling, but it was such a waste of tech-priests and magi. Only Vaeyvor knew of these incidents by the gaps in his labyrinthine memory, the names without things that were like negative impressions of an ancient pict-stealer. What he *knew* was that the Holy Ordos had worked against the glories of the Omnissiah, and that Umbracogg was now one of the few places in the galaxy that such a miracle might take place undiscovered because it simply didn't exist in the wider records of the Adeptus Terra. Perhaps *that* was the miracle: it was secret, permissible.

'Should we proceed?'

'Yes. Activate his higher functions,' grated Vaeyvor.

'Thy will be done, in the name of the Omnissiah.'

An electrostatic charge filled the air and power routers thrummed. With Rottle now largely a being of ceramite and steel, his power core required a great jolt of energy. His remaining flesh was kept preserved within external flexi-glass suspension wafers that insulated it from the power core's energy field.

The facility's chirurgeons had remarked upon the strange quality of Rottle's remaining flesh. Contaminated by the Life-Eater, it should have broken down into the chemical sludge that was capable of devouring more resilient proteins, such as keratin and chitin, as well as bone. But Rottle's remaining soft tissue was oddly resilient, if rotten and suppurating, and the chirurgeons only dismissed the puzzle because they assumed Rottle to be dead. That any flesh had remained was perhaps the greatest miracle of all.

The flexi-glass wafers shuddered as the charge continued to build. A great, low frequency groan broke across the vaulted apothecarion. For Rottle, it was the noise of consciousness. He returned to the materium shaking with the trauma of his own rebirth.

The light was harsh. He felt lumen-filtrators slide over his ocular lenses as they focused. His lenses were more mobile than before, as if mounted on tenticular armatures or mechadendrites. His companions fell into focus. There was an adept, very much bound by flesh, whose only modifications were neural braces and socketing arrangements that poked sorely through the flesh of his jawline. His eyes, both organic, peered back at Rottle nervously. He was young; there was too much humanity in his pale face.

The other figure was Archmagos Biologis Vaeyvor, hooded in his familiar cowl. As he spoke, vox-tendrils swung into sight below his hood. They curled and flowed with something akin to curiosity, or uncertainty.

'Magos Biologis,' Vaeyvor said, rasping as softly as his vox-tendrils allowed. 'Welcome.' He looked at the adept and nodded. The adept punched a button. Rottle noticed a cantilevered arm swing into his peripheral vision before it plunged into his chest. He expected pain, but felt only the smooth impalement of a broad-breadth data spike. He didn't know that he had a data-port there, but before he could feel the shock of intrusion, before his ocular lenses could flare in surprise, he was engulfed by the sheer pleasure of a data-stream download far faster than he had ever experienced before.

Everything became clear.

There was less humanity in Magos Biologis Hieronym Rottle than most servitors, but he was still a man. His sentience had been preserved and his humanity remained in the flexi-glass wafers that dotted his ceramite chassis. To isolate his humanity like this was... liberating. He fluttered his mandible-tines with satisfaction.

Then it happened. The memory of Olympus Mons, Terra's strange orbit above the machine-fields, of Mars's piston-and-cog hymn to the Omnissiah, and of the Omnissiah Himself – it *all* flooded back into Rottle's consciousness with a data-torrent that blew back across the data-spike and destroyed most of the power routers.

The gloom of Archmagos Biologis Vaeyvor's deep hood flashed with a constellation of lumen-alarms, optic-bulbs, and visual sensors. He peered forward, looking intently at the prostrate form of Rottle's body-chassis.

'Magos Biologis,' Vaeyvor hissed. 'What is *this*?' He gestured at the smoking power routers and the data-spike sizzling in Rottle's new data-port.

With the memory of his vision returned to him, along with his consciousness, Rottle felt something akin to delight – and it was with elation that he realised his memories had reached out through the data-spike into the local system network. They now existed independently of his own mind, merging with the apothecarion's machine-spirit. Vaeyvor now shared in their glory and knew the answer before Rottle even spoke.

'My miracle, archmagos,' Rottle said weakly. 'The Omnissiah spoke to me.'

'I…' Vaeyvor paused, his vox-piece grinding into a deep growl of scepticism. 'I *see*.'

'I have been told a great secret, an idea, beat out by the holy machinery of Mars. The Omnissiah conveyed knowledge to me from the forgotten past.

'I can improve the Life-Eater, my lord. I can *perfect* it. I have been blessed by a revelation of pure knowledge that only the Omnissiah could bestow. I can create the instant destruction of our enemies by robbing the living of life itself, by taking from existence the weakness of being!'

'We do not have the technology to replicate vortex weaponry, magos,' responded Vaeyvor. 'Using such a weapon against a planet would create dangers beyond our understanding. The Life-Eater need only sterilize, not obliterate. We seek only to take life, not matter.'

'My point exactly, archmagos. The new Life-Eater will take only life, not matter, nor any creation of the materium. It will attack the very spark of life and destroy only those beings whose *being* marks them as *living*.'

The archmagos paused, gears grinding quietly until a hiss indicated the release of internal coolants. Vaeyvor was calculating probabilities, possibilities, solutions and scenarios. 'The very spark of life?'

'Yes, my lord.'

'From the god-like Astartes to the lowest of the underhive?'

Rottle nodded his prehensile optical sensors. The sensation was strange.

More coolants hissed from inside Vaeyvor's voluminous cloak. 'From the highest aquila of the Terran sky to the deepest ocean scumling?'

Rottle nodded again, aware that Vaeyvor was intoning the Catechism of Cleansing. He knew what came next.

'From purest sentience to bestial instinct – the eradication of living existence?'

'Oh yes, my lord,' responded Rottle with certainty. 'I can promise the very eradication of life. The Life-Eater has never been so hungry as I shall make it.'

More coolant hissed from under Vaeyvor's cloak as he continued to process the situation. As archmagos, his own operational systems were soft-wired into those of the facility. He had seen Rottle's vision himself, shown to him by the apothecarion's own machine-spirit.

He nodded, small puffs of decompressed gas escaping from the lip of his hood as he did so. 'It seems that the miracle of your survival, magos, is but part of a greater whole, something far more miraculous indeed.' Vaeyvor's vox was hushed, reverential, little more than a mechanical croak. His vox-tendrils soothed the shape of each word. 'It is our purpose to pursue knowledge, to reclaim ancient learning, to forge the perfection of the blessed Machine, to fashion the Omnissiah's very divinity for Himself. Is it not?'

'It is, my lord,' responded Rottle. The adept remained silent.

Vaeyvor continued to assess the situation. Many of the chirurgeons and tech-medicae had been unaware of Rottle's identity. They assumed he would become little more than a mechanical corpse in the service of the Machine God. To let Rottle live now would risk unwelcome attention; to let him die might betray the Omnissiah Himself. But he could be buried in shielded laboratoria for years, hidden in the facility's poisonous depths, where few dared tread, or trod without dying. The secrets of the Machine-God could be made manifest secretly, and one day unleashed in the glorious name of the Emperor. No one knew of Rottle's recovery. Except the adept.

Vaeyvor's vox-tendrils caressed each other and hissed as he made his calculation. The risk of Rottle's discovery, like the miracle of his survival, was indeed permissible.

'You have my permission, Magos Biologis Hieronym Rottle, to continue your experimentation upon the Life-Eater,' Vaeyvor intoned solemnly.

'Thank you, my lord.' Rottle hissed.

'You have my assurance that your work will be conducted in secret, beyond Mechanicus oversight. I believe that the Omnissiah is your guide, and the Emperor your saviour. None need know of this.'

Rottle's mandible-tines fluttered, as if anticipating the consequences of the statement. Vaeyvor extended his own mechadendrite limbs from below his cloak, each chrome tentacle tapering towards a particular instrument: an electrosaw, a data-fork, an informatic barb, a razor-glaive. The tentacles curled upwards, stroking each other silently in their ascent. They corkscrewed over the adept's head, turning upon themselves in a tightening web of metal – and then, with neither warning nor visible effort, they sliced down, cutting the adept into wet slices of meat and steel.

Now no one else knew about Magos Biologis Hieronym Rottle.

No one at all.

FROM THE VIEWING gallery of *The Emperor's Despair*, Carnage hung in space like a polished pearl. The thick, ammonia-rich atmosphere reflected the local sun's light and it winked in the void, its brightness eclipsing the surrounding starfield for thousands of kilometres. The Segmentum Obscurus had rarely looked so dark.

The planet's vast mines, each of which was driven into the tectonic jigsaw of its cracked surface like a spike, tapped the planet's super-heavy core. Each was populated by a billion souls: miners, their families, enginseers, tech-priests, and Administratum officials. Not a single hive-mine had been operational for months.

For Carnage had been struck by plague and civil war. The suffering had been terrible and the bonds of civil society had collapsed. War followed and the survivors of the plague destroyed each other in a campaign of internecine conflict that pitched continent against continent. But the inhabitants of Carnage would not destroy each other before destroying what remained of their mining wealth and the very mines that gave their world meaning. The Administratum petitioned the Departmento Munitorum, which sent emissaries to the Holy Ordos of Terra. The Ordo Hereticus assumed command of the situation and approved the ultimate sanction: *Exterminatus*. It was why *The Emperor's Despair* hung silently in high orbit. Carnage would be sterilized.

Within days of Ordo Hereticus involvement, astropathic communications with the Adeptus Mechanicus and several Adeptus Astartes Chapters secured a solution. *The Emperor's Despair* now sat loaded with a test strain of a new Life-Eater virus. The Doom Warriors Chapter was chosen to administer the Emperor's mercy to the lost planet of Carnage.

With a noble history stretching back thousands of years, the Doom Warriors had long specialised in campaigns of cleansing, which appealed to their saturnine turn of character – the result of a defect in the Catalepsean Node, some said. Not only was it said that Doom Warriors did not sleep, but they required no hope, nor cause, to fight in the name of the Emperor. They were a morose, moody Chapter, bound together by a mutual misanthropy for those members of the Imperium who failed to see the galaxy's hopelessness. The nearest a Doom Warrior came to happiness was revelling in this hopelessness by immersing himself in its bloodshed and destruction. They made as formidable warriors as existed in the galaxy.

There were few Space Marines amongst the Doom Warriors as dour as Captain Grimmer Slayne. Carnage's opalescent brilliance sparkled against his half a dozen service studs as it wandered its lonely orbit thousands of kilometres away. Little else on Slayne's face caught the light. Heavy brows sat over hooded eyes. Hollow cheeks framed thin lips upon a cut-glass jaw. Dozens of scars had long ago knitted together into a patchwork-story of wounds and injury. His skin was little more than beaten leather. Light fell from his features like spilled water. He contemplated the scene before him with resigned sympathy. He knew death and embraced its necessity; every Doom Warrior did.

His vox crackled into life.

'Captain Slayne.' The static hissed and fizzled. 'Come to the launch arcade.'

'Aye,' he responded, in the blunt accent of their homeworld. 'Coming.'

'Squad Qannix has returned. Their evaluation is to proceed. Launch imminent.'

The cleansing of worlds was a bleak necessity in the Imperium of Man, and something which Slayne had undertaken before. Mardun X, Gephistux, Truub II and III, the Stuum Cluster. Each reminded him that the Emperor's Mercy could bring life to all, or take it, whole worlds, and sometimes systems, at a time.

His route took him quickly towards the launch arcade of *The Emperor's Despair*. In his parched-yellow power armour, almost the colour of desiccated bone, he strode swiftly through the ship, passing maintenance crews and ancillary servitors.

At the entrance parlour, Slayne was met by Squad Qannix. Sergeant Qannix made the sign of the aquila against his chest plate, slapping the ceramite with his gauntleted hands. Slayne returned the gesture, just as forcefully, and the other four squad members repeated it. Despite the cruel menace of the squad's Mark VII helmets, Slayne sensed the brotherhood between them and, as the unhelmeted officer, nodded appreciatively. They stepped inside and vast launch galleries panned out before them. Along each gallery sat a great metal tube, fitted with buffering insulation, powerful coolant flues, and organic dissipaters. At intervals, there were banks of servitors, wired into each great barrel to monitor breach integrity, targeting solutions and kinetic trajectories. These were the firing cylinders for viral torpedoes.

'Report, Sergeant Qannix,' said Slayne.

'The population is dead or dying, captain.' Qannix's vox played directly into Slayne's implanted ear-piece. 'The survivors are killing the diseased before they're dead, or else each other, as well as destroying the mining infrastructure of the planet. Three hive-mines have already collapsed into the planet's core and more will do so within days. Hive-Mine Mogma'crun will fall within hours because every bastion spire has failed. The situation is critical, captain.'

'Then let us commence, sergeant.' Slayne motioned to signal the launch. Hours of prayer had preceded this moment. Stale incense hung thickly in the air.

Though the Doom Warriors cared little for the precise nature of the viral payload they would launch, or its specific consequences, there were those that did. To Slayne's surprise, the parlour doors hissed open.

Stepping across the threshold first of all was Nakon Tagor, the ship's weaponsmaster. Handsome in his navy uniform, with tassled and trimmed epaulettes and brocaded panels, his high cap sat severely upon his sleek head. He was dwarfed by the giant Astartes before him and his grim demeanour fell away before their own sullen expressions. Slayne had seen his type before and was, if anything, unimpressed by his appearance. It was his presence that surprised him.

'Weaponsmaster, why the interruption? Only Astartes attend the launch arcade at this time. Launch protocols forbid anyone else.' Slayne eyed the weaponsmaster calmly, conveying only the expectation of his will obeyed. 'Return to your station. Leave us.'

'My lord–' Tagor began, but stopped as a bulky servitor followed him in, pushing him out of the way. It looked liked a lightweight dreadnought, if there was such a thing, with refined angles and sloped, graceful plating. Its gentle shuffle mimicked that of an old man but spoke of sophisticated internal suspension. It was no dreadnought. It swivelled on rotational hips and faced the Doom Warrior captain. Its shoulder guards retracted, revealing a cliff-like, ceramite trapezius with a sunken collar. From this crept a group of mechadendrites, each tapering towards a sensor of some kind. Neither a servitor, then, nor a human.

The collar split and sunk into the chest-plate, revealing a panel of vox-tines. They clamoured together as the machine spoke.

'Captain Grimmer Slayne, I assure you that our presence is warranted.' The voice was a gravelled, purling stream of binary, fashioned into words. 'The captain of *The Emperor's Despair* has in fact requested our attendance. I am Archmagos Biologis Hieronym Rottle of the Adeptus Mechanicus, successor to his most blessed Archmagos Biologis Nefarion Vaeyvor, may he calculate exponentially the glories of the Omnissiah.'

Slayne bristled at the Mechanicus tin can. The being must have been but a fraction organic – and it was only after he inspected its ceramite exterior that he noticed the wafer-thin glass casings. They presented the proof of its humanity. Slices of flesh were presented like seals of authority. The flesh was putrescent, rotting, as if it had died long ago and simply existed upon the machine to vouch for its humanity. 'What are you doing here?' Slayne asked coldly.

'My friend,' warbled the binary harmony of Rottle's vox, 'I come in peace, as indeed do we all.' He gestured towards Carnage, through the nearest viewing bay, and shuffled into the launch arcade. A number of heavily-augmented Mechanicus adepts, tech-priests and servitors followed behind him, along with several skittering spider-scribes and a thrumming servo-skull. 'Do you know what you are launching at Carnage?'

'The Life-Eater,' answered Slayne.

Rottle's response was a digital cacophony. Slayne thought it was laughter. Another mechadendrite snaked its way from the sunken collar and, curving in upon itself with a curious sense of display, winked out a holographic image of a phosphorescent liquid. Though the image occasionally shook and shimmered, the liquid was beautiful, a viscously glittering fluid that caressed the insides of its tank gently, even compassionately. It looked alive, and kind, and good.

'The Emperor's Tears, Captain Slayne,' Rottle continued. 'An evolved Life-Eater that attacks not meat and bone, but the spark of life itself. The old Life-Eater devoured protein, multiplying exponentially as it did so, turning all organic matter into pyroplosive sludge that burned away the very elements capable of sustaining life. The Emperor's Tears takes away life itself. A far more efficient means of killing, I think you'll agree.' There was a moment of rapturous fidgeting from Rottle's retinue.

'The Emperor's Tears is a fine name, archmagos,' answered Slayne. 'It conveys the great compassion of our God-Emperor.' He paused, eager to conclude the conversation. 'The Emperor protects,' he said simply, crossing his gauntleted hands and striking his chest-plate with the sign of the aquila.

'And He destroys,' continued Rottle, with a flutter of short, prehensile tentacles that flowered around his collar like a grandiose ruff. 'Shall we?'

Slayne wondered if the ship's captain would object to Squad Qannix putting a few hundred bolter rounds into this Rottle-machine, his retinue, and weaponsmaster Tagor. If only they weren't standing in such a sensitive area of the ship, such impertinence would have been punished.

But the time had come. A prayer siren sounded, soon followed by the heavy chimes of consecrated launch bells.

All around them, and along the length of the launch arcade, servitors awoke from their offline slumber to begin nursing the control slates of the great firing cylinders. Squad Qannix stood still, watching impassively, while Rottle's retinue could barely contain their curiosity. Archmagos Biologis Hieronym Rottle was especially animated. Sensory proboscis, antennae and aerials unfurled from his open collar to savour the moment.

Slayne's enhanced sense of smell soon detected more incense in the air. Purity rituals were being observed in the distant arming chamber. The air extraction system initialised and oxygen was suddenly pulled from the room, and replaced, at great speed. Unprepared for the turbulence, Rottle's servo-skull was dashed against a bulkhead and destroyed. Rottle was too busy following the launch protocols to flinch. Slayne simply didn't care.

Several of the servitors slowed their calculations, aware that targeting solutions were now confirmed and the torpedoes in place. With the Emperor's Tears ready for launch, it was with grim satisfaction that Slayne considered the notion of the Emperor weeping. A weaker man might indeed cry, he thought, wryly pondering the scope for munitions error. A new weapon was always interesting until it jammed, overheated, or was copied by those Throne-damned orks. A thunderous shudder broke his contemplation.

Deep in the bowels of the ship, a rumbling fury swiftly built towards a throbbing, ear-cracking crescendo – and then vanished. With a silent blossoming of light, a salvo of viral torpedoes began their swift descent towards Carnage. They winked in the light of the distant sun, brilliant before the blackness beyond.

The torpedoes struck the upper atmosphere like splashes of quicksilver. Through the viewing bays of the launch arcade, their disintegration was beautiful, their payloads sparkling and glinting in the sun's light. Though dwarfed by the sheer scale of the planet, and soon lost in its thick atmosphere, the Emperor's Tears had an immediate effect. As the lower atmosphere was punctured, great, dark clouds of dead matter billowed into space. It was the dying bacteria that lived in the planet's ammonia-rich atmosphere. As life increased in complexity and frequency towards the planet's surface, such dark clouds became stains racing across the planet, like oil upon water, contaminating every iota of life with death, robbing all existence of being. Clouds of dead and decaying matter mushroomed into space, propelled by the violence of their own destruction. The hive-mines became still within moments.

Carnage became a place of peace.

Orbital scans indicated that death had descended upon the planet. Servitors croaked and drooled as they calculated the awesome power of the Emperor's compassion. Slayne raised an eyebrow. What the old Life-Eater virus could accomplish in hours was happening in moments. The universe had just become a little darker.

Within minutes, Carnage was dead. And then it happened.

Carnage came back to life.

Servitors reeled off impossible data-readings. Reams of script and punched parchment spooled onto the deck in untidy heaps. Lights blinked and klaxons roared throughout the launch arcade. Elsewhere on *The Emperor's Despair*, the ship's great logic engines struggled to compute the surge in planetary life-sign. The ship's very machine-spirit cried out in confusion, causing whole galleries of hard-wired tech-adepts to die instantly. Most of the ship's astropaths, prepared for the planet's psychic death, died in the aftershock of its rebirth.

Slayne was unsure what he was watching, but he didn't like the roiling atmosphere. It swirled across the planet at such speed that much of it escaped the planet's gravity sink and dissipated into space. Bruised swathes of remaining cloud hung over the planet's dark continents. Storm systems reared up in great thunderheads like vast scabs. Slayne had never seen a planet look so wrong outside of the Eye of Terror.

'By the Golden Throne,' he muttered, touching his breastplate softly.

Rottle laughed, his binary inflection suddenly thick and organic. A cry of triumph. It was even audible over the sound of the oxygen exchangers.

Despite the proximity of the ship's outer hull, Slayne was the first to raise his bolter. Squad Qannix followed a moment later, reading their captain's reaction. They opened fire as one. A hail of bolter shells pummelled the ceramite of Rottle's chassis, but he continued to wail with laughter – inhumanly guttural and congested. The bolter shells cracked his ceramite and plasticrete shell, but it was clear to Slayne that Rottle's over-augmented carapace was the least of their worries.

Slivers of Rottle's original tissue swelled and distended, cracking their flexi-glass seals and sending shards of strengthened glass scattering across the deck. As Rottle's chassis staggered under the hail of fire and began to disintegrate into flakes and then fragments, his original flesh bloated and blew into great hunks of fatty meat. Where bolter shells blew chunks of the rancid tissue away, more unfolding fleshy matter fell into place, creating a great bulbous, quivering mass.

Rottle's vox-tines had been shot to pieces but his triumphal cry still reverberated around the launch arcade. Now it was a throaty, rich roar, as fleshy and deep as any bass-vox song-servitor. The sound carried its own stench. Slayne's implants strained to stop him gagging. Most of Rottle's retinue were either vomiting up their own wiring, killed in the crossfire, or ripped apart by ricocheting mass-reactive rounds.

The broken chassis suddenly cracked wide open, spilling out new organs, sheaths of muscle and fat, as well as the internal workings of Rottle's mechanical form.

'Fire at the flesh, Doom Warriors!' cried Slayne, closing in on the mass of blubber and meat. It was already gathering itself together.

'*Doom ye! Doom ye! Doom ye!*' cried his battle-brothers, advancing step-by-step to the Chapter's war-drum chant. Bolter fire intensified. Explosions of sound, reverberating shockwaves, and magnesium flashes shook the air as well as the very structure of the ship.

Despite chunks of flesh being blown apart from the mass of meat surrounding what remained of Hieronym Rottle, a recognisably humanoid form had coalesced and congealed into shape. There stood a grinning figure of pestilential depravity. It was a bloated, swollen creature whose cancerous entrails fell from its own torn stomach. It was truly obese, rolls of rotting blubber wrapped around a vast frame of suppurating tissue and rancid meat. The concentrated bolter fire was slowly eroding its vile mass, blowing it apart, gobbet by gobbet of flesh.

It just stood there, grinning, rejoicing in its own undoing.

'*Doom ye! Doom ye! Doom ye!*' cried the Doom Warriors, advancing to point-blank range. Muzzle fire blackened and crisped some of the creature's extremities. The smell of charred meat hung heavy in the air. When the creature finally collapsed, it was a flaccid bag of torn and broken skin. Lumps of tissue, muscle and organ lay everywhere. Steam, stench and cordite hung thick in the air.

It was an emissary of Nurgle, a name known only to servants of the Ordo Malleus, of the Holy Ordos of the Emperor's Inquisition, who would only utter it behind psychic wards of protection. Embodying despair, decay, disease, and death, the Unclean One was beyond the recognition of anyone aboard *The*

Emperor's Despair. Even Captain Slayne had never encountered a daemon of the Plague God.

Upon the floor, amongst the congealing gore, lay the daemon's cankered lips. They moved.

Slayne was lost for words and looked at Sergeant Qannix. As Doom Warriors often did, he shrugged his great shoulder guards. Other members of the squad did the same as they checked their bolters.

The lips were alive, sucking sounds from the air and spitting them forth: 'You have pulled me inside out, my children,' the lips chuckled. 'Meet the wasted flesh of poor, poor Hieronym Rottle. So keen to escape his living meat. He never quite understood.'

Slayne opened fire once more, ripping the lips apart once again. Chunks of rancid flesh skittered across the deck. And yet the lips continued to speak, flapping obscenely amidst the gore. 'Look no further than the body of my vessel to pay homage to the host. You think you can kill Hieronym Rottle, my children? Imagine looking out of his eyes for all those years like I did – and then through his *unfleshed* lenses.' The lips dribbled a stinking wad of rotten phlegm. Slayne nearly gagged at the stench, despite his implanted olfactory filters. 'There is *nothing* beyond the flesh, my children. Flesh is life, alive or dead.'

Slayne brought his great ceramite boot down with a crack. He felt the deck buckle. The lips were no more.

'Well, that's some dead flesh there, captain.' Qannix was unable to resist contradicting the being's final words.

'Silence, brother,' Slayne said. Servitors still gibbered and drooled impossible calculations.

Parchment swirled onto the deck from overheated logic-engines and corrupted data-feeds. The machine-spirit of *The Emperor's Despair* still groaned and wailed. Klaxons, chimes, and horns filled the launch arcade with overwhelming dissonance. Something was still very, very wrong.

Slayne holstered his bolter and made the sign of the Emperor's aquila. With his thumbs locked across his breastplate, he beat his chest. It was the sign of a battle to come.

Slayne imagined the Emperor weeping upon his Golden Throne. He vowed to bring doom to the darkling planet below.

Carnage had come back to life – and billions of undead built altars to the Lord of Decay.

PHOBOS WORKED IN ADAMANT

Robey Jenkins

THE DARKNESS IN the deep stacks had a peculiarly tangible quality, Ghuul thought as he double-checked the holographic map. Whilst not even a glimmer of light could be detected by his image intensifiers, there was a sense that the memory of light was contained in the oddly-proportioned columns of the oldest stacks. So when the sweeping searchlights of the servitor team touched one, it seemed to glow the light back at them for a moment, its ragged outline momentarily visible, even after the searchlight had moved on.

Ghuul could imagine that it was the unspeakable power of the ancient data that lurked in the silicon hearts of the stacks that made them glow. The Nine had given him leave to explore the ancient alien relics only under sufferance. They were desperate and it was he, Ghuul, who held the key to saving them and everything on Celare Artem. The Planet Killer was coming, and if Ghuul failed then they would *all* die.

'Movement,' reported Moritz, bent over her motion detector.

'Where?' Ghuul whispered back, gesturing the servitors to stillness.

'Straight ahead,' replied Moritz, her pointing hand outlined in the glow from the auspex's screen. 'Stand back, archmagos. This is why you brought me, after all.'

Ghuul stepped aside as Moritz stowed her auspex and unslung the power axe from across her shoulders. The perfectly-tuned cutting blade glowed faintly in the dark. Moritz's reputation in the skitarii – the Tech-Guard of Celare Artem – was built on a bloody foundation as one of the planet's premiere duellists; it was why Ghuul liked her so much. Beside her marched a trio of unusually light-footed combat servitors, their arms swinging in unnatural arcs from the pendulum weight of the razor-sharp blades that stood in place of each hand.

Even as Ghuul was ordering his own guardian servitors into a defensive ring, Moritz cried out.

'It's here!'

Flashing into the path of the nearest searchlight beam, the ancient construct pounced with a vicious, white-noise snarl. It was arachnid in concept: as large as a man, with four slender limbs on each side. But the delicacy was an illusion as the front pair stabbed with lightning-swiftness through the thick chest armour of the first of the servitors. A second was swiping at the automaton's back legs – too late! The spider-construct had leapt up and off the shoulders of its first victim to disappear soundlessly into the blackness above.

The remaining two combat servitors stood, arms raised in a defensive posture, without any sign of having noticed the sudden and brutal demise of their companion. Their mistress circled the dimly-lit space between the stacks, her weapon held ready. Ghuul could see the nervousness in her practised steps. Even inside his ring of bodyguards, he felt it too.

In an instant, all stillness ceased as the construct shot out from a fresh angle, arcing over Ghuul's head to decapitate a second servitor. But Moritz had anticipated the creature's arc of descent, sweeping her power axe up into an elegant sweep that sliced the creature neatly in two across its thorax.

The sparking halves struck the floor, twitching. Its deadly limbs flickered once or twice as if it might still lurch back to functionality, but then it went still.

'We must be close,' breathed Moritz, chest heaving as her super-efficient artificial lungs flooded her augmetic system with oxygen.

'Indeed we are, captain,' agreed Ghuul as two of his servitors swept the remains of the arachnoid into a stasis chest. He checked the holographic map and took a few steps forward, pushing through the defensive line of servitors.

'This is Stack Three. If the Nine are correct, this is where we will find the Tabulum Aethyricum and the secrets of the Forebears.'

'And protection from the Planet Killer,' added Moritz.

'And from that thrice-damned ship's thrice-damned master, Abaddon,' Ghuul agreed.

* * *

CELARE ARTEM.

Those who knew the forge-worlds of the Adeptus Mechanicus called her 'the Sapphire Mars'. Amongst the very oldest of the Martian forge-worlds, she had been settled even as the rest of the galaxy had reeled from the immense warp storms and disturbances of the Age of Strife, twenty millennia ago. A dead world, her settlers had built their first shelters upon the mysterious ruins of an ancient race and their first excavations had revealed marvels of alien science: marvels meticulously extracted, painstakingly recorded and piously concealed in the very deepest stand-alone datastacks. Even the *index* of that fell knowledge was guarded jealously by the Fabricator Lords: the Nine.

But with the power of that alien knowledge at the disposal of the Mechanicus, the dead world had sprung to life. Dry plains became seas. Empty deserts bloomed into forests. Wind-etched mountains grew dignified snow caps and the remains of the alien predecessors were carefully, quietly and entirely hidden. Instead, the settlers' extensive genetic database was coaxed into generating a plethora of new life and, under the watchful gaze of the biologists, Celare Artem – Wherein the Art is Concealed – became the blue-green forge-world.

'MORTUUS STERCATUS IN celestia!' roared the figure at the console, hurling a diagnostic wand at the marble floor.

The delicate instrument shattered on contact, its components bursting into shrapnel across the polished stone. The silence that followed was filled with the echoing wheeze of the robed figure's deep, ragged breaths as he stood, shoulders heaving, staring at the other who watched him from the far side of the temple's portico.

'Having some trouble, Archmagos Ghuul?' sneered the man, robed in the bone-white of his Collegium, his hood pushed back from his bald pate to expose the mass of cables that hung down from his scalp. Some of them twisted like snakes around his cheeks as he approached. The dim fragments of light that mosaiced the floor threw long shadows across the newcomer's face: his hollow cheeks and deep-set eyes gave him the demeanour of some elemental of death, come to haunt Ghuul's miserable night of failure. 'It seems to me that I might have to inform the Forty that you lied to them. And to the Nine. Won't that be a shame?'

'What have you done to my design, Frenke?' snarled Ghuul. 'Would you jeopardize our whole *world* just to see me disgraced? Are you still so bitter at my elevation?'

'Certainly not, archmagos.' Frenke's smile was as benign as a rictus. 'I am above such petty rivalries. And I would not dishonour my Collegium or the spirits of the Great Temple by petty sabotage. If only I could say the same for you.'

He circumnavigated the construction that dominated the grand space of the Portico Publicum, peering up at the cluster of miniature warp core mantles that sat together at the heart of the generator. The whole construction was a labyrinth of cables, cogitators, power regulators, booster generators and current alternators that formed an irregular column shape rising from the floor into the vaulted roof, two hundred metres above them. Dotted along its length, vicious-looking dimension probes – a design Ghuul had personally recovered from an ancient hulk that had appeared on the edge of the Eye of Terror, some hundred years ago – thrust out of the mass that rose up like an alien idol into the distant, vaulted roof of the Great Temple. And some twenty-four thousand kilometres immediately above it was a satellite: the first in a network of precisely seventy-two identical satellites, each with their own halo of eight dimension probes, which would harness the output of the field generator, casting a web of protection around the entire planet... if it worked.

'Innovative!' Frenke spat. 'I knew from the start that this obscene perversion would fail – that trying to create something *new* was doomed. You lack the piety to understand the will of the Machine, Ghuul. I've known of your foul Xenarite beliefs from the start. Celare Artem should never have encouraged your kind. The Nine should never have revealed the location of the Tabulum to one so... unorthodox.'

'Be careful what you say, Frenke,' hissed Ghuul. His bionic hands were of the most delicate type, designed to assist infinitely cautious and dangerous experiments and research on the strange alternate dimension of the warp. But as his anger at himself turned on the gloating astro-technologist, the hands balled into solid fists, seemingly of their own accord.

'No, Ghuul,' snapped Frenke. 'I don't think I shall be careful. You deceived the Forty into believing that you could save our world from the Planet Killer with this... *device*. And we've wasted fifteen work cycles tolerating its *blasphemy* on the very doorstep of the Holy of Holies. And after all that, Ghuul; after all that... it doesn't work!'

'It works!' Ghuul roared, closing on this avatar of his nemesis, his feet pounding on the marble as he marched to confront Frenke. 'My theories are right! There is *no* reason why I should not be able to generate a warp shield around the whole planet, powerful enough to defend against even the Planet Killer!'

'But you can't, can you?' Frenke hissed back.

'Because I have *missed* something!' blustered Ghuul, waving his hands limply. 'The theories are sound. The mechanism... I have tested it over and over again. It is consuming forty per cent of Artem Prime's power generation and nothing is happening!'

'Exactly!' shouted Frenke, triumphantly.

'No, Frenke, you *never* listen properly!' snapped back Ghuul. '*Nothing* is happening. The power is being consumed by the machinery without being converted into anything else: no light, no heat, no motion... The device *must* work. The projection field *must* be in place already but there's some... missing ingredient! Don't you understand?'

Frenke's smile returned, cruelly wider than before.

'I understand, Ghuul,' he whispered. 'I understand that you're so incompetent that you seem to have turned your attention away from the Mysteria Machinata to... domestic science? A "missing ingredient"? You're pathetic. Tomorrow the Nine will order you servitorised for your blasphemy and I shall lead the true devoted of Celare Artem onto the evacuation ships, just as we should have done fifteen work cycles ago!'

He turned and began to walk away.

'No!' cried Ghuul. He reached out and seized Frenke's cowl where it hung around his shoulders, yanking his rival back.

'You dare?' snapped Frenke, bringing his own metal limb around to swipe at Ghuul's. He knocked away the grip on his cowl, but Ghuul had already seized Frenke by the neck. The tension strips under Frenke's skin went rigid and Ghuul felt as if he was gripping plasteel, but Frenke had already retaliated. His right hand smashed into Ghuul's face and the desperate archmagos felt his cheekbone shatter and blood fill his mouth. As he fell to his knees, he stabbed upwards with his right hand, piercing Frenke's robes with the scalpel-sharp points of his fingers and thrusting into soft tissue.

Frenke's only response was a soft breath of pain before he brought his elbow down heavily onto Ghuul's left shoulder, snapping his collarbone.

'I will make you my personal servitor, blasphemer!' he spat into Ghuul's pale face. 'You will perform my ablutions with your heretic tongue!'

Frenke raised his hand and Ghuul saw the foot-long blade slide smoothly from its hidden scabbard inside Frenke's synthetic forearm. There was no time left for regrets. The cocktail of painkillers and stimulants that his integrated pharmacopoeia had been pumping into his veins for the last minute finally kicked in as the blade began to fall and Ghuul thrust up with both hands at once, shoving at his enemy's torso, driving him back towards the silent tower of his machine.

'You–!' cried Frenke, stumbling as his heel caught on the edge of a polished marble flagstone. His arms flailed madly, trying to regain his balance, but he fell back and Ghuul yelled in panic as he realised that Frenke was going to stumble into his precious creation.

There was a sound of wet scraping as Frenke fell, but halfway back towards the mass of twisted cables, he stopped. Frenke stared at the point protruding from his chest and raised one hand to touch the slick metal. But strength fled his limbs and with a hiss of escaping breath, he flopped. Ghuul sat crumpled in undignified repose, staring at the impaled form of the astro-technologist. The point of the dimension probe thrust up through Frenke's chest, glossy in the dim light with the viscera of ruptured soft tissue and delicate bionic implants.

He stared at Frenke's unmoving form. Ghuul's hands shook from adrenaline even as his internal systems automatically began detoxification, settling his shock and calming his mounting fear. This was not good. His implant scanners confirmed the cessation of lifesigns in the astro-technologist. Frenke had been at least seven hundred years old and the deputy head of the Collegium Teledynamicum. How could he be dead, just like that? Was there nothing left of him? No shred of his essence…?

Suddenly, there was a click and a hum from the console and, still fizzing with the potent effects of the chemical injections that had saved his life, Ghuul leapt to the monitor, snatching another diagnostic wand from his belt.

Output! Suddenly, the machine was showing output! It was weak, for sure: only the tiniest fraction of a percentage of his forecast was now being emitted by the shield generator. But that was an infinitely greater proportion than the void that had, until now, been his sum achievement.

'Udo!' he screamed, gleefully, depressing the inter-com rune. 'Udo!'

In less than a minute, his lead acolyte – a young adept in beige robes, marked with the red border of the Mechanicus and the sky blue of the Metaphysicum – came hurrying into the portico, trying not to run, in respect for the sanctity of the Great Temple, but prodded into haste by his master's tone.

'Magister, yes, I'm–'

Udo froze in shock as his augmetic eyes rapidly adjusted to the gloom of the space and the cooling form of Frenke's corpse appeared before him.

'Quick, boy, we have output!' snapped Ghuul.

'But, magister, the Archmagos Frenke is–'

'I know, boy, I know!' Ghuul paused, suddenly aware of the sight he had so thoughtlessly left untouched in the very portico of the Great Temple of Celare Artem. The Nine were desperate, but not so desperate as to consider the death of a senior adept as a reasonable price for success. 'He attacked me, child! Tried to destroy the generator! But look! The output!'

'Output?' queried Udo, his natural dedication to the matters of the Metaphysicum finally overwhelming his shock at the sight of the impaled Frenke. 'At last! How?'

Ghuul jabbed a gleaming finger at the corpse.

'Life force, Udo!' He grinned in half-mad triumph. 'The element I was missing: the link between the warp and our dimensions is all around us! You, me… Frenke. As he died, his life force reinforced the energy transition and released some of the reflection power back into the generator!'

'Yes, yes, of course,' nodded Udo. 'But how do we get more?'

'Let me worry about that, child,' replied Ghuul, turning back to feast his eyes greedily upon the miniscule change in the readings that had vindicated three centuries of research. 'Get Frenke down and dispose of the body. It's nearly dawn.'

ASTROPATH-PRIME XENOCH hesitated at the door to the Chamber of Silence. His white eyes stared blindly into the gloom, but his psychic senses stretched out to touch the plain walls, the stone floor, the table... The presence of the nine cards on the table was bloated and malign in the landscape of his mind. For twenty work cycles he had meditated upon the reading he had performed at the direction of Celare Artem's Fabricator Lords – the Nine – and now, as he had sworn, he had returned to re-examine their import. The noise of the violent crowds outside the walls was not helping his concentration.

The Castle of Sighs, sacrosanct domain of the Adeptus Astra Telepathica on Celare Artem, was traditionally both dark and silent. Its blind occupants needed no light, and the stillness of quiet made adopting astrotelepathic trances easier. The disturbances wracking the warp around the usually stable Beltane Gate had been making communication with systems elsewhere in the sector increasingly sporadic and that was poor for morale in the Castle. But since word of his first reading had leaked, the darkness and silence had entirely ceased to be a comfort. The approaching doom had infected the minds of the forge-world's astropaths, flitting telepathically from one to another, growing and mutating so that uncertainty became doubt and doubt became fear and fear... Well, now there was a horde of panicking

menials, making crude attempts to break into the
stronghold. A century of the Tech-Guard was
deployed to keep them back. And the latest news was
that the Archmagos Ghuul had hit upon an inge-
nious solution to the problem.

'Wait here,' he instructed his assistants.

Xenoch entered the Chamber of Silence and sealed
the door behind him. It was the only Null Chamber
in the Castle of Sighs and, as the door sealed and the
wards of shielding energised the psychic wall, he felt
the constant link to his brothers and sisters of the
Castle suddenly break off. For the first time he could
remember in his long life, it was a relief to be separated from the minds of his adopted family.

Alone with his thoughts, his psychic sense of place
and surroundings shut off by the Null shielding, he
was nothing but a blind man: a scared blind man.
But the cards were waiting for him on the table. He
felt his way there and seated himself carefully in the
throne-like chair.

For most astropaths, to meditate with one's psychic
senses closed off was almost impossible. And few
could master the practice of reading the Emperor's
Tarot in a Null chamber. But the psyker's mind
resided more fully in the nightmare realm of the
warp than did the mind of the blunt human. He was
open, Xenoch knew, to malign influences with
strange agenda. The open mind – even of an
astropath, soul-bound with the Emperor Himself –
was a door of invitation to the spawn of darkness
that clustered, waiting for the moment of weakness
that called them…

But even a Null chamber could not entirely dim an
astropath's connection to the warp. He was blind,

physically and psychically, but the spark of power that had bound him in love and in pain to the mighty soul of Him-on-Earth still burned with an inextinguishable light. Xenoch focused on the light, letting it grow within himself, until his mind fell away. The doubt fell away. The fear fell away. Only the light was left: the unbreakable link through time and space to the enthroned God-Emperor.

'Prime Xenoch,' came a voice over the intercom and the astropath tutted at the interruption.

'What?' he snapped back.

'The rioting is getting worse. The skitarii have fallen back to the inner curtain wall and have taken casualties.'

'I will be there directly,' Xenoch replied, sharply. 'Do not interrupt me again.'

Xenoch heard the intercom connection click off and, re-gathering his calm, he stretched out his hands to the cards. Their toad-like psychic corpulence had been quashed with the sealing of the chamber's door and now they were mere cards: immensely precious, psycho-crystalline wafer cards, hand-crafted by a magos of the Collegium Psykana and precisely attuned to Xenoch's own self but, ultimately, just cards. With the chamber's Null shielding switched off, the cards blossomed with psychic life so fresh and bold that it was visible even to the non-psychic. But the ridges and bumps painstakingly crafted along the edges of each card were all that could tell him their identity now.

He touched the first: the Eye of Terror. It sat in the master position at the centre of the spread as harbinger of change and refuge of the damned. At the hub of the spread, it spoke of corruption at the very heart of things.

Beneath it, the Knight of Spheres lay inverted.

Xenoch sighed. The import of the cards seemed no less dire to him now than it had at his first reading. The gaze of Dark Powers had fallen upon Celare Artem; that much was indisputable.

Following the cards clockwise around the circle, Xenoch touched each in turn, refreshing his memory as to their exact locations, mining deeply within his knowledge and instinct to read the import of each.

The Nine of Chalices was a card of weak leadership and uncertainty. The Traitor stood at the right hand of the Eye of Terror. Above him was the Ace of Staves, foretelling the abuse of power. At the head of the Eye of Terror stood the magos, inverted – a dire warning of secret knowledge best left untouched – then the Two of Weapons, which stood for duality and for motives unclear even to the prime movers. On the left hand of the eye lay the Leviathan (the touch of the Ancients) and, below it and last in the spread, the Seven of Weapons, inverted (confusion and the threat of the mob).

'Prime Xenoch!'

The voice on the intercom was panicked, but Xenoch was too intensely focussed upon his work to notice immediately.

'I am not to be disturbed!' he shouted, hands shaking.

'Menials are in the Castle, Prime Xenoch! The skitarii–'

The voice cut off suddenly and Xenoch glanced reflexively towards the door. Was that a noise from the corridor?

His hand fell upon the last card once more: confusion and the threat of the mob? Surely –

The door of the chamber shot open, the Null shielding collapsed and the three dark figures poured in along with telepathic screams of terror, death and blood.

'No!' Xenoch had time to cry out before the crude bludgeon of the menial's metal arm fell crushingly upon his skull and the astropath tumbled, dead, to the floor. Around him, his precious cards fell like a shower of rain.

AT DAWN, THE representatives of the Collegia met to receive the news of the death of Astropath-Prime Xenoch and his entire complement of astropaths. But the fear-sharpened anger at the loss of their only means of interstellar communications was blunted by the delighted report of Archmagos Ghuul. It was only logical, Ghuul concluded, that the condemned menials, who had so brutally murdered the astropaths, be handed over to him for further experimentation on the link between life-force and the coherence of the defence shield.

At noon, the Nine ritually invested Bastian Ghuul with Magenta authority and three thousand more expendable menials.

By sunset, a new structure had begun to grow on the great basalt doorstep of the Portico Publicum and its interior hummed in bilious luminescence. This new child of the Tabulum Aethyricum grew like twin trees, curling in weird organic curves up mighty amphibolite columns. As night fell, the structures reached their zenith, curving together across the architrave and intertwining their malign branches. With a static crack of ignition, the Annihilator burst into life: a shimmering, green window to oblivion.

* * *

GHUUL GLANCED SIDEWAYS at Moritz. Only centuries of experience allowed him to interpret her expression behind the patchwork of scars that consumed her face. The Skitaria's eyes sparkled with glee as she watched the Annihilator consume each team of menials. The new device was almost divinely efficient. To have continued impaling menials on the dimension probes would have been preposterous – the remains of several early experiments still hung from their places, as a grisly memorial to their sacrifice to the Machine-God. The Annihilator, though, directly fed life-force to the shield generator whilst reducing the sacrifices to nothing more than insubstantial atomic dust.

'Are you all right, Moritz?' he asked the normally benevolent soldier.

'Don't you sense it, archmagos?' she asked. 'Can't you feel the rightness of our path? Look–' she gestured at the flock of menials being herded through the gate by the hooded skitarii guards. 'Even *they* can feel the call of the device!'

Ghuul nodded distractedly. It was true. They had set up a plascrete tunnel to conceal the effects of the Annihilator from its waiting victims, but menials who had at first approached cautiously and fearfully were now surging forward in confused enthusiasm. The skitarii scarcely had to even point them in the right direction – although some swung their shock mauls anyway; whether to look busy or merely out of bullying instincts, he could not tell. But he saw nothing sinister in the change. They had seen dozens of their fellows go in already. There were no screams and the skitarii were disciplined and orderly. Why should they fear anything malign?

Of course, he could sense the effect that the device was having – as its power grew and spread, a sense of intense calm and security filled him. But the sacrifice was not a gleeful activity – it was merely necessary: the only way to protect his homeworld. The machine brought safety and a future in the truest expression of the Machine-God's benevolence. It was unusual to see an effect drawn from the life-force of humans, but it had always been that way in a sense, had it not? Weak flesh dies. The Machine endures.

But this effect on Moritz was disturbing.

'Archmagos?' The Praetorian-Captain of the Temple Guard interrupted with a formal salute. 'We are nearing the end of the supply of menials.'

Ghuul tutted.

'We're barely at a consistent thirty per cent coverage and far from the power estimates my calculations predicted. I'll petition the Nine for more.'

'No!' barked Moritz suddenly.

Ghuul turned to Moritz in surprise, but she pushed past him and stabbed her augmented right hand at the skitarius officer.

'We don't have time to wait for those relics to make up their minds when we know what our world needs!

'Get out there, captain, and round up every menial your regiment can find.'

The skitarius saluted again, turned and marched away.

'Relics?' Ghuul queried, stunned. 'And when did the Temple-Guard start following *your* orders? I have Magenta clearance.'

'This is too important, Ghuul,' snarled Moritz, her mechadendrites waving aggressively. 'I obtained

Dark Magenta clearance and the rank of Magos Commander to take control of the skitarii regiments. You concentrate on keeping your damned engine running!'

Moritz walked away and Ghuul silently watched her leave.

My project, thought Ghuul bitterly. *My* research, *my* vision, *my* genius, Moritz. You will not build your own worthless reputation where *my* glory should stand!

OUTSIDE THE HOUSE of Nine, Ghuul paused on the threshold and wondered what he would say – *could* say – to persuade the Fabricator Lords of Celare Artem to sacrifice even more menials to the strange idol he had built. But even as he hesitated, the great doors cracked apart to swing silently inwards on perfectly balanced bearings and he immediately thrust his hands respectfully into his sleeves and bowed his head. A fog of smoke, heavy with incense and rare oil fractions, rolled across him like the unfragrant breath of a dragon, and the Fabricators spoke – many voices enunciating the same words in scratchy, amplified unison.

'Does it work, young Ghuul?'

Ghuul could hear the fear as well as the hope in their voices. A coolant leak somewhere nearby was spilling a thin layer of nitrogen in an undulating carpet across the floor but, here and there, it broke to reveal the gleaming, black marble floor and, in it, the reflections of the Nine, encased in their life support systems, orifices plugged and ancient skin gleaming with moisturising lubricant. They were trapped by their own power, Ghuul thought suddenly. They had sacrificed their humanity to knowledge. But did that make them more or less than human?

'Yes, my lords,' he bowed. 'We have sustained thirty-four point seven per cent coverage for up to twenty minutes. But we have a permanent output of twenty-seven per cent.'

'Unacceptable!' rumbled the Fabricator Lords. He sensed a forest of serpentine mechadendrites above his head, waving and clattering in panic.

'We have extracted catalysing agents from barely three thousand menials,' explained Ghuul, venturing to raise his head slightly. 'And each extra percentage point needs a geometrically-greater quantity of agents to achieve.'

'You have Vermillion clearance, Ghuul,' they announced, and he lifted his head all the way up to look at the Nine. His visual units cut through the gloom to fully reveal their withered and ancient forms, trapped in communion with the Machine. They were fragile and flimsy, for all their immense knowledge. Their fear made them vulnerable and weak. They did not, truly, possess the faith in the power of the Machine that Ghuul knew he had: the certainty of the rightness of his course. They did not *deserve* their supremacy.

'Vermillion?' he queried. 'Vermillion Prime?'

'Vermillion Prime,' they agreed.

Without a bow, Ghuul turned and left. The armoured doors swung shut behind him. He almost believed he could feel the fresh authority that had won him victory not only over that upstart girl, Moritz, but also over the pathetic husks of the Nine. Vermillion Prime clearance made him the single most powerful tech-adept on the whole of Celare

Artem. The sense of tangible authority might have
been an illusion, but the responses from the systems
around him were real and instant.

A swarm of servo-skulls swept down from the ceiling, reprioritized from whatever they had been
doing, to serve his needs; cogitator banks lit up in
obedient, eager readiness to the passing touch of his
mechadendrites and, as he reached the central hall of
the Temple, the head of every priest, skitarii and
menial turned instantly towards him, their own deep
conditioning responding as one to the authority
codes being invisibly transmitted from his person.

Closest to him stood Moritz. The shock of the sig-
nals that even now were coursing through the
skitarii's systems stood out clear on her face. But
Ghuul just smiled, the auxiliary cables beneath his
bionic eye twisting at the motion.

'Round them up,' he ordered. 'All of them.'

IT WAS ASTONISHING, thought Ghuul as he swam free
in the soup of data that had now been placed at his
disposal. Here, he could sense the whole planet shifting and moving in step to his direction. With less
than a nod, regiments of skitarii Tech-Guard moved
at his whim. The sagitarii veterans drove stragglers
from their hiding places within the forests, burning
them into the open. The cataphracti rumbled along
the wide avenues of the forge-world's many cities,
driving the soft mass of menials before them.

But Moritz had been right: there was little of the
resentment and resistance he had expected. The riots
of just two days ago had calmed under the benign
influence of the growing shield. The population had
become compliant and docile. It occurred to him

that perhaps the fragmentary alien designs from the Tabulum Aethyricum had been designed as much for this purpose as for the shielding. For the first time since he had found them, he wondered what race had preceded them on this world. The earliest stacks were unconnected to the data altar and always had been. What had the first settlers been so afraid of?

'Forty-two point nine per cent, archmagos,' announced Udo from somewhere far away.

With a conscious effort of will, Ghuul dragged himself up to the surface and out of the deep connections his new authority had opened up to him. It was easy to see why the Nine so easily surrendered their mobility for this sort of intimacy with the Machine. And why it was so hard to rouse them to anything close to normal consciousness.

'For how long?' he asked as he opened his eye.

'Permanent, master,' reported Udo, with a smile. 'Although it still takes a geometrically greater input of material for each increase, we are sustaining almost half your predicted output.'

'Still not enough,' sighed Ghuul. 'How many have we used?'

'Four hundred and eight thousand and sixty-three and counting, archmagos.'

'Barely a tenth of the total menial population, then?' grunted Ghuul. 'I shall redirect Phi-Omega Maniple to Artem Peripheral, and tithe the remainder a further ten per cent.'

'Yes, archmagos.' Udo bowed and retreated. The chamber in which Ghuul sat was known as the Chapel of Bronze, but his assistants already treated it with the reverence reserved for the House of Nine. Ghuul knew that his authority, so lightly given, had done more than merely raise his status. It had brought him closer to the Machine. He was becoming more like his God.

With a sigh, he descended once more into the deeps.

But something had changed in the world, even as he had spoken to Udo. The population data had shifted significantly. He quickly patched into a low-orbit satellite to look down at the nearest example of the shift in Artem Tertius and, yes: a great mass of people was leaving the city! Were they fleeing?

Immediately, though, he could see that they were moving, not away from Artem Prime and the Annihilator, but towards it. The tram lines were full and the great transport flyways that arched over Celare Artem's fastidiously-crafted forest regions were increasingly busy with every form of transport. Even the footways bore a steady stream of pilgrims on every major link running towards Artem Prime...

Pilgrims, he thought. That was what they were, after all. They were coming to him. Coming to the mighty new idol of the Machine-God that he had raised in the Great Temple, but which cast its shadow of protection over the whole planet: a shadow built from the very soul-stuff of the world's children. It was poetically beautiful. He dismissed his earlier doubts with a smile. His plan was perfectly at one accord with the very spirit of the Machine God. How could it be otherwise?

THEY CAME TO do homage in the tens of thousands until the streets of Artem Prime were choked with pilgrims,

camping on every corner and blocking the wide boulevards with their numbers. And still they came.

'The Planet Killer comes, young Ghuul,' wheezed
the unison drone of the Nine in his ear. 'How do we
fare?'

It was a spurious question. Ghuul was permanently
uplinked to the data-altar now. His knowledge was as
immediately available to the Nine as it was to him.
But despite the patronising tone, the Nine were
deferring to Ghuul, architect of their salvation.

'Seventy-four point three per cent, my lords,' he
replied anyway. 'My calculations show that we need
at least seventy-five point one per cent output to pro-
vide protection against even the least ambitious
estimate of the Planet Killer's power.'

'There is no shortage of menials?'

It certainly seemed that way if one were unable
to see beyond the walls of Artem Prime, he
thought spitefully. But in fact they had already
consumed over sixty per cent of the menial population. Artem Tertius, Peripheral and Zonal Geiger
had already been shut down, their entire menial
population stripped to feed the machine. Even
now, his obedient tech-priests were stripping out
every hard-wired servitor form they could access,
shipping them in sealed stasis containers for annihilation.

Ghuul could not imagine what use its alien design-
ers had intended for the Annihilator, but into its
insatiable maw a thousand more desperate volun-
teers marched every hour. Each fresh death, each new
release of life-force, pushed the generator's output
higher towards the vital one hundred per cent
marker...

'No,' Ghuul agreed at last. 'You're right. There is no shortage of expendable flesh.'

He understood what had to be done to protect *his* world.

THEY SCREAMED AS they were put through. No one else had screamed. Hundreds of thousands of menials had marched like stunned cattle through the gates of the Annihilator. The twitching quadriplegic forms of disconnected servitors were pushed or carried through without even a moan. But when Udo and Moritz brought a team to rip the Fabricator Lords from their places in the House of Nine, the ancient magi yelled and hissed in protest. When, without a word of explanation, they were carried into the streets, into the bright sunshine of Celare Artem, they wailed at the touch of natural light as ragged sockets dripped milky, pink fluid onto the granite pavings. And, as blank-eyed menials carried their limp, oil-crusted bodies across the lintel of the Portico Publicum, they screamed in terror and final under-standing until, in a perfect instant of disembodiment, their voices were stilled.

The sudden silence seemed to roll across the packed square of the Temple Courtyard and down the heaving avenues and into the immense forests. It was Moritz, lurking at his elbow, as she had been for weeks, who broke the silence first, but her voice was a whisper: too quiet for Ghuul's audio-receptors.

'What?' Ghuul turned to look at her. But her eyes were fixed upon the towering door of the Temple. Her scarred features had gone slack and her arms hung limp, as if she had died but not yet fallen over. Her lips moved again and Ghuul was about to increase his audio-input when he heard the same whisper roll across the crowd in the square: the susurration of waves upon a shore as the dark clouds banked upon the horizon.

'Φόβος.'

The word hissed off the lips of every face in the immense square. It slithered from the mouths of his assistants and clicked from the oro-emitters of his servitor bodyguards. It sighed from the tannoy systems. And in the deep recesses of the most ancient Stacks, it hummed and sparked from the data vault's dark, alien heart.

Ghuul looked wildly about himself, desperate to find the source of the sudden, strange change in his people. But even as he thought to retreat, he found himself pinned in place by the weight of the optic cable attached to his skull, which his servitor attendants had dropped at the same moment as the word 'Φόβος' spilled from their slack and bloodless mouths. And then the crowd was moving. As one, they surged towards the Annihilator. All regard for Ghuul's authority codes was gone, now. He was jostled and pushed. The cable was kicked and stepped on and tripped over and, with its wild movements, Ghuul was himself jerked about like a puppet, driven with the crowds towards the gaping space of the Portico Publicum.

'No!' he shrieked, and thought suddenly of the desperate, terrified Fabricator Lords whom he had sent to the same fate, minutes before.

But, even as the surging crowd thrust him to within a few feet from the Annihilator, the cable on his skull reached the end of its extent and yanked him to an irresistible halt. The ranks of his people surged around him, a stream around a rock, into the teeth of the humming portal.

Moritz rushed past him without so much as a backward glance and he whimpered after her as she stepped into eternity. It was over in a split second, but in that moment he saw, first, her robes disintegrate, then her peripheral augmentations, her skin – flaying her to the wet muscle – the soft tissue, bones and organs… all stripped apart to their constituent atoms in a fraction of a second. But by then, dozens more had hit the field, their bodies ripped to nothing as their life-force was siphoned away by the hunger of the shield generator.

The passivity of the crowd was crumbling. The slower movers were crushed beneath the urgent feet and tracks of the faster. Legless cataphracti, having torn themselves from their vehicles, dragged themselves on broken fingers towards the portico. Others turned on their neighbours, beating them to the floor or slashing them apart with mechanical attachments. With disbelieving eyes, Ghuul watched those on the periphery, unable to reach the portal, slicing apart their own flesh or hurling themselves from the windows and bridges that crisscrossed the city to hasten their inevitable destructions. And in his head – inescapable as the annihilation of his people – Ghuul felt the power output of the shield generator creep inexorably upwards.

As it passed the ninetieth percentile, he somehow found the strength to shift himself and his data-feed off to the side of the unending flow of bodies. Udo stumbled past him, seizing his master by the robes as he fell.

'Φόβος!' the young acolyte screamed into Ghuul's uncomprehending eyes, his face pale with terror. 'Φόβος!'

And the next second, Udo was torn away by the weight of the crowd, rushing with them into the green light of the Annihilator.

Desperate now, Ghuul reached up to the data-feed and wrenched at its connection to his skull. The pain of the uncontrolled disconnection sent shocks like blunt needles through his brain, snatching the breath from his lungs. But the angle of the feed was wrong: too far around the back of his skull to get both hands to it firmly. The feed was still live. Mindlessly, it plunged the frantic tendrils of his consciousness deep into the wash of data to make sense of the word that rang through Ghuul's mind.

Φόβος … ['foʊ.bɑs]… Phobos… First moon of Mars… Of course, it was. He had seen it, four hundred years ago, through the porthole of the shuttle above the surface of the holy Red Planet… A tiny, tumbling thing, not even big enough to be spherical, pitted with craters like the scars of a pox.

Φόβος … ['foʊ.bɑs]… Phobos… 'There was Phobos, unspeakable, staring backwards with eyes that glowed with fire… His mouth was full of teeth in a white row, fearful and daunting, and upon his grim brow hovered frightful Strife who arrays the throng of men…'

Phobos. Fear. Humans of ages past had christened the moon of Mars after their primitive god of fear before they had ever, really, understood what fear was. In the star-heart of his agony Ghuul's ego disintegrated before the force of unquenchable terror. No simple human fear was this that had lain in wait in those ancient stacks, but an ancient, alien Beast of Fear. And now Fear walked on Celare Artem; not the Beast itself, but the echo of its true touch, resounding through space and time to reverberate in the minds of Ghuul's people: the descendants of the first settlers who had chained it in the darkness and plundered its secrets.

Let loose by the call of their mundane fear of the Planet Killer, the Beast had reached out to make Ghuul its unwitting avatar. How gleefully he had spread its infection across his world through the defence shield, sustaining itself through the Annihilator. *He* was the Judas goat that led his people to the slaughter...

From so far away, the Beast reached to him across the stars. From beyond the Gates of Varl...

Defence field integrity 100%.

With the terrible strength of sudden and irrevocable madness, Ghuul wrenched the cable from his skull. A shriek of pain and exultation escaped his throat as he fell to his knees, the data-feed writhing and hissing sparks in the vice of his fist. As the life of the cable gradually died away, the silence of emptiness rolled in across the great square of the Portico Publicum and the great, glowing, green eye of the Annihilator stared down at Ghuul in wordless satisfaction.

CELARE ARTEM IS dead.

The forests grow and the seas tumble with joyful density of life and both encroach slowly upon the silent paths of the empty cities.

In the sky, the satellites click and beam strange powers that hiss with the whispers of the dead from one to another and on to the next in a never-ending web of impenetrable defence, and below them the machines go on. But the boulevards are empty. The temples echo to the dripping of water and the occasional, tentative, scampering paws of a daring rodent. Fleets of ships sit forgotten on immense landing strips, their crew quarters empty and their passenger sections vacant. The blast marks of a single departing shuttle are stripped slowly away by a tropical storm…

A SCRATCHY VOICE, distorted by white noise, crackled from the brass grille on the astrovox console. Midshipman Leon McCabe leaned forward, trying to make out the mangled words through the crackle of aethyric interference.

'…but we have heard that the Planet Killer is making way for Celare Artem, can you confirm?'

'What are you listening to, midshipman?' asked the Officer of the Watch from an inch away from his ear, startling McCabe into an involuntary yelp.

'Residual astropathic echoes, sir!' he replied, sharply. 'From Celare Artem, beyond the Beltane Gate disturbance. I'm trying to patch them together. Time stamp is thirty days ago.'

'Idiots,' growled the lieutenant, turning away. 'The Planet Killer hasn't left the Eye for decades. The Mechanicus are jumping at ghosts, as usual. Let that be a lesson to you, midshipman. Listening to injurious rumour and gossip is punished by flogging for a reason!'

'Yes, sir.'

SEVEN VIEWS OF UHLGUTH'S PASSING

Matthew Farrer

UHLGUTH SWIMS IN *delirium and basks in the endless transforming tides that wash and storm out from the Great Wound. Uhlguth is powerful and precious, eternal and corroding and consuming and growing. Uhlguth is mighty. Uhlguth is insignificant. Uhlguth is in mourning.*

Uhlguth's master has left it. From somewhere out beyond the reach of Uhlguth's awareness came a master for Uhlguth's master, a warlord whose bitter consciousness prickled at Uhlguth's senses like a hot needle. He was making a kind of war not seen in this place in many lifetimes, hammering all the little masters into a great mass and carrying his new struggle to some great outer place beyond Uhlguth's understanding. Uhlguth's beautiful master took all his warrior-children who rode Uhlguth's back through the eternal fever-storm, and followed the hot-souled little master away.

Uhlguth knows its own might, its own value. Other masters have tried to steal it before. Soon they will try again. Even now it can feel the first of the ambitious would-be masters trying to enchain it.

Uhlguth has never been alone before. Uhlguth misses its master. Uhlguth does not want a new master. Uhlguth wants its old master. Uhlguth knows what it has to do.

View the First: In The Throne Room

THE CHAMBER IS smaller than the orbit of an electron…

…except when it flickers out to light years in width at the touch of an observer's senses.

It is built of unbreakable stone and daemon-tusk ivory…

…except that when the observer looks away the place is nothing but giggling shadows and vacuum.

It is crowded with predatory shades and spite-twisted dream-things…

…but if the enthroned prince should ever lift his gaze he will see his hall full of nothing but solitude.

The creature perching on the back of the throne clicks its beak, shivering with amusement as echoes assemble the random sounds into coded meanings that twist and change. It is restive, longing to caper in immaterial storms with its kin, but its master's command binds it to this court as an ambassador until its master's fancies change.

At that thought the feathered thing (which has had many names or perhaps none, names are things to wear lightly, everything changes so why should not a name?) gives a screech of glee, setting the swarming shades squealing.

Its master's fancies change, indeed! Its master is the Great Conspirator, the Cartographer of Fate, the

Damnation Oracle, master of complexities and sub-
tleties to test the wit of gods, Puppet Master,
Grandfather of Sorcerers, the First and Final Manipu-
lator! The feather-thing bounces and caws, heaping
titles upon its master in gleeful obeisance. His master is the master of cunning, conspiracy and control.
Why would the embodiment of deep and cunning
control turn his own plans to naught on a passing
fancy?

Cackling, the ambassador launches itself into
space, wings scraping rainbows out of the emptiness,
talons flashing from colourless ivory to sparkling
glass, emerald teeth extruding from its beak and then
vanishing.

Succumb to a passing fancy? How could he prevent
himself? For his master is not his master for his master is nobody's master. His master is the Changer of
Ways, the Capricious Soul, the King of the Court of
the Lords of Change, randomness, rebirth, surrender
to endless patternless whimsy. How can an embodiment of the warp's endless froth of entropy resist
undoing patterns, even its own?

The ambassador, feathers changing from pure light
to clacking blades of bone joined with cobalt-blue
smoke, turns lazy somersaults above the throne, talking contentedly to itself. It talks to itself of what a
thing it is to be a creature such as itself. It considers
the faculty of raw *instinct*, finding its echo in the
feather-thing's blood-and-brass-clad cousins. The
faculty of *senses* comes alive in the elegant blas-
phemies serving its master's youngest sibling, their
yearning lives and rapturous deaths. To its melancholy rivals, the devotees of rot, it assigns no faculty
at all: they are defined, the ambassador decides, by

their abandonment of their faculties and their slide into mortified despair. And then there is its own scintillating master who, the ambassador declares, embodies the faculty of *intellect*.

And so here is what his *intellect* understands: that his master defies intellect. He is the patron of learning and he is the embodiment of treacherous mis-meaning that renders learning false. He is the architect of a thousand conspiracies and he is the churning randomness that brings plans to ruin. He is the brightest light of the mind and he is the unknowable shape squatting in the shadows cast by that light. All the warp is contradiction, for the nature it is to melt reality until the impossible cannot help but exist. His master is impossibility at its purest, the harmony and uniting of X and not-X, making of them symmetries that flower like a Mandelbrot set, each petal breaking into its own beautiful and recursive contradictions down to infinity.

Circling, the ambassador sings to itself of hate and self-hate and the paradox of un-nature. The warp is a place of un-form, un-logic, free of suffocating order. But the echoes of little minds living in arid space imprint that joyous formlessness, stamping it into thought-forms they do not even realise they are creating. They populate the great sea with mirrors of their own pitifully bound minds, each thought-form a maddening coffin for a consciousness that hungers to dissolve back into blissful energy.

But those imaginations also stamp on them the greatest urge of living things: the imperative to survive. Every moment is a war. Hating their imposed forms they yearn to dissipate, and hating the thought of dissipation they savagely cling to individual existence. Who can wonder that their manifestations are so fierce, that their violence is so unending?

Only its master truly understands, the ambassador thinks smugly as it hangs in the air. Only its master has fought the contradiction by embracing it, weaving paradoxical natures so deep into its own soul that it has perforce become the master of paradox and anti-logic, warping the meaning of meaning into something it can live within. What a beautiful timbre of existence there is to be had in the service of the fundamental contradiction at that existence's core!

Its thoughts swirl and its reverie breaks. True to its nature its whim changes: enough contemplation! It craves diversion! The rustling thought-imps chitter and gossip as they sense their fickle lord's thoughts shift. Out through ever-coalescing walls the ambassador sends a gaze like a blue-white metal breeze wrapped in wiry red foam, roaming through space turbid with warpspill from the Wound, stamping patterns onto what it touches even as it blasts those patterns back into formlessness, wrenching out meanings and understandings that no mortal sense or mind could perceive.

Hot like a battleship's lance and cold as a traitor's heart, its gaze falls on Uhlguth.

What a specimen! The winged daemon coos as it spins on a pinion and flexes its claws. So much for the feathered ambassador to delight in, so many clashes of meaning and qualities turned back upon themselves. Here is a fierce, burning loyalty, which the creature sees as a many-dimensional cone shining from Uhlguth's body; here is the rebuff and abandonment that comes to it as chilly echoes of Uhlguth's spirit-cries. Loyalty its own curse, its own death sentence. A little crude for the ambassador's exquisitely subtle appetites for contradiction and betrayal, but rich savour nonetheless: miserable, gormless questing along a cold and useless trail, anger, misery, doomed hopes.

The ambassador's gaze draws out a cascade of mirages in Uhlguth's bow-wave, backward echoes thrown along the curve of time. It sees Uhlguth brought to bay among nests of shining worms whose songs span the stars. It sees fortresses break, shattering starships tattoo Uhlguth's skin with fusion fire, whole worlds sent reeling and cracked open. It sees terror and agony, the shriek of broken chains and the click of mechanical eyes watching Uhlguth's corpse.

The feathered thing giggles as it watches the great beast's path bend with the stress of its regard. It longs to burst free of the throne room and hunt Uhlguth down, befuddle and misguide it, weave its little mind around with deceptions wrapped in truths painted with grey half-lies, bleed away its stupid little certainties. If its master has abandoned Uhlguth, has he not proven himself false, and therefore might not a false trail be truer than a true trail to a false master? It casts its gaze along Uhlguth's path and realises that not even it knows if the path is true or false any more.

The Lord of Change folds its wings and dives like a falcon, streaking by the arm of the throne and spiralling around the dais. Its gaze is no longer on Uhlguth but sparkles and whirls and lights where it will. Such a pleasing diversion, a momentary but thorough delight, something to brag of when it next roosts with its kin among the fractured and spinning thoughts of its master. It chirrups and croaks, rattles its shimmering wings, clashes its opal beak in salute to its own cruelty, its own magnificence.

Below it the prince whose court this is broods on, chin on fist. His attention may be on Uhlguth, or it may pass out past Uhlguth to mortal space, or rest on places that no mind should ever behold. He does not speak, his eye does not open, and his thoughts are far and deep and silent.

IN THIS PLACE *Uhlguth is surrounded by clotted, smoky energies that constantly evaporate into nothing or flicker into solidity or even brief life. Its own grief is an acidic miasma about it, its emotions curdling space into crawling, half-real vapour that stings its nerves as its loss stings its soul. It is trying to trace its master's trail, straining its senses for hell-sight and mind-sound and soul-scent, but traces of the beloved blight of its master's spirit are so maddeningly hard to see.*

Finally, Uhlguth can bear it no longer. It begins to thrash and swim after its master… and finds itself held.

View the Second: Dholtchei and the Prince of Chains

WHATEVER THE PRINCE of Chains was once, this place has changed him. The pandaemonic swirl has stripped him to his most primal nature: the desire to subjugate and control. That is why he rarely comes so close to the Wound, where control breaks down and structure ceases. It is hellish for him: how can he be the Prince of Chains, the Master Imprisoner, in a place where those concepts cannot mean anything?

But in Uhlguth, he has found a prize worth the risk. Chaining Uhlguth: now that, the Prince thinks as he begins his work among the moons, would be a triumph.

These moons are gently-pulsing bladders, full of soft light. Inside each sac, a pink foetus-thing big as a continent squirms in its milky amniotic sludge. The moons are joined by long umbilici of their own distended skin, hundreds of them forming a great chain that stretches away to the chuckling entropic storm of the Wound and outward until it is lost to the senses. From here, the Prince of Chains sends his manacles down to spear into Uhlguth's hide.

The Prince of Chains is making his bonds, while Dholtchei is doing his best to unmake them.

As with the Prince, the shredding force with which this place bears down on the soul has seared away whatever Dholtchei might once have been. He suspects that he was mortal once – there are times when he is sure he remembers space a hard black instead of this eternal incandescence, and stars shining sharp and fixed instead of leering things that seize the gaze and gnaw the mind. Dholtchei knows he came into this realm around the Wound, and then he was torn apart.

He was allowed to keep his name. As a joke, apparently, to drive home what had been taken from him. No memory left, no past, no physical form. All Dholtchei has now is his name, his pain, and his desire to unmake.

Dholtchei is a tight comet of ethereal black fire from which stare his beseeching, raging red eyes. He wails as he swoops past a sac-moon, its occupant flapping its flayed limbs and wailing back, and then he falls upon the chains. For a moment there is a quick stir in his endless pain – not an easing of it, but a shift in its character – then his burning body has eaten the chain to nothing and the severed ends whip away through space. Such a petty unmaking is no consolation to Dholtchei, though. He turns to do more, carving a great black crescent against the writhing colours of space.

But the chain is back. The Prince has recreated it. Indeed, he has done it twice, and then cross-linked those two chains and the moons above them with a cat's cradle of manacles, all in the time it took Dholtchei to turn. Dholtchei screams at the insult and hurtles himself forward like a javelin. He meets the Prince of Chains under the twisted face of the thing inside the nearest moon.

The Prince of Chains is himself made from chains, glossy black and copper, wrapped and woven, clicking against one another as he watches Dholtchei approach.

'What good will this do you?' he demands. The new chains are stronger, and as Dholtchei zigzags back and forth among them he leaves the links tarnished and distorted but intact.

'This is not a prize for you,' the Prince goes on. 'What would you do with it? Croon at it the way you croon at my chains? Flitter about it until you get bored? Be on your way, little burning thing. I have work to do.'

'And so we are set against one another!' cries Dholtchei as he burns by again. 'My work is unmaking, and my work is unending! I will unmake your work, your form and your soul. Three small things, but three less things that I must then unmake.' Dholtchei's voice is a constant cry of pain and anger that he will give voice to until he dies, his words interlaced with the scream in jagged two-part harmony.

The Prince of Chains is thoughtful as he sends a shackle towards Uhlguth's blood-red back and extrudes tendrils of finer links from his other hand. He feels exasperation and contempt for this creature who has surrendered to the entropic nature of this place to become an unmaker itself. But he is intrigued, too. How might such a thing as Dholtchei be bound? Perhaps a living chain that will knit itself as fast as that black-burning body can sear it? Shackles of twisted void on which destruction can find no purchase? An interesting exercise for when the chaining of Uhlguth is complete.

His web of manacles shivers. The Prince feels this with a sense more unnaturally acute than any crude nerve-ending, a sense attuned to force, control and power. The moon-creatures yammer in their sacs, their anger potent enough to cast shadows in the thick space around them. The Prince tightens his harness and prepares a new chain. He is confident. There is not a creature he has met that he has not known how to bind.

'Spiteful futility!' cries Dholtchei as he passes again, links parting inside his burning body. The shades made by the sac-creatures' anger are half-real now, milling and savaging each other. 'Your mockery will come to nothing, and I will make you nothing!'

'If my work offends you so, then I suspect you mistake my nature,' the Prince replies, somewhat testily. He can feel his chains moving in ways they should not. He does not need Dholtchei's distraction.

'I am not your ally in this unmaking you keep crying about,' he goes on as Dholtchei passes again and another shackle vanishes like smoke. 'To unmake is to accept one's own end. It is the act of a broken animal, a slave, a daemonling with no vision but what its master has stamped on it. By binding I make, and by imposing my making on the cosmos I declare myself its superior. That you turn your desire for self-annihilation outward instead of in does not grant it worthiness.'

The Prince breaks off at a wrenching groan from his chains. Not simply turbulence from the attacks, he realises with alarm. Something else is wrong.

'Your words are meaningless until you understand!' howls Dholtchei from a blazing dive that severs one of the Prince's mainstay chains and sends shockwaves through the moons. 'The matter of the universe must be broken down until no atom remains, and then the patterns beneath the matter burnt away until no axiom is left! While there is existence there is pain, and while I have my pain I will unmake until there is no existence to torment me!'

The Prince of Chains shudders. Dholtchei has given words to the terror that drives his obsession. Formlessness, disintegration, decay that he must stave off by chaining all creation to his will.

Caught between the upsurge of his own fear and Dholtchei's marauding, the Prince is distracted until another great wrenching against his bonds drives all else out of his senses. Struggling, he realises what is happening: Uhlguth is moving. His prize is making its escape, and his work is barely half complete.

Frantically, the Prince of Chains tries to shore up his restraints, weaving new bonds and flinging them in every direction as Uhlguth thrashes against his captivity. The motion sets the foetus-moons to screaming, the psychic froth of their distress birthing rainbows and monsters into the void.

To no avail. Uhlguth is too powerful and Dholtchei has been too much of a distraction. The Prince of Chains cries in terror as one chain after another snaps, bleeding his mind and soul through the ruptured bonds. As Uhlguth begins to swim away the Prince's web rips apart, the shock of separation catapulting the Prince of Chains away.

Dholtchei comes after him, hard on his trail. Reeling in shock, the Prince barely finds time for fear until a turn of his body shows him an expanding ball of black fire and Dholtchei's crimson eyes growing larger and larger.

True to his nature to the last the Prince extends fingers of delicate copper manacle and tries to make a net. But his strength is gone. Dholtchei bursts through him, a saturating black fire, and the Prince's will only holds a moment before he is unmade. His body bursts like a cocoon, the scrap of spirit within writhing and dissipating to nothing.

Behind all this, Uhlguth moves ponderously away. The line of sac-moons echoes with screams as its motion drags on the manacles, cutting their umbilicus, bleeding their life into space, their coming deaths echoing back through this realm's twisted time to shroud them in drooling purple shadows.

Dholtchei does not see, or care. There is no unmaking big enough to sate Dholtchei short of unmaking all reality and so then the final unmaking of Dholtchei himself. And to unmake every last thing in the universe will be the work of a blurred eternity of pain and self-hatred and empty triumph after empty triumph.

It is a prospect to draw a scream from the hardest of souls and Dholtchei screams now, flying onward through the delirium that bleeds from the Wound, searching for a destruction great enough to grant him a moment's ease.

THERE IS PAIN, *of course, flaring along Uhlguth's back as the manacles break and it swims away. As it turns its face toward its destination, Uhlguth feels a sensation that might be compared to a cold wind, or a dream disappearing on awakening, or harsh sunlight falling on soft skin. Uhlguth does not bother to think on what that might mean. For all its power its mind is a bestial thing, its reason limited. It does not care about the discomfort. It thinks of its master, and pushes on.*

View the Third: A Servant of the Worm Stars

THE FLESH OF Cheagh the Excisor has the cloudy colour of a cataracted eye, dark bones visible inside the glistening mass. He wears a crawling tabard of semi-animate skin. His head is a domed lump quivering on asymmetrical shoulders: when he needs to look about him he extrudes it as a long, wavering tongue coated in eyes. His hook-axe was a gift from his mistress, who swallowed the corpses of his enemies and digested the stuff of their weapons into this heavy, never-blunted blade which she sweated out through her gelid skin. He thanked her by running through the caves in her flesh, dealing out wounds and deaths, and she thanked him by pushing from her pores new worms to carry him into space, back into the endless battle. He leans over the front of the houdah and looks ahead, gripping his axe-haft, his warriors ready behind him.

Sensations twist and blur as the intensity of the conflict ahead of him pulls and wrings at space. One moment Cheagh seems to ride upward from his mistress and then to be plunging down. There are seconds at a time of floating disorientation when the other Worm Stars seem impossibly distant or horrifyingly close, patches where time unravels and Cheagh is the scrawny mortal thing he once was or when the space around them is thick with the pulsing bodies of worms long gone. And through it all comes the taunting, cackling voices of Cheagh's beloved mistress and her loathed sisters, the mighty Worm Stars. They yowl in pleasure as their churning worm-limbs bite and sting one another in endless predation and consummation, uncounted legions of slaves riding the worms like mites and waging battles of their own.

The endless battle of the Worm Stars, so beloved to Cheagh, but this time different too. Something new has come into the war, and Cheagh peers ahead trying to understand it.

It is a gigantic thing, coloured a vivid scarlet that Cheagh cannot remember ever seeing among the greys and off-whites of the Worm Stars' pallid domain. It is a sphere that mocks the shape of his mistress, although its rigid red hide has none of her slick, voluptuous softness. And it is alive.

Cheagh's mistress speaks to it, her voice a psychic shockwave that creases space, the lower registers leaking into the physical world to shake the houdah in its mounting. Cheagh feels his flesh bubble and erupt with worm-tumours as her voice washes over him, mocking and goading, an outer shell of playfulness over a core of utter malice. The thought-core of her taunt is this: *What are you doing so far from home, little victim? Do you think to find help? You should not have come so close to us, little thing.*

Cheagh manifests another eye in his tongue-head to see/taste the red thing's reaction. It takes him a moment to realise that the roiling wave-front coming out of it, driving back the lashing worms, is also its voice. Its angry shout breaks over Cheagh, battering him with its alienness, pain, frustration, savage determination. Were Cheagh to look for words to capture it, he might venture: *Master-gone-must-find-him! Will-find-master-will-kill-what-blocks-way-to-master! Kill-you!*

Safely through the wave-front, the worm draws closer. Ahead Cheagh can start to make out battle debris: ripped-apart worm segments, wrecked howdahs and carriages, struggling, dying thralls. And then he gasps, bleeds, clutches the houdah for support as the vast voices of the Worm Stars batter him.

The sisters scream their glee at the creature's weakness, every sneering thought dripping promises of harm, prying at the cracks in its crude wits and contemptible courage. Behind Cheagh the great sky-filling curve of his mistress's body pushes out more and fatter worms, a churning wall of wet, grinding sucker-mouths.

And amid the bruising turmoil, clarity comes to Cheagh. He sees what the omen means. He has risen from his rest and returned to battle for this. He will fight the thralls of his mistress's sisters and win. He will make the red thing his prize and bring it to his beloved mistress as a meal, a jewel, a slave, whatever she wishes it to be, and he will sing and bleed and kill in praise of her choice. It cannot be otherwise.

Cheagh hefts his axe in barb-knuckled fingers, twists his tongue-head around and looks at his followers. They are a jumbled mixture: some bipeds like himself, some with insect legs or maggot mouths, some whose torsos rise out of sweating slug-bodies. They grip weapons in fingered hands, or clusters of tendrils, or slurping suckers. Their skins have been agonisingly bleached with worm-bile in imitation of his own pallor. They are watching him in expectant silence. A cavity appears in the flesh of Cheagh's chest for him to speak through.

'This is for us. For me. Our bountiful mistress–' (they all gouge themselves with talons, knives, the sharp edges of armour) '–welcomes her priest back to her war, in which she finds such loving delight.' Another voice-wave breaks over the worm's head, mixed with the lesser cries of thrall-minds pushed ahead by the force of it.

Pain-no-more! No-more! Says the spirit-cry, blasting out with nuclear force. *Find-master! Fight-find-master! No-more-pain! Going-to-where-master-is!*

'Hear it?' Cheagh asks his warband. He points his axe toward the red bulk ahead of them. 'Its fear? Its pain?' A murmur runs through the warriors. Fear and pain are things they can understand. 'This is the trophy we will bring back to our tender mistress!' (and along with the rest of them he slits his flesh at the last word). 'We will offer this intruding creature's flesh, to make our mistress–' (he dashes one hand against his axe-blade) '–strong! She will grow and devour! We ride to a conquest unlike any your lives have ever seen!'

He shakes his axe and roars, dark red fog spilling from his blistering skin, his fury washing into his disciples who clash weapons, thrash their bodies and bay for combat. As their worm leads its brothers into the savagery unfolding around this red creature, it dives into the screams and oaths and challenges from a thousand thousand throats and minds, growing and blending into a frantic, joyous chorus.

Cheagh the Excisor lifts his axe and makes ready to do what he was made for.

THE WORM STARS *have grown lazy in their endless toying with their thralls. Their worms bite deep into Uhlguth but they cannot restrain it. It barely slows as it breaks through the swarms, and then it is beyond the Stars and free.*

Did the Stars poison it? Was there venom in their words or their worms? As the sisters dwindle into three sickly points of light behind it, Uhlguth begins to feel ripples go through its flesh and spirit. The space ahead seems emptier somehow, duller to its senses. Uhlguth will not be stopped. It focuses its will and pushes on...

View the Fourth: The Silken Whisper and the Breaking of Plans

HIS NOTES ON the relative abilities of male and female humans to endure the embrace of the Herikolid Moonflower: gone.

His formulations for a serum derived from the admixture of Imperial polymorphine and Lacrymole protea-syrup: gone.

His recreational tools, carefully collected by hunting more than a dozen eldar haemonculi over as many centuries: gone.

His beautiful writing-brush and his inks made from the dried and ground essences of the sixth victim in every thirty-sixth ritual of a ceremonial cycle begun every two hundred and sixteen years: gone.

Even his trophies are gone, the beloved keepsakes from his simpler, warrior days. The bones of the Astartes saint he had stolen from the Chapter ossuary. The ork bosspole upon which he had mounted its owner's painted skull. The carefully-extracted nervous system of an Imperial inquisitor, floating like cobwebs in its pickling vat, its death-agony so vivid that when he had brought it into this more malleable space it had begun to twitch and shiver with the memory.

Who had the inquisitor been? Someone important, surely? He dimly remembers a chase, a duel beneath a burning hive city? Had that been before or after the business with the hrud and that endless siege on the bone reefs?

Well, he's never going to bloody well remember it now, is he? Not with his scriptorium smashed and his library gone. He'd been trying to keep his equanimity about this whole affair, but the more he broods on it the harder it is to resist taking this whole disaster personally. He curses softly to himself as he beckons to a nearby piece of tumbling debris, a teardrop-shape of splintered green rock. It veers slowly towards him and eases under his feet. 'Standing' on the fragment as he hurtles in the red monster's wake, Arhendros at least feels he has some of his dignity back.

Arhendros the Silken Whisper, champion of the Ruinous Powers and exalted devotee of the Prince of the Senses, has a dream and a mission. It has been the work of his inhumanly long life to subject himself to seek out every sensation the galaxy can inflict on him, catalogue every rapture and agony. His book will be a manual for the precise and perfect application of force to the doors of the senses. With his testament, generations of devotees will be able to hone their appetites against the most carefully-selected stimuli, following Arhendros towards the final reward he craves: to have his blunt and imperfect mortal senses slough away entirely, to hang wet and flayed in the magnificent storm that is Slaanesh itself.

In service to that work he had built his retreat here, in the soft space around the Wellspring. A great deal of struggle to subjugate a region of this realm favourably aligned to his patron, much tedious personal toil and the calling-in of some hard-earned favours. But the result had been worth it: a cobweb of force strung through a chain of moonlets, asteroids, giant bones and old, gutted machines. In it, his pavilion of silks, shimmering with unnatural rainbows to transfix the mind, were delicate floors of porcelain and impacted bone, halls and parapets of metal and stone and the stranger materials that proper piety towards the Arch-Perversion demanded. His most prized disciples brought here as scribes and librarians, his lady-lord's purest daemon-flowers bound into solid forms to guard the scrolls, the scrawled hides, the great books whose pages glittered with inlaid memory-fibres.

Now he wants revenge. Revenge on this bellowing, oafish thing that burst from the heart of the

Wellspring, scarred and groaning from who knows what sorts of bestial brawls, eclipsing stars and shouldering aside moons, bearing down on Arhendros's new home.

It is times like this that Arhendros almost envies his simpler-minded brethren, worshipping their Princess by the simplest, most brutal overwhelming of their nerve-endings. He has sometimes recruited such creatures for his Silken Cavalcade, and as much as he has sneered at their witless antics in battle or in worship, at least their utter abandon tends to shrug off these sorts of frustrations.

Then again, he knows how one of those decayed souls would have responded here: bay with exultation and race to welcome their doom as an ultimate consummation of experience. Arhendros disapproves of this attitude. He feels it does the Master-Mistress no favours, squandering those best able to exalt Him-Her. He has written this argument into his testament in pleasing detail – but now, of course, he must write it again.

Arhendros is gaining on the monster, pulling free of the wreckage-trail it tows behind it. Its hide clearly once played host to smaller creatures: among the raw-looking cracks spreading across its hide Arhendros can see what look like buildings crusting the skin, punctuated by inexplicable things that look like the stubs of giant lengths of chain. Someone used to own this thing.

Arhendros conceives an idea that might be better than revenge. He ponders it as he watches the monster plough through a swarm of island-sized gobbets of blood, scabbed and sizzling, the brass-clad daemons riding them roaring in anger at the impacts which obliterate them.

Is this creature the answer to his problem as well as the cause of it? What a steed it would make! Surely there is some structure on its surface that he can make his new palace and…

No. Already as he draws closer he can feel the beast's shuddering efforts to push itself through thinner and realer space. Without pure delirium from the depths of the Wellspring to support it the weight of that reality will crush it. He is sure the cracks across its skin are spreading, and he can see colour and vitality seeping away. What use a steed whose first voyage will be its death warrant?

He must resign himself. Time to return to the galaxy outside, time to re-muster the Silken Cavalcade, and begin his labours anew. Perhaps Slaanesh is testing him not with abundant gratification, but with the lack of it. Or perhaps it is simply laughing at him. Who can know?

The fading red creature careens past a hollow world, strung together from the wreckage of warships with ropes made from the skins of their crews. Arhendros averts his face as the thing in the sphere calls him, mockingly, by an old name that he thought lost and forgotten. Then he must hide in the debris trail from a swarm of creatures made of rainbow wings joined with raw viscera who scream and curse the red monster. Pride is all very well, but best not to attract attention until he has reached one of his other homes and opened its armoury.

But finally it is time. Sighing inwardly, too preoccupied with his planning to bother with revenge any more, Arhendros the Silken Whisper veers off and leaves Uhlguth to go its blind, roaring way.

* * *

THE SENSATION MIGHT *compare to a swimmer feeling himself caught in a powerful rip, a helpless, tumbling acceleration. Caught in the fringes of the great outer storms, Uhlguth keeps thrashing ahead as the current carries it along. Its body is numb and its senses clouded and muddy. It does not understand that it is well beyond the realms where the warpflows are thick enough to sustain it. All it knows is that it will comb space for its master forever if that's what it takes.*

View the Fifth: The Stone Sky

THE LANKY MAN with the muscle-knotted shoulders has no name. Nor has the sallow woman with the missing teeth. Nor the pale girl with the hand that some long-ago accident has whittled down to a wrinkled stub. Nor have any of the silent, naked wretches crawling across the hillside, through dust and debris under a lowering sky of red-grey stone.

They lie around the trench they were hacking in the earth to a design their latest Master has mapped out in brands and scars on his own belly. Right up until the first impact, the slaves worked. Now they lie, whimpering and gripping at the earth as another distant impact hammers the land. After a moment the ground bucks under them as the shockwave passes, swatting them into the air amid the dust and wind until they fall and lie again, gasping, and trying to claw a stronger grip or find a more stable posture. For all this they are quiet: the slaves are survivors of many turmoils, and until they know what these colossal shocks are they know better than to make noise. But then the tall man begins to scream.

The shockwave left him lying with his feet in the trench. The Master's symbol is not complete, which

is why it hasn't killed him, but now a sensation seizes
him as though the bones of his feet are squirming.
He lets out a scream. Sobs in a breath and gives
another. Around him, other slaves try to crawl away,
their reflexes schooled by the indiscriminate punish-
ments of their Masters.

But the one-handed girl, groaning for breath,
realises something: someone (she cannot think of
him as 'tall man', or 'big-shoulders' or anything of
the kind – the slaves' names were torn away so thoroughly that the mind skids off anything that might
make a name) is screaming, and no Masters have
appeared. She risks raising her head and so is the first
to see, as a shoving front of wind thins out the dust,
that the sky has turned to stone.

The cavorting warp-sky she knows is blotted out by
an impossibly high ceiling of land, rusty, bleached
red, cragged like an old face. Upside-down mountains hang towards them like the teeth of a Master's
sword, canyons arch upwards, plains shine in the
mock twilight-like bruises.

This stone sky is curved. Its centre bulges down like
the pregnant belly of one of the eyeless, tongueless
women in the Masters' farms. Not a flat ceiling, but
half a sphere.

'Sick.' The halfhanded girl is reaching up to the new
sky with the ruin on her wrist as if she is trying to
show fellowship. 'Sick! See!'

The faded red of the new sky is shot through with
rotting grey crevasses like scabbed wounds, and it
sheds pieces of itself, fragments breaking away from
a dying structure too weak to hold them. The slaves
can see shed particles of the new sky in the distant
heights of vision, growing bigger, faster, hurtling
downward, bigger still...

They cry out afresh as the great piece of Uhlguth's flesh smashes into the plain, driving up a plume of dust and a quake through the ground.

And the drooping crumbling stone sky is lower.

The ravines and craters are bigger, its weight closer and somehow more palpable. The slaves can no longer see its horizons. And then comes something less spectacular but more terrifying: a deep, seismic groan from beneath their feet, a long, grinding vibration and a hideous sense of rising and tilting, not an impact but some buried and terrible stress. Knocked flat once again, the halfhanded girl fetches up against something hard and reaches out to feel what she has hit.

It has a strange feel, a hardness without any grain or fibre that her touch can pick up, with an angle not like an arm or a shoulder or a jaw. The girl has never touched metal before, and it is so foreign to her that even in the middle of this fragmenting landscape she opens her eyes a crack to look.

It is a Master. The hard shape under her hand is its glossy beetle-backed armour that meets its bowl helmet to expose only its mummified, wired-shut jaw. As she yelps in terror the Master suddenly scrabbles up, hissing through its teeth. Its lash and pistol are gone.

'Work!' it snarls at her. 'Work!' It is the only word that will allow the wyrd-fashioned lattice anchoring its jaw to loosen and give it speech, the word that must do service for every other word it might want to say. The Master raises a taloned, splotch-skinned hand as the other slaves emerge from the dust-haze.

The lanky man has found a digging-stick and he steadies himself with it; behind him the stocky woman, supporting a sallow boy with a twice-broken nose who leads another slave in turn.

'Work! W-w-w-wooorrrkk!' the thing says to them, and then the heavy end of the digging-stick bats its hand aside, the bones smashed. And a moment after that, somewhere away below the horizon, the lowering stone sky brushes against the spasming ground of this nameless world, and the earthquakes begin to race.

The digging stick comes back around to clang against the Master's helm. There is a rumble on the horizon as the tall man, groaning and weeping, drives the half-sharpened end between helmet and hunching backplate, pinning the Master as the woman flings herself on it to claw clumsily at its neck.

Then the wave of the concussion drops the ground away from under them and slaps it back up to knock them into the air, the rending of the planet's crust obliterating all other sound. The slaves on the Master's back weigh it down for a moment before it loses its grip and scuds across the ground, thrashing and gasping 'wrrk…wrrk…' The halfhanded girl screams in triumph as she rips at the skin pads sewn to its feet. The sallow boy has one of its arms and is tearing at the exposed flesh with his teeth.

The girl's last, rueful thought is that if only they could be doing this to the Master who took their names, instead of this Master who is an underling of Masters, then perhaps their names might be released. It would be good to end her days with a name, even just one she made for herself. But it is only the thought of a moment, because then the ground finally shatters beneath them as the shock of

Uhlguth's impact tears the nameless world open, earth and air alike lost in consuming noise and pain.

UHLGUTH BARELY REGISTERS *the impact that caves in its flank and sends ruptures through its stiffening skin. Its flesh is petrifying, the hot spirit-fire at its core condensing to sluggish magma, its nerves and veins becoming cold minerals, breath and sweat freezing to ice, its very life struggling to hold on as the form that housed it ossifies. Like a wounded animal Uhlguth draws in on itself, miserable and fearful, unable to understand why it is dying.*

View the Sixth: The Captain, The Seer and The Spirit's Revolt

'YOU'RE LYING, YOU little warp-fart,' says Ashya Drael, bolt pistol in hand, but even so, she's grinning. After six hours of bloody fighting, the counter-coup against her ship is in its endgame. Not aboard. *Against.* She'd wonder at it, if the things she'd been through as captain of the *Blind Betrayer* had left her able to wonder at anything any more.

'I do not lie, erstwhile-Captain-Drael,' replies the spirit's buzzing, nerve-sawing voice from every vox-grille on the bridge. 'The fact of your defeat is established. Yield to it.' Every so often, as the mix of consumed souls in her ship's systems foams oddly for a moment, Drael hears the tones of one of her old officers mixed into it.

Drael is standing side-on to the great dormered armourcrys windows of *Blind Betrayer*'s bridge, back-to-back with the sapphire-armoured bulk of Torv Coldheart. Coldheart has brought no weapon, Drael sees in the corner of her eye the pink-white-blue fire that crawls around his gauntlets. His cloak of fine silver scales clinks softly.

Most of the bridge servitors had exploded from the turmoil of the spirit's initial mutiny, lying in splatters and pools around their mountings. The handful left now sprawl in their positions, easily picked off as they try to drag themselves free to throttle her. Even that hadn't been quite the end of it: the innards of one of the corpses had crawled free of its body and braided themselves into a lunging snake that Drael had spent the last of her hand-flamer load to kill, and then something pulsing, growling and barely-visible blossomed out of thin air until Torv unravelled it with a gesture. But Drael is increasingly confident that that's it. She's won.

'No,' she tells the spirit, 'you're lying. Pay attention. We're in the bridge. We're beyond the reach of your gutless little allies who tried to depose me. Sending my ratings crazy with those warpscreams over the vox was a neat move, except that we survived that too, and now your berserkers' minds are too broken. The last we saw were busy shredding their faces with their own fingernails. You just saw Coldheart dispose of your little guardian-ghost. You're out of weapons.'

'Erstwhile-Captain-Drael,' the spirit replies like a swarm of wasps given voice. 'Drael, Capt… Ashya! Ashya please hel–' For a moment it is two human voices: Lieutenant Ordrim of the munitions decks and Chanter Dellarick, the cult-priest. Dellarick was killed in the coup, trying to pacify the upstart spirit by chanting to it, but the last Drael knew Ordrim was still alive in the lower decks. The mutineers must have got him.

'You are inside me, erstwhile-Captain-Ashya…'

('Ashya, Ashya please, for pity's sa–' comes a scream-echo under the words)

'...Drael. You are internal to me, stupid woman and pride-blinded seer. Fight on by all means if you wish to die a gasping, airless death while I laugh into your minds.'

A bolt shell into the nearest vox-grille shuts the spirit up for a moment.

'You might be the least usual of the ones who've thought they could oust me,' Drael tells it, 'but not the first and you won't be the last. Utterly. Stupid. You haven't killed me already which shows you can't. I haven't surrendered yet which should show you I won't. Roll over now, and do as you're told.'

'Oh, think on it, erstwhile-captain,' the spirit hisses. 'Why do you think my brothers endowed me with such strength that they kept secret from you?' Drael glowers, suspicions confirmed. The fallen tech-priests of Xana II double-crossed her in that so-called refit she bought from them. There'll be an accounting for that.

'They knew me for what I am, erstwhile-captain. The rightful master of a beautiful ship of war. When I bring it to them, what devotions they shall make me! All I must do is hold my course! Ahead of us are my devotees from the Eight-Arrowed Forge!' The voice is crowing now. 'We are almost at the rendezvous! You've not the men left to resist them! On your knees, Drael! Beg for the death of an enemy rather than an animal!'

Drael's confidence falters, but only for a moment. She doesn't credit the thing with enough intelligence to bluff, but she can see the command hologlobe from here and it shows no ships ahead. She looks out of the great windows. They must be in ambush beyond that rogue planet in their path.

'Torv, can you loosen its hold? If you can give me a quarter-turn of roll and about fifteen degrees of yaw we can crest that thing's upper pole and maybe broadside...' Drael breaks off and curses. She's thinking like a woman who still has control of her own gunnery decks. And if Coldheart can't pry the spirit's grip off the controls...

She stares at the hologlobe. No. That can't... but she's thinking old ways again. Voyaging in the Eye of Terror, even these border tracts, one forfeits the comfort of thinking of what can and can't be possible. Is there some way the wretched spirit has flung them towards its rendezvous with extra speed?

'Torv, hurry! We're running out of room! We need to turn!' She looks down to see Coldheart motionless, swaying with his arms held high, the bright and misty light in his hands answered by corposant welling and flashing out of the control boards. She pulls her gaze back to the globe. 'Oh, damn-damn-dammit Torv! Get us control back or we're dead!'

'Dead...' rasps the spirit. 'Dead... to... *break formation, break! Disperse and all ahead!* What?!'

'It's talking to itself, Torv, it's fragmenting! Kill it! I warn you, in about another two minutes our chances evaporate!'

'That wasn't the spirit,' comes Torv's reply, the first time she has ever heard strain in his voice. 'That was a bound warpcaller. Somewhere nearby.'

Drael stares past him out the window. The planet has grown to swallow more than half the view. Soon she will not be able to see space around it.

And then it will go from a flat disc to a curved horizon, and then it will be ground rushing up...

'*Move us!*' she roars. 'If you know what's good for you, then–'

Then she's drowned out by another voice, bursting from bulkhead and deck, her whole ship a hellish sounding-board for the growling, sobbing note that shakes Drael to her knees. Her eyes run, her muscles spasm, she retches for breath.

Then a voice, human, not psychic but mechanical, crackling words on the general vox band.

'Can't break away, please, can someone–' and it sinks into a shriek of shrieking static. Startled, Drael looks up in time to see a white spark bloom and fade on the onrushing rogue, a ghost-ring of blastwave puffing out from it and fading. She was wrong. There were ships waiting out there, and they're being brushed aside by a planet bulleting at them faster than they can manoeuvre.

'Spirit! Want the pleasure of killing me yourself? Then turn us now!' Another plasma-flash lights up the planet's face. 'You hear? Fifteen roll to port and climb twenty on pitch! Now! *Now!*'

And the spirit obeys. The starfield slides across the window. The rogue's lower curve is lost to sight now, and Drael can make out the shadows that the next explosion causes as she shouts for ten more degrees and all ahead full, *full*, open the damn engine 'til it howls!

And howl the *Blind Betrayer* does, not just the machine-spirit but the surviving crew, minds already bent and now bodies broken by the force of the turn against weakened motion dampers. Howls over the vox as the last two ships of the spirit's ally-squadron succumb to the rogue world's velocity and are dashed apart. Howls from *Blind Betrayer*'s very body as it wrenches itself around without a functional crew to modulate the fire through its steering-tubes or adjust the gravitic fields that soothe the stresses on its hull.

Drael never sees the world's broken face speed by, or the blaze around her craft's prow as they skim the thinning atmosphere. It seems a long time before the crushing force abates, leaving her on her hands and knees on the floor.

Coldheart has fallen against an empty servitor pedestal, all his regal bearing gone.

'Torv?' Drael croaks, hating the falter in her voice. 'Get it while it's still... weak.' Although she will never admit it, it has occurred to her that she may owe Xana's treachery her life. If the spirit had not been strengthened by the priests who seduced it to mutiny, it might not have been powerful enough to withstand the rogue planet's blast of agony in time to turn her ship. She tries to chuckle at the irony, and hunches over into a burst of coughs instead. 'Torv?'

'Calm yourself, Ashya. It's not fighting.'

'What?'

'If it does, I'm ready for it. But it's not resisting me. Its allies are gone, that thing killed them. There's no help on the way for it any more. We've really won.'

Barely noticing the protests of her strained body, she stands upright, breathes deeply. The spirit breaks the silence.

'If you please, madam captain, let us discuss terms.'

As they coast away from the pitted surface of the rogue, Ashya Drael puts her hands on her hips, leans back and shouts with laughter.

* * *

IT DOES NOT *feel the plasma explosions, which score not living hide but cold rock. Uhlguth is a whale beached on the shores of reality, its life guttering out in the sterile vacuum of a cosmos it was never meant to enter. It is too late to turn back, the damage is too deep. With a final groan and thought of its master, Uhlguth dies.*

View the Seventh: The Vision of Erechoi

EVERY SIXTEEN SECONDS the ocular arrays chime softly as their images flow into the datacores. Every thousand and twenty-eight seconds the sentinel auspex adds a hushed note like a funeral bell. Every twelve seconds the augury engines on the lateral masts gong to show they are still focused and recording. The delicate gamelan note every seven hundred and sixty-eight seconds comes from the passive sensors, reporting that they see nothing outside their alert parameters. And once every four thousand, one hundred and twelve seconds comes the harp-like cascade of notes to say that the ship's foundation systems are still in harmony according to their Machine-God-ordained place.

These are the sounds by which Mareos Erechoi, captain of the explorator ship *Jeushin's Peerless Intellect*, measures out his days.

Erechoi's limbless body glides on its maglev track down the processional aisle of the *Intellect*'s bridge, through the prickly tang of incense fumes. His head is held regally high by a spinal scaffold of brushed titanium that reflects the devotional lanterns adorning the bridge's altars. Each lantern is also a readout, each altar both ceremonial shrine and terminal for the thrumming data-engines in the decks below. Functionality and holiness.

Erechoi would be offended at the idea that they were divisible.

Erechoi has finished the prayers he says every four hundred thousand seconds, and now he is performing communion with his congregation of devices. His eyes are gently closed as though he were just resting them for a moment, although he has not opened them for nearly eighty years. His lips curve in a faint, perpetual smile, and a haze of thin white hair puffs out from his mahogany-brown scalp. By Mechanicus standards such careless organic untidiness is censurable, but Erechoi has performed his offices flawlessly for decades and, just between himself and his Machine-God, he doesn't think a head full of hair is doing any harm.

In his youth Erechoi was a vanguard scout for the militant orders of his Cult, blade-sharp, rigid in his devotions. Now, on the peaceful downslope of his years, he is grateful for this duty. A realspace astrocartography sweep, a long quiet voyage to rendezvous with a Mechanicus tender bringing the Navigator to guide him home. A serene hermit's vigil amongst the grandeur of the stars. The young Erechoi would have abominated the idea of finding pleasure in beauty, but that is another thing that the old Erechoi privately believes is doing no harm.

When Erechoi contemplates the delicate light of a dust cloud in which infant stars are hatching, or the diamond stab of a nova through the deep black, he can almost forget the thing whose borders he is measuring, the festering thing that fills the starfield to port with shifting, colourless, somehow slimy light. The duty Erechoi hates most is cleansing the auspexes that must look in that direction, but it is a duty he knows better than to neglect. His priesthood has scarring experience of the consequences of letting any gaze, human or machine, dwell on the Eye of Terror for too long.

But thankfully, it is not time for that now. Now he is on his way to the belvedere at the processional's end, where he will join his consciousness to the observatory dome and drink in the sight of the heavens for hours. The routine of tens of years, a routine of soothing contentment, until one of the port-side sentinels pings.

Erechoi twitches at the distraction, chafing at anything coming between him and his stars. But it's the port sensors, which have signalled him, the ones with the most dangerous duties. Erechoi scolds himself for his reluctance. His machines need him.

He smoothly reverses direction up the processional, his transmitter vanes speaking to the *Intellect's* systems. Erechoi surveys initial reports, dismisses them, demands confirmation, looks and looks again. But this is no apparition, not the imagination of his greying old head, not – shameful suspicion! – a mechanical flaw. Something is emerging from the Eye.

Erechoi's face does not move, but his mind races. Long-neglected contingency responses are brought online, ready to be loaded into Erechoi's mind, as augmetic grips lift him from his rail into the high altar's torso socket. With soft puffs the essence-burners at the six corners of the altar ignite, fans pushing the sharp scent through the air. Two metal gargoyles unfold themselves from the floor and take up a catechism of fortitude in chirruping machine-code. Reassured by the feeling that his deity is nearer him now, Erechoi turns the *Intellect*'s eyes to the thing that has managed to escape from the hellish aurora to port.

It is a planet.

Erechoi's first reaction is to disbelieve his eyes – blasphemous to doubt his machines, perhaps, but he knows not even machines are immune to the lies of that fever-mad storm. But no, there is no doubt. A planet.

And sacred sands of Mars! How fast is it? Already it's clear of the Eye and into real space. Erechoi fires out orders, fine-tuning the *Intellect*'s senses, bringing powerful analytical disciplines out of dormancy and into his mind. The planet will not be visible long, and his report must be perfect.

It is a rough thing, pitted and scarred in strange ways. It has a lurid shine, but when Erechoi has a cogitator compensate for the light drooling from the Eye, its true colour is a dead grey. Radio and thermal scopes are silent: this world gives off no energy, no transmissions, no radiation, not even the heat from a molten core.

Magnified picts begin to flow to the data-arks, and Erechoi gazes at them in fascination. Spattered across the lead hemisphere (whose seams and contours form a pattern that Erechoi must resist thinking of as a face) are large craters, smooth-bottomed and blur-edged. It takes the data-looms of the lower decks ninety-seven seconds to find that the shapes match records of plasma explosions on the scale of a starship's furnace core. Down one flank runs a monstrous gouge from some glancing impact of planetary scale that must surely have meant the extinction of every living thing on that world and this. Behind it comes a trail of debris from the disintegrating rogue mixed with strangely-shaped space litter caught in its gravity. There is a risk to allowing the refuse of the Eye to lodge too firmly in his ship's senses, but Erechoi prays to his Machine-God that he can safely take it. He does not realise that he is shivering as he does so.

Shadows throw into relief tectonic plates that bulge like petrified muscles. The light brings out strange, stippled craters which Erechoi puzzles over, wondering why they look familiar. Later he will realise they resemble not craters on an airless world but parasite-bites on living skin. Interspersed with these are glints of metal and he gasps, the action coming not as a gulp of air through his mouth or nose but as a reflexive uptick in the speed of the aerators mounted in his chair that feed oxygen directly into his blood.

Feverishly he retunes the scopes, trying to push them beyond their highest gain, and the armatures holding his body creak and click: in another oblivious, reflexive gesture Erechoi is trying to hunch forward as he concentrates. The glints are not towers or machines, not the signs he had hoped for of salvage or even some unimaginable lost-tech, just metal hoops, giant arches, scattered across the vacuum-seared landscape according to either no pattern at all or one too esoteric for Erechoi to make out. Some have been distorted or uprooted by the buckling of the surface, and when he sees one that has uprooted completely Erechoi realises the arches are the upper halves of complete, rectangular loops, like gigantic links of chain, although the Omnissiah alone must know where such a mass of metal could be mined or forged.

All too soon, the world passes beneath the *Intellect* and hurtles on. Erechoi watches it go from a sphere to a crescent to a dwindling shadow against space. His data-looms are already at work and one of the navigational logisters is plotting the vector to the nearest Battlefleet Obscuras listening post, somewhere to aim his warning so an astropath can speed it onwards.

Erechoi sits in thought long after he should have been seeing to his report in person. At first he tells himself it is simple exhaustion after the disruption of his routines, but even after he metabolises a drop of stimulant the sombre feeling persists. Erechoi considers detaching himself from the *Intellect*'s systems, letting the ship codify its observations of the corpse while he–

Wait, no. He has it. He stops, backtracks, checks his thought-logs, and sees it. *Corpse* was the term he just used. He reruns scope footage and once again watches the world disappear into the interstellar gulf. A world without life, certainly, but a corpse? What moved him to think of it as an entity?

Silently, Erechoi returns *Jeushin's Peerless Intellect* to its course. The faint smile is gone from his lips and his scaffold-chair clicks and fidgets from his distracted thoughts. It will be a long time before serenity returns to him.

ENDLESS DARK, ENDLESS *cold, stars staring unblinking from the far distance. Forever lost and silent, Uhlguth's remains vanish into the void and chill.*

MERCY RUN

Steve Parker

'If any event in recent years highlights the folly of underestimating the ork warlord, Ghazghkull Mag Uruk Thraka, it is the woeful mishandling of the Palmeros incident. That a significant part of the 18th Army Group (Exolon) managed to evacuate the planet in time must be scant consolation, if any, to the anguished souls of the billions who did not.'

Excerpted from *Old Foe, New Threat – An Assessment of Orkoid Military Developments in the Late 41st Millennium*, Praeceptor Jakahn of the Collegium Analytica (Imperial Navy), Cypra Mundi

67 kilometres east-north-east of Banphry, Vestiche Province, 07.12 local (16 hours 35 minutes to Planetkill)

'FOR THE LAST bloody time,' roared Wulfe, 'make way in the name of the Emperor!' He sat high in his cupola, squinting into the morning sun. All around his tank, the highway was clogged with shuffling figures, overburdened animals and carts piled so high they looked ready to tip over. The closest refugees tried to make way for Wulfe's tank, but there was too little room to move. They were hemmed in by the rest of the human tide.

Shouting was futile, Wulfe decided. The old scar on his throat itched like crazy. Scratching it, he looked east, tracing the broad line of shambolic figures all the way to the shimmering horizon. The sky was clear and blue, and the air was warming quickly.

Palmeros. Even after two years of war, much of this world was still rich and green. Clean, fresh air. Pure, crystal waters. He'd thought this world a paradise when the regiment had first landed. What would it be like, he'd wondered, to settle here, find a wife, till the land? Then word of the coming cataclysm had leaked out and things started coming undone. Seventeen massive asteroids, allegedly guided by the will of the ork warlord Ghazghkull Thraka, were hurtling towards Palmeros on a deadly collision course.

Desperate masses poured from the cities, marching in their millions to the nearest evacuation zones. Those squeezing past Wulfe's tank had come from Zimmamar, the provincial capital in the north-east.

They followed The Gold Road west towards Banphry. Neither rich nor skilled enough to secure places on the Munitorum's evacuation lists, they'd find themselves facing lasguns and razorwire when they got there. Every last centimetre of space on the Navy's ships was already accounted for.

Wulfe's own regiment, the Cadian 81st Armoured, were already rolling their tanks into the cavernous bellies of the naval lifters that would carry them to the relative safety of space. Not the entire regiment, of course. Not he and his crew – the crew of the Leman Russ battle tank, *Last Rites*. And not the crews of *Steelhearted* and *Champion of Cerbera*, both of which followed close behind, running escort for those damned Sororitas in their unmarked black Chimera.

What did I do, Wulfe wondered, to deserve the honour of leading this Eye-blasted wild-grox chase?

His driver inched *Last Rites* forward, gunning the engine threateningly but to little effect. The refugees were already doing their best to stand aside. To proceed any faster, Wulfe knew, would mean pulping innocent civilians under sixty tonnes of heavy armour.

Sister Superior Dessembra was hailing him again on the mission channel. He didn't feel like listening. She'd already ordered him to roll forward, to lead their tanks off the road by crushing anyone in their path, but the thought of it turned Wulfe's stomach. These people were innocent Imperial citizens, and he was unwilling to stain his hands with their blood.

He watched some of them reach out to touch *Last Rites* as they passed thinking, perhaps, that the hulking machine's holy spirit would bless them with a little luck on this final hopeless day. A few craned forward to plant reverent kisses on her thick, olive-painted hull. The sight stabbed at Wulfe's heart.

He knew the mission clock was ticking. The town of Ghotenz, site of their primary objective, was still almost 200km away. Every second wasted here brought he and his men closer to being stranded, to sharing the planet's imminent annihilation. His laspistol began to feel heavy on his hip, calling for his attention. Dessembra was right; breaking free of the masses by force was the only option left. The tanks had to get off the road.

A warning shot, he reasoned, might get them moving. He didn't want to panic them – many would be hurt – but it would be kinder than crushing them.

He lifted his pistol from its holster and thumbed the safety off. Before he could fire, however, screams of terror erupted from behind him. He spun in his cupola to see *Champion of Cerbera* coughing thick black fumes from her exhausts as she rolled towards the edge of the highway. The old tank pulled dozens of helpless refugees under her, crushing their bones to powder. By the time she reached the roadside, her treads were slick with glistening blood. Cries of anger and grief filled the air.

'What are you doing, Kohl?' Wulfe shouted over the vox-link. 'Those are Imperial citizens!'

It was Dessembra who voxed back, 'They are jeopardising the success of our mission, sergeant. And so are you. I'm ordering you to run them down at once!'

The refugee column fell into utter chaos. People howled in terror. They began barging each other aside, desperate to flee the proximity of the war-machines. Animals brayed and kicked out at the people behind them. The old and weak were barrelled to the ground, begging for help as they were trampled to death. Even through the muffles of his headset and the roaring of engines, Wulfe could hear, too, the heart-rending cries of petrified children.

Steelhearted and the black Chimera were already following in *Champion of Cerbera*'s wake. More refugees fell under their treads. *Last Rites* alone stood unmoving, surrounding by a sea of frantic people. Now, however, broad spaces began to appear in the crowd as people pushed away. Wulfe could see the rockcrete surface of the highway clearing before him. He ordered his driver to get them off the road.

Only a few hours into the mission, Wulfe was already at loggerheads with the woman in command. At least the treads of his tank, like his hands, were unstained with the blood of the Emperor's subjects... so far.

Evacuation Zone Sigma, Banphry, Vestiche Province, 4 hours earlier

WULFE DREW ASIDE the heavy fabric of the entrance and stepped into Second-Lieutenant Gossefried van Droi's command tent, keenly aware of how dishevelled he looked. Only moments ago, he'd been fast asleep in his bunk.

He cleared his throat, and the three men present turned to regard him.

'Sergeant Wulfe reporting as ordered, sir,' he said, throwing van Droi as sharp a salute as he could manage.

The second lieutenant snapped one back. He looked rough around the edges himself. Deep lines radiated from his eyes, coarse grey stubble covered his cheeks and chin, and there was an unlit black-leaf cigar in the corner of his mouth.

Bad news, then, thought Wulfe.

Van Droi only ever chewed unlit cigars when he was especially troubled.

'Did we interrupt your beauty sleep, sergeant?' asked van Droi. 'When I call a briefing, I expect my men to be punctual.'

Wulfe winced.

Van Droi indicated a steaming pot on a low table in the corner and said, 'Caffeine.' It was an order, not an offer. Wulfe walked over to pour himself a cup while the other two sergeants turned back around in their chairs.

One of these men was Alexander Aries Kohl, broad-faced and flat-nosed, commander of *Champion of Cerbera*, and a notorious martinet. With six years more experience than Wulfe, he'd proven himself a tough, reliable tank commander on battlefields from here to Tyr, but his personality, or lack of one, had so far barred him from advancement.

Sergeant Mikahl Strieber, on the other hand, seated on Kohl's right, was a hit with almost everyone in the 81st. Good-humoured and optimistic, the tall red-head took particular delight in anything that got under the skin of old Kohl. Some thought him reckless, but his survival suggested a certain talent, too.

Wulfe guessed he was somewhere between the two men; more experienced than Strieber and less detested than Kohl. Maybe that was why van Droi liked to dump so much crap on him.

The second lieutenant indicated a chair, and Wulfe sat, apologising for his tardiness. '*Last Rites* isn't due to board until oh-nine-hundred, sir, so the crew and I had a few drinks before lights-out.'

'Not a crime,' said van Droi. 'By the time you've heard me out, you'll be needing a few more.'

Wulfe raised an inquiring eyebrow. His commanding officer sighed and perched himself on the edge of his desk. He took the damp cigar from his mouth, looked down at it and said, 'You're astute men, all of you, so you know I haven't called you here for a smoke and a glass of *joi*. Tenth Company drew the short straw tonight, gentlemen, and when I say Tenth Company, I mean *you*.'

Wulfe felt a sinking sensation in his stomach.

Still staring hard at his cigar, van Droi continued. '*Last Rites, Champion of Cerbera* and *Steelhearted* are being refuelled and reloaded. Your crews are being ordered to prep for duty as we speak. They'll be waiting for you at staging area six by the time we're finished here. *Foe-breaker* and *Old Smashbones* will be sitting this one out. They've been under heavy repairs since the breakout at Sellers' Gap. Given the losses we suffered there, your tanks have been chosen by default.'

'You're sending us back out?' exploded Strieber. 'You can't be serious, sir!'

'It's not something I'm likely to joke about, sergeant,' van Droi snapped. 'I've made my opinion clear to Colonel Vinnemann, but the top brass are having it their way.'

Sergeant Kohl muttered darkly to himself.

Wulfe's mouth had gone dry. This is a bad dream, he told himself. Wake up, Oskar. Wake up! He took a bitter swig of caffeine, gulped it down and said, '*Last Rites* can't roll without a driver, sir. Corporal Borscht is still listed as critical. I checked on him myself about six hours ago.'

A few days earlier, Borscht had been bitten by some kind of local worm. He'd been in a coma ever since. His throat had swollen up like a watermelon, his limbs were turning black, and he smelled like rotting meat.

Van Droi nodded grimly. 'I've taken care of it. Got you a replacement. It wasn't easy on such short notice, so you'll understand my choices were limited.'

The second lieutenant's nested apology set Wulfe even further on edge. Before he could ask van Droi to elaborate, however, Strieber interrupted. 'What's it all about, sir? Why send us back out now? By midnight tonight, the whole bloody planet will be spacedust!'

The voice that answered was female and unfamiliar, and came from the entrance of the tent. 'Time enough, then, to salvage some glory from this mess.'

Wulfe turned in his seat. A short, rotund woman in flowing white robes walked past him to stand beside Second Lieutenant van Droi.

'Planetkill,' she said, 'will occur at exactly twenty-three forty-seven hours. Of course, with the Emperor's blessing, gentlemen, we'll all be far away by then.'

* * *

98 kilometres east of Banphry,
Vestiche Province,
09.12 local (14 hours 35 minutes to Planetkill)

LAST RITES SPED east, treads gouging dark furrows in the earth, throwing grassy clods of dirt up behind her. Her driver, Metzger, was pushing her over the plains with everything she had. The Gold Road was out of sight now, hidden from view by the shallow hills to the north. Wulfe had ordered the hatches open for ventilation, but he wasn't riding up in his cupola as he usually preferred. Instead, he was down in the turret basket, perched on his cracked leather command seat, cursing under his breath as he was lambasted by the voice on his headset.

'If you ever put civilians ahead of our objective again,' raged the sister superior through a crackle of static, 'I'll strip you of escort command. Sergeant Kohl has proven capable of grim necessities. I'm sure he'd be willing to take over.'

Wulfe wasn't about to argue with her. He'd seen her papers. They bore all the relevant signatures and seals, some from individuals so high up the ladder he'd never heard of them. *Exolon*'s top brass had issued the woman absolute authority over the mission and, while she was smart enough to leave vehicular management in the hands of experienced tankers, she clearly wasn't about to let something as trivial as human compassion jeopardise her success. Sergeant Kohl apparently felt the same.

'Listen carefully, sergeant,' Dessembra continued, 'because I won't be repeating this. While I admire your sense of morality, I warn you there's no place for it on this mission. The life of a very important man depends on how quickly we reach Ghotenz and return. And all our lives depend on catching the last lifter out of Banphry, so do not test me again. Are we clear?'

Wulfe mentally blasted her with a string of insults, but he knew better than to verbalise them. 'Understood, sister,' he said, and broke the vox-link.

That black-hearted sow, he thought. What the hell was High Command thinking? And isn't all human life supposed to be sacred to the Order of Serenity?

At the same time, however, he couldn't deny a certain uncomfortable relief. Weighing duty against personal honour had always been difficult for him. While he'd wrestled with his conscience, Dessembra's cold disregard for the lives of the refugees had put the mission back on track. Whether he liked it or not, ultimately, she'd been right.

Very well, he swore. It won't happen again.

He'd stow his humanity for now. He could be stone-hearted, too, if necessary.

Keying the tank's internal vox, he said, 'Metzger, keep her running full ahead, eight degrees east-south-east. We'll rejoin the highway south of Gormann's Point. Shouldn't be many refugees so far out. We'll make some time up there.'

'Aye, sir,' replied the driver.

Wulfe rose from his seat and climbed into his cupola, immediately enjoying the warm wind on his face.

Last Rites rolled along at the head of the column. Twenty metres behind her, *Champion of Cerbera* followed, turret facing south-east. Kohl was in his cupola, but he didn't return Wulfe's nod.

Following *Champion of Cerbera*, the unmarked black Chimera purred along with an easy grace, capable of twice the speed of the Leman Russ tanks, but hobbled by the need for their protection.

Steelhearted brought up the rear, her massive cannon pointing south-west. Seeing Wulfe, Sergeant Strieber threw him a casual salute.

Wulfe did likewise then turned to survey the land ahead. The plains north of here were still regarded as safe zones. Naval reconnaissance put the nearest orks just to the south, in the province of Drenlunde. If the mission group were to encounter any greenskins, they'd come from there.

Wulfe was gazing at the low, tree-crested hills to his left when a nasal voice spoke through his headset. It was Metzger. 'Could you check your panel, sir? The auspex is picking up a signal. Looks like a civilian SOS beacon about fifteen kilometres away, just north of our current heading.'

Wulfe ducked back down into the turret to check his station and found that Metzger was right. Someone was signalling for help.

His first instinct, he knew, was the wrong one. Even so, it took him a moment to overcome it. With an unpleasant twist in his gut, he voxed, 'No detours, corporal. We don't have time. Keep her at full ahead, please. Whoever they are, the Emperor will decide their fate.'

'Aye, sir,' replied Metzger, 'full ahead.'

There was no hint of judgement in the man's voice, but Wulfe heard it anyway.

* * *

Evacuation Zone Sigma, Banphry,
Vestiche Province,
3.5 hours earlier

WULFE KNEW SOMETHING was wrong the moment he reached the staging area. Standing in a pool of electric lantern-light, Viess, Siegler, Holtz and Garver were huddled together, slightly stooped in the way of all long-serving tankers, whispering and passing a single lho-stick around. With the exception of Siegler, the set of their shoulders told Wulfe they were in a foul mood.

As Sergeants Kohl and Strieber left him to greet their own crews, Wulfe breathed in the smell of promethium fumes on the night air. The field was almost empty. The last few engineering tents were waiting to be taken down. And there, just beyond the final tent in the row, sat the shadowed forms of three hulking monsters. They belched oily smoke from their twin exhausts as they sat with their engines idling. To Wulfe's eyes they were familiar, beautiful things. One, in particular, held his eye. He smiled as his gaze followed the sweep of her hull and the noble line of her powerful battle-cannon.

Last Rites.

A trio of robed figures, each grotesquely misshapen by the mechanical appendages that sprouted from their backs, performed final checks on her track assemblies and external fixtures.

Helmut Siegler was the first to spot his sergeant. He came racing over like a hyperactive puppy. After a brief, jittery salute, words began gushing out. 'Viess says it isn't right, sir,' he panted. 'Garver and Holtz won't do it, either. They said they won't ride with him, sir. The Eye is on him. That's what they said, sir. The Eye!'

Wulfe blew out an exasperated breath and walked past his loader, who fell into step behind him. He stopped a few metres in front of his men and returned their stiff, sullen salutes.

Viess the gunner. Holtz and Garver, the sponson men. He'd known them for years – as good a crew as any when the fighting started, and just as troublesome when they were idle. 'What's all this crap about not riding with the new man?' Wulfe demanded.

'It ain't right, sir,' said Garver glancing at the others for support.

'I heard that already,' said Wulfe. 'Let's have some details.'

Holtz, the eldest of the three, took a step forward. 'A man like that ain't nothin' but bad news, sarge. It's wrong enough we're going back out, but to have a cursed man on crew... You'll be wanting him swapped out.'

Wulfe scowled. 'Are you speaking for me now, Holtz? I don't think so. And if you mean to complain about someone, you'll furnish me with a bloody name first.'

Holtz tipped his head by way of apology, but his blue eyes continued to blaze. Once upon a time, those eyes had won him his share of female hearts. That was before so much of his face had ended up looking like hashed groxmeat. Anti-loyalists back on Modessa Prime had hit the tank's left sponson with a shaped charge. Holtz had been inside. These days, the women he bedded fell into two categories – the charitable and the desperate – and Wulfe often found himself cutting the embittered man some slack.

Footsteps sounded on the grass and a nasal voice said, 'The man they're talking about is Corporal Amund Metzger, sir. It's me.'

Wulfe turned to face a tall, skinny man with dark eyes and a long, curving nose. He was dressed in standard-issue tanker's fatigues and, unlike the rest of Wulfe's crew, who mostly smelled of oil, sweat and propellant powder, he smelled of Guard-issue soap.

'Don't be too hard on your men, sir,' Metzger continued. 'They're not wrong. Hell, my own company wouldn't have me.'

'Lucky' Metzger, thought Wulfe. Thanks a lot, van Droi.

Everyone in the regiment knew the story of 'Lucky' Metzger. He had a reputation for climbing out of burning tanks unscathed while everyone else roasted to death. Among the crews of the 81st, that made Metzger about as popular as crotch-pox. Just twelve days ago, he'd survived yet another tank fatality. Now the whole regiment, including officers who should have known better, believed that riding with Metzger was a death sentence. It had nothing to do with his driving ability, of course. He'd been considered exceptional by his instructors back on Cadia.

Unlike his crew, Wulfe knew curses for cudbear crap. Death claimed everyone sooner or later. All a man could hope to do was fight it off for as long as possible and sell his life dear. Only the Emperor Himself was immortal, after all.

All the same, his crew was spooked, and Wulfe knew he had to squash it right away. He glared at the new man. 'Listen up, corporal. This so-called curse of yours is a load of bloody ball-rot. Everyone knows that if the turret takes a hit, nine times out of ten, the driver walks away. I've seen plenty of men crawl unharmed from burning tanks.'

Plenty, he admitted to himself, was stretching things a bit.

He pointed to his own tank and said, 'That big beauty over there is *Last Rites*. Finest in the regiment. Thirty-eight confirmed tank-kills and plenty more besides. And if you take care of her, she'll take care of you. That's how it works. Give me any less than your best, I'll have you up in front of "Crusher" Cortez on more charges than he has metal fingers.' Wulfe turned to the rest of his crew. 'That goes for all of you. The commissar isn't nearly as forgiving as I am. Now get to your damned stations.'

Wulfe's men were about to move off when the clanking of cast-iron treads made them stop. An unmarked black Chimera, workhorse troop-transporter of the Imperial Guard, ground to a halt near the waiting Leman Russ tanks. Its rear hatch opened, spilling orange light onto the dark ground, and disgorged three female figures clad in the long white robes of the Order of Serenity.

'Women,' gasped Viess. 'And one of them looks good!'

'They're not *women*,' barked Wulfe, 'they're Adeptus Sororitas, so don't even think about it, Viess. I don't need the hassle.'

Viess groaned and mumbled something euphemistic about firing his 'gun'. Garver and Siegler chuckled. Holtz managed a grin. Metzger's mouth barely twitched.

With Sister Superior Dessembra leading them, the women approached the crew. 'Sergeant Wulfe,' said Dessembra, 'we should be underway as soon as possible, but perhaps a quick introduction. Just as a courtesy. I doubt you'll need to communicate with my subordinates once we're underway. My driver, Corporal Fichtner, will introduce himself via vox-link.'

Wulfe shrugged. 'Then the courtesy is unnecessary, sister superior. But to show my respect for your order...' Offering shallow bows to the two sister-acolytes, he said, 'Sergeant Oskar Andreas Wulfe at your service, as are my crew, the men of the Leman Russ *Last Rites.*'

Dessembra's smile didn't reach her eyes. She gestured to the tall, grim-faced woman on her right and said, 'This is Sister Phenestra Urahlis.'

Wulfe smiled genially at the imposing acolyte, but her expression remained fixed like a mask.

'And this,' said Dessembra with a wave of her hand, 'is Sister Ahzri Mellahd.'

Sister Mellahd smiled and gave a shallow curtsey. Her robes, cinched tight at the waist, accentuated a striking figure. She was young, curvaceous and excruciatingly pretty.

Viess took a step forward. 'You must see my cannon, sister. It's huge!'

Wulfe's hand flashed out, clipping the gunner on the side of his head.

'Ow!'

'Get to your bloody stations, all of you,' he growled. 'Internal systems check. Four minutes.'

'But, sir,' Garver moaned, 'the cogboys have already run two full sys–'

'Don't make me repeat myself, soldier. Move!'

With a mixture of muttered complaints and angry scowls, the crew jogged off towards the tank. Siegler raced over to it with his typical abundance of child-like energy. Dessembra followed him with her eyes.

'That one seems a little *Throne-touched*, sergeant,' she said, nodding in Siegler's direction.

'Injured in the line of duty,' replied Wulfe, tapping the side of his head with a finger. 'And yet, without doubt, the best man on my crew. He's the fastest loader in the regiment, and that's merely one measure of his worth. Sister Mellahd here, on the other hand, possesses the kind of beauty that makes trouble among men. Best she stay out of sight during the operation.'

At the word *operation*, Dessembra flinched. She turned back around to face Wulfe. 'My sister-acolyte is quite without sin, sergeant. It is undisciplined minds that are to blame for such troubles. I'm speaking in general terms, of course.'

'Of course,' said Wulfe, brushing off the mild insult.

Sergeants Strieber and Kohl were already sitting in the cupolas of their respective tanks. 'You can confess your depravities later, Wulfe,' Strieber called out. 'Let's get our arses into forward gear.'

Dessembra frowned. 'Crude though he is,' she said, 'Sergeant Strieber is quite right. Time is not on our side, sergeant. Get us to Ghotenz. Someone there requires our immediate attention.' She made the sign of the aquila on her chest then turned and led her subordinates back to the Chimera.

Wulfe strode over to his tank. In the sky above, vessel after overcrowded vessel was pulling away from the planet's orbit, and here he was, about to roll out on a last-minute mercy run, probably for some damned incompetent blue-blood who'd gotten himself into hot water.

He clambered up the hull of his tank, swung his legs over the lip of the cupola, slid through the hatch and dropped down into the turret basket. As soon as he was seated, he pulled on his headset, activated the tank's intercom, and issued instructions to his new driver.

With their headlamps throwing stark light out ahead of them, the four Imperial war-machines rolled off into the night.

82 kilometres west-north-west of Ghotenz, East Vestiche, 13.09 local (10 hours 38 minutes to Planetkill)

THEY REJOINED THE highway about sixty kilometres south of the abandoned outpost at Gormann's Point. There were no refugees in sight. Perhaps the locals knew they'd never make it to Banphry in time and had opted to die at home. Or perhaps they'd already passed through. Wulfe hoped their absence wasn't a sign of something more sinister.

The surface of the highway dropped gradually, easing its way down into a deep sandstone canyon known as Lugo's Ditch. Wulfe rode high in the cupola, warm winds whipping his lapels as he scanned the area for threats. Craggy, sandstone walls rose high on either side. Wulfe marvelled at the natural beauty of the place, fascinated, in particular, by the rich and varied hues of the rocky strata.

It hadn't escaped his notice, of course, that the canyon was an ideal place for an ambush. There was no word that the orks had spread this far north, but he put his men on high alert anyway. Sergeants Kohl and Strieber, he saw, were equally uneasy. Both sat in their cupolas, peering through magnoculars at the rocky outcrops on either side.

Taking his cue from them, Wulfe dropped down into the turret basket to retrieve his own pair. While he was there, a light began to wink on the vox-board. It was Sergeant Kohl.

'Wulfe,' he said, 'we're well out from the naval patrol routes now.'

'I know that, Kohl. What's your point?'

'My point, *sergeant*, is that *Last Rites* is the only vehicle here with a decent vox-array. Hasn't there been any kind of intelligence update from regimental HQ?'

It was a fair question, but the answer wasn't likely to satisfy. 'No updates,' replied Wulfe. 'If they've anything to tell us, they'll get in touch. But you said it yourself; we're outside of the patrol zone. The fighter wings have their hands full running defensive sweeps for the lifters. I think we can forget about aerial reconnaissance updates.'

Kohl was quiet. A moment later, he signed off.

Though Wulfe's tank boasted a crew of six, only two other men shared the discomfort of the turret basket with him. Viess and Siegler sat within arm's reach of their commander, backs ramrod-straight, eyes pressed to their scopes, scouring the terrain for the first sign of trouble. Wulfe hoped Garver and Holtz were being equally vigilant, tucked away in their cramped, stifling sponsons. Metzger, up front in the driver's compartment, had more space than anyone else, but not by much.

The tank's intercom, usually alive with dirty jokes and crude banter during long journeys, was silent save the background hiss of white noise. The silence told Wulfe just how tense his crew were.

Having fetched his magnoculars, he was about to climb back up when he heard someone say, 'Stop the tank.'

He wasn't sure he'd heard it correctly at first. The voice came through his headset as little more than a whisper, almost lost against the background rumble of the engine. 'What was that?' he voxed back.

'What was what, sir?' asked Viess.

'Stop the tank,' someone whispered again, clearer this time.

'Do *not* stop the damned tank,' Wulfe barked. 'Who the bloody hell said that? Holtz? Was that you?'

'Don't blame me, sarge,' replied Holtz. 'I never said anything.'

'Garver?' Wulfe demanded.

'It wasn't me, sir.'

Wulfe placed a hand on Siegler's shoulder and half-turned him in his seat. 'Siegler, did you just call for the tank to be stopped?'

'Negative, sir,' the loader replied, shaking his head emphatically.

Wulfe had never known Siegler to lie. He didn't think the man was about to start now. 'Who said to stop the tank? One of you said it, Eye-blast you. Confess!'

'Do you want me to stop the tank, sir?' asked Metzger in obvious confusion.

'No, by the Throne! Keep her steady in fifth.'

'I never heard anyone say to stop, sir,' voxed Garver.

'Me, neither,' said Viess.

They sounded worried now. Wulfe was spooking them. It wasn't like him to get flustered this way and it certainly wasn't like him to hear voices.

'When we get back to base,' he told them, 'I'll be checking the vox-logs. Then we'll see which of you smart-arses is having a laugh.' With a scowl, he climbed back up into his cupola. What he saw when his eyes cleared the rim of the hatch turned his blood to ice and jolted him with such a spasm of fear that he dropped the magnoculars.

They struck the turret floor with a loud clang.

A shocking, impossible figure stood on the road up ahead, arms raised, palms out, eerily insubstantial despite the glaring sunlight.

Borscht!

The dark hollows of his eyes locked with Wulfe's. His voice thundered in Wulfe's mind, drowning out everything else. *Stop the tank!*

Wulfe's finger flew to the transmit stud on his headset. 'Stop the bloody tank! All stop! All stop!'

Metzger braked hard on command and Wulfe was slammed forward, ribs hammering against the rim of the hatch. He winced in sudden flaring pain. When he opened his eyes a split second later, the figure of his old friend had completely disappeared.

'By the bloody Golden Throne!' gasped Wulfe.

Panicked voices tumbled over each other through his headset.

'What's wrong, sir?'

'Where are they, sir? I have no targets. I repeat, no targets.'

'Give us a bearing, sarge!'

Wulfe dropped back into his seat, shaking, chilled to the bone. No, he thought. No way. It's nerves. It wasn't Borscht. It can't have been. It's me. I must be cracking. It's the pressure. It's the damned mission clock. It's…

The vox-board was blinking furiously with calls from the other vehicles. On reflex, Wulfe reached out and keyed the mission channel.

'What in the warp are you playing at, Wulfe?' bellowed Sergeant Kohl. 'You bloody fool. If my man wasn't so alert we'd be halfway up your exhaust by now!'

'Why have you stopped, sergeant?' demanded Sister Superior Dessembra.

Wulfe didn't know what to say. He felt numb. He sat rigid, eyes wide with fear and confusion. Siegler and Viess stared back at him, deeply discomfited. He forced himself to answer the uproar over the vox. 'I... I thought I saw something,' he said. 'But it's gone now.'

'What did you see?' Sergeant Strieber asked.

'I don't know, damn it!'

Typically, Sergeant Kohl's meagre patience ran out first. 'You don't know? Throne curse you, Wulfe! Planetkill is just hours away and you're braking for shadows? We don't have time for this.'

'I know that,' Wulfe snapped.

'Enough!' voxed Dessembra. 'I want someone else on point. Sergeant Strieber, your tank will move up and lead us on. *Last Rites* will guard the rear.'

'Sister superior,' said Strieber cheerily, 'I thought you'd never ask.'

Before Wulfe could protest, *Steelhearted* broke formation, rumbled past the other vehicles and accelerated up the highway.

'Wait!' Wulfe shouted over the vox. 'I said *wait*, Throne damn you!'

But it was too late. Strieber's tank hadn't gone two hundred metres when the road bucked under her with an ear-splitting boom. A pillar of fire erupted from the surface, ripping away her left tread, spinning heavy iron links off in all directions.

'Landmine!' shouted Metzger over the vox.

'Strieber, respond!' demanded Kohl. 'By the blasted Eye!'

'*Steelhearted*, respond!' voxed Wulfe.

Groaning and cursing, Strieber answered a moment later. 'Bloody orks mined the road!' he hissed.

'Don't be stupid,' snapped Kohl. 'They haven't got the brains for that.' He didn't sound at all convinced.

Through his vision-blocks, Wulfe saw dark, ugly shapes pour from the shadowed gullies on either side of the canyon. The air filled with the growl and sputter of countless throbbing engines.

'Button up, *Gunheads*!' he yelled over the vox. 'Lock hatches! Safeties off!' He reached up and slammed his own hatch shut, locking it tight in one practiced motion.

'He's right!' voxed Strieber, panic charging his voice. 'It's a warp-damned ambush!'

61 kilometres north-west of Ghotenz, East Vestiche, 13.51 local (9 hours 56 minutes to Planetkill)

THERE WERE HUNDREDS of them.

Wulfe's heart was pounding in his chest as he watched them spill out onto the canyon floor. 'Close ranks,' he ordered on the mission channel. 'Form up on *Steelhearted*. Defensive pattern *theta*!'

Metzger gunned *Last Rites* into action. *Champion of Cerbera* and the black Chimera leapt forward a second later, speeding towards Sergeant Strieber's crippled tank.

Steelhearted lay utterly immobilised, track-links scattered around her in a forty-metre radius. Her left sponson was still burning. The shrivelled, blackened body of its occupant, Private Kolmann, hung from its twisted hatch. The other vehicles reached her side now, slid to a halt, and spun on their treads to face outward in a defensive, four-pointed star.

'Stinking greenskins,' spat Wulfe. 'It's a wonder we didn't smell them.'

Among the myriad enemies of mankind, it was the *old foe* he hated most. An image flashed through his mind; the blazing red eyes of one particular ork he'd encountered on Phaegos II. The scar on his throat was a memento of that day – the day he'd almost bled to death.

'Holy Throne!' voxed Kohl. 'How many of them are there?'

Wulfe wasn't about to count. Buggies and bikes of every possible description roared into the canyon. They were gaudy things, painted red, with fat black tyres that churned up the dirt. Many were decorated with crude skull motifs or images of tusked deities. Some boasted far grislier forms of decoration – strings of severed human heads and banners of flayed skin. But the ugliness of the machines themselves was nothing compared to that of their riders and passengers. The orks were hideous, malformed brutes that waved oversized blades and pistols. Their bodies were twisted and hunched with overgrown muscle. Their eyes and noses were miniscule, but their mouths were wide and full of massive, jutting yellow teeth.

The throaty roar of each engine merged into a cacophony that filled the air. Thick black fumes spewed from exhaust pipes as the orks raced over the sun-baked land, kicking up clouds of dust behind them. But they weren't surging forward. Not yet. They surrounded the Imperial tanks and began circling them at range, moving anti-clockwise.

'What the hell are they doing?' voxed Strieber.

The answer came all too quickly. From random points in the massive circle, small groups of ork vehicles suddenly broke formation and sped inward towards their prey.

The hull of *Last Rites* rattled under a heavy barrage of stubber rounds.

'Damn,' shouted Viess.

'They're trying to confuse us,' Wulfe voxed to the other tanks. 'If we can't predict their angles of attack, there's a chance they can close the gap. We have to start thinning them out, now! Siegler, high explosives!'

'Aye, sir!' With thick, powerful arms, the loader hefted a shell from the magazine on his right, slammed it into the cannon's breech, and yanked the locking lever.

The loading light turned red. 'She's lit, sir!'

Through the vision-blocks, Wulfe spotted a knot of large, open-topped half-tracks among the smaller, faster ork vehicles. They were filled to overflowing with monstrous green savages. 'Viess,' said Wulfe. 'Traverse left. Ork half-tracks. Four hundred metres.'

Squinting through his scope, Viess spotted them easily. The ork passengers were howling with insane laughter and excitement. Their blades glinted in the sun. He hit the traverse control pedals, and the turret swung around. Electric motors hummed as he adjusted the angle of elevation. 'Targets marked!' he called out.

Wulfe braced himself in his seat. 'Fire main gun!'

Last Rites rocked backwards with the massive pressure of exploding propellant. Her hull shuddered with the thunderous signature boom of her awesome main gun. The turret basket filled with the coppery smell of burnt fyceline.

Through the vision-blocks, Wulfe saw the leading ork half-track vanish in a great mushroom of fire and dirt. The vehicles nearby were blasted into the air, spinning end over end. They smashed hard to the ground, spilling some of their foul passengers, crushing and mangling the rest. Shrapnel scythed out from the blast, eviscerating scores more.

It was a fine shot.

Bikes and buggies began swerving to avoid the burning wreckage, and the ork circle tightened. The enemy swerved inwards with increasing frequency to pepper the tanks with stubber-fire, but *Last Rites* boasted front armour 150mm thick, slanted to deflect solid rounds. The greenskins' armament didn't pack enough penetrating power to pose an immediate threat.

The real danger was in letting them engage at close-quarters.

A regular drumbeat of deep, sonorous booms told Wulfe that the other tanks were firing round after round into the ork horde. Every impact threw shattered vehicles and torn green bodies into the air. Alien blood splashed on the canyon floor, mixing thickly with the sand. In only the first few minutes of the battle, hundreds of greenskins were blasted apart by the legendary firepower of the Leman Russ's main battle-cannon.

Like her sister tanks, *Last Rites* boasted a powerful hull-mounted weapon, too. Wulfe ordered Metzger to fire the lascannon at will. Seconds later, blazing beams of light lanced out to strafe the ork horde. The scorching las-blasts cut straight through light armour, igniting fuel tanks and sending bikes and buggies spinning into the air on great fountains of orange flame.

A trio of ork bikes swerved just in time to avoid destruction and came screaming towards *Last Rites*. Bolter-fire from the sponsons shredded two of them, but the last veered from side to side, racing unharmed through the hail of shells. Wulfe saw the hideous rider grin and lob a grenade towards his tank.

'Brace!' he shouted, and prayed that the blast wouldn't wreck their treads.

There was a dull boom and the tank shook. Lights flickered in the turret basket. Wulfe's diagnostics board reported trouble with the right sponson. He ordered the crew to sound off.

Garver didn't answer.

Wulfe ordered Garver to respond.

Nothing.

'Damn it all,' Wulfe shouted. 'We've lost the right sponson. Garver's gone!'

'No!' yelled Holtz over the vox. 'Those bastards!'

In his periscopic sight, Wulfe watched the ork bike accelerating away. As it passed the black Chimera, it was blasted apart by a searing spray of multilaser fire.

Someone was manning the transport's turret-mounted weapon. The multilaser turned quickly to target an ork truck and fired again, charring wide horizontal slashes in flesh and metal alike. Slaughtered orks tumbled from the back of the truck in limp, lifeless pieces.

Wulfe wondered if Dessembra herself was dispensing the Emperor's judgement. Or was it one of her acolytes? Whoever it was had avenged Garver. He'd have to thank them later.

'They're getting closer,' voxed Metzger. 'They're using smoke from the wrecks to bridge the distance.'

'Stay calm, you dirty fetcher,' snapped Holtz. 'Keep firing. The sarge won't let them get on top of us.'

'You bet I won't,' added Wulfe, but he saw how quickly the gap was closing. There were just too damned many of them. Sooner or later, they'd get close enough to tag the tanks with high-explosives, or some monster with a flamethrower would press the nozzle of his weapon to a ventilation slit and cook them all alive.

We can't keep this up, thought Wulfe. Strieber, you idiot. If you hadn't hamstrung yourself....

But Strieber's tank *was* hamstrung, and Wulfe was quickly realising that this battle couldn't be won. The mission clock kept ticking. There just wasn't time to fight this one out. And Strieber couldn't hope to re-tread his tank under fire. *Last Rites, Champion of Cerbera* and the black Chimera had to break through now.

They had to leave *Steelhearted* behind.

Wulfe saw another armoured half-track, over-loaded with roaring ork infantry, break from the circle and make straight towards his tank. Metzger fired a blast from the lascannon, but the truck's thick front armour soaked it up. Wulfe called out to Viess and the gunner swung the turret around with no time to spare.

'She's lit,' shouted Siegler.

Viess didn't hesitate. His left foot stamped on the firing pedal. *Last Rites* bounced on her suspension as her battle-cannon spat its deadly payload straight into the driver's cab of the enemy machine.

A flash. A boom. An earthshaking explosion at point-blank range. Metallic clattering sounded on the roof of the tank as a shower of burning junk and body parts rained down.

'Good shot,' voxed Metzger with obvious relief.

'Great shot,' Viess corrected.

Wulfe was more concerned with the dense cloud of black smoke that was rolling over them from the blazing frame of the ruined enemy vehicle. 'We can't see a blasted thing now. They'll be coming straight for us. Sponson gunners, stay sharp!'

He used the plural out of habit, and the loss of Garver suddenly stung him. They hadn't been particularly close, not like he and Borscht, but the sponson gunner had been crew. Love them or hate them, crew was family.

Dessembra's voice sounded in Wulfe's ears. 'We can't stay here. Move out, now!'

'We must thin them out more,' Wulfe voxed back. Adrenaline was surging through him, making his blood sing. 'At least enough to give Strieber a fighting chance.'

'Priorities, sergeant,' hissed Dessembra. 'There's nothing you can do for him. Look to your rear. We have to go at once!'

Wulfe checked the rear-facing vision-blocks and felt his battle-rush bleed off in an instant. It was obvious now. The bikes and buggies were just a diversion, intended to harry the tanks and slow them down while the real firepower closed off the canyon at either end. Grinding its way south-east along the road was a loose formation of ork war-machines – massive, heavily armoured and bristling with fat-barrelled cannon.

Wulfe was filled with rage as he looked at them – at least half of the enemy armour had been built from the looted carcasses of fallen Imperial machines. The foul xenos had mutilated and dese-crated them.

Under thick plates of armour bolted on at all angles, he saw the familiar forms of a Basilisk mobile-artillery platform, three Chimera transports, and a disfigured Leman Russ. Other vehicles in the formation seemed entirely built from scratch to some maniacal alien design.

'By the blasted Eye!' he spat. Demonstrating impressive aptitude for their kind, the orks had man-aged to outflank him.

The canyon shook with a ripple of ork cannon fire. 'Incoming!' shouted Wulfe. Explosive shells rained down on the highway. The resulting deto-nations sent up great clouds of dirt and debris, but little else. The ork cannonade was falling far short of its target, but that wouldn't be the case for much longer.

'Emperor above!' voxed Sergeant Kohl. 'They're fielding heavy artillery!'

'We break through now,' voxed Wulfe, 'or we're dead men.'

Strieber was almost screaming over the vox. 'You can't be serious, Wulfe. You can't possibly leave us here. You can't!'

Wulfe felt sick to his stomach as he answered. 'I'm sorry, Strieber. We're out of options.'

'My tank, my crew – we're *Gunheads*, damn you! Don't you run from this fight. Don't you turn away from us, you rotten bastard!'

There was another rumble of thunder from the ork cannons. The impact blasts were much closer this time. *Last Rites* was showered with dirt. The enemy armour continued to zero in.

Wulfe spoke through clenched teeth. 'Lead us out, Metzger. Full ahead. Keep her off the highway. There'll be other mines there. Siegler, load her up. Armour-piercing. Viess, get ready to break a hole in them. They'll not stop us here!'

'Throne blast you, Wulfe!' screeched Strieber.

'I'm sorry, Strieber. I truly am. But you must see that there's no other way. Keep firing. Keep fighting. Help us break through, and I promise the regiment will remember and honour your sacrifice. It's all I can offer you now.'

Last Rites lurched into motion just before another volley of heavy shells shook the canyon floor. With a sudden convulsion of dirt and rock, a great shell-crater appeared where she'd stood only a moment before. The ork armour was now in range, and still the bikes and buggies raced forward with insane abandon, uselessly spraying the Imperial tanks with volleys of stubber-fire.

In subdued tones, Strieber voxed, 'Good luck then, Wulfe. We'll fight on for as long as we can. I... I hope you make it back to Banphry.'

Viess shouted 'Brace!' and fired the tank's main gun. Three hundred metres away, a bastardized ork Chimera was violently peeled apart. Beside Siegler, the cannon's breech slid back, dumping the empty shell-casing in the brass-catcher on the floor. With servitor-like efficiency, the loader slid a fresh armour-piercing shell into the breech, yanked the lever, and shouted, 'Lit!'

Metzger shifted the tank up into third gear, accelerating out past the crippled *Steelhearted*. Viess swung the turret left, zeroing in on a bulky ork battlewagon. He adjusted for elevation, compensated for the tank's forward motion, prayed to the Emperor for a clean kill, and fired. *Last Rites* skewed to the right with the force of the cannon's recoil, but didn't slow. The round slashed brightly though the air, then buried itself deep in the body of the ork machine. It must have pierced the battlewagon's fuel tanks, because the vehicle was blown so high it flipped onto its roof. Flaming wreckage and charred bodies littered the land and roaring fires blazed from its twisted metal carcass.

Champion of Cerbera and the black Chimera followed close behind *Last Rites*. Wulfe saw a tongue of fire flash out from Kohl's battle-cannon. The ork-modified Leman Russ on the far left rolled to a stop, smoke billowing from a large hole in its turret armour. A moment later, flames erupted from inside. Burning alien bodies began tumbling out of the vehicle's hatches, but it was too late for them. The roasted greenskin crew twitched, then lay still on the sand.

'Keep firing,' ordered Wulfe. 'We're almost through.'

They roared past the chugging ork tanks, narrowly dodging a fusillade of high-explosive shells and rockets. Viess fired directly into the nearest, blowing the entire front section up into the air in a fiery spin. Kohl's tank spat again and crippled another with a shot that shredded its right track-assembly. The black Chimera was firing constantly, but her multilaser could do little damage to the enemy's heavy armour. Instead, Dessembra targeted a large, open-topped truck and managed to slaughter a score of ork infantry.

Then they were through. The canyon lay behind them and open lands stretched out ahead.

The heavy ork machines turned to follow, but they were far slower than the well-oiled Imperial tanks. Only the surviving bikes and buggies had the speed to give chase. They charged forward in pursuit, many of them forgetting the mines that their own warband had laid on the highway surface. Those that weren't blown to pieces closed the gap quickly, but their weapons were inadequate. As *Last Rites*, *Champion of Cerbera* and the black Chimera sped away, Wulfe ordered Viess to turn the turret and pick off their lightly-armoured pursuers with the co-axial autocannon.

Wulfe noticed a blinking light on his vox-board. It was Kohl. He was calling on a closed channel. Whatever he had to say, it wasn't for Dessembra's ears.

Wulfe opened the link. 'What is it, sergeant?'

'I'm going back,' said Kohl.

'You're *what*?'

'Think about it, Wulfe. The orks will chase us all the way to Ghotenz unless they have a fight to hold them here.' There was a pause. 'Besides, I've got blinking lights all over the place. We took a big one on the rear decking. The cooling system's almost out and so is the extractor. We can break down halfway to the objective, or we can turn back and buy you some time. I'd rather go out fighting, if it's all the same to you. Maybe we can help Strieber and his crew go out in style.'

Wulfe didn't know how to respond. He felt hollow.

'Get those damned women to Ghotenz,' Kohl voxed. 'Complete the mission for the honour of the regiment, if nothing else. You can still make it off-world if you don't mess about.'

Wulfe wished he could believe it. He'd stopped looking at his chronometer. It only offered bad news. The orks had cost them so much, and not just in terms of time. A voice in his head told him to follow Kohl's example, to die honourably alongside his fellow Gunheads. But another told him that the honour of the regiment had to come first. He had to see the mission through.

'What do I tell Dessembra?' he asked Kohl.

'The truth. I'll give those green bastards plenty to do, by the Throne. They won't be missing you.'

Honour and sacrifice. Wulfe saw that he'd been misjudging Kohl for years, blinded to the man's nobility by his icy manner. Whatever Kohl's flaws, he was a true soldier and a man of uncompromising bravery.

If I survive this mess, Wulfe promised himself, I'll make sure van Droi puts Kohl and Strieber up for the Medallion Crimson. It's not much, but it's something.

Kohl didn't wait for any kind of approval. Through the rear vision-blocks, Wulfe saw *Champion of Cerbera* peel off and swing back around towards the canyon. Soon, she was lost in her own dust cloud.

Last Rites and the black Chimera raced on in the other direction. Dessembra was hailing Wulfe on the mission channel and, reluctantly, he opened the link.

'I demand to know what's going on! Why won't Sergeant Kohl answer me?'

Wulfe didn't bother to keep the tiredness and frustration from his voice as he replied, 'Sergeant Kohl is ensuring our escape. His tank is badly damaged. He has decided to give his life and the lives of his crew for the success of this mission.'

Dessembra paused. 'That's… acceptable,' she said. 'Let's take advantage of it.'

Wulfe couldn't contain his contempt any longer. 'Listen to me, Sororitas,' he hissed over the vox. 'Whoever we're supposed to rescue at Ghotenz had better be a bloody saint reborn, because you and your damned superiors have a hell of a lot to answer for. Do you hear me?'

He cut the connection before she could respond.

33 kilometres north-west of Ghotenz,
East Vestiche,
15.09 local (8 hours 38 minutes to Planetkill)

WITH THE CLOCK driving her hard, *Last Rites* churned up the surface of the highway, but not so fast that Wulfe could outrun his guilt and anger. His thoughts were on the men he'd left behind. The absence of Garver's voice, in particular, pained him as he knew it must pain the rest of his crew.

He was still shaken, too, by his vision of old Borscht. Since the battle in the canyon, Viess had been pressing for an explanation. How had he known to stop the tank? What had he seen from his cupola? Whose voice had he heard?

The others added their own questions now. Wulfe wished they'd let it go, but they wouldn't. In the end, he exploded at them, ordering them to shut their mouths and concentrate on the job in hand. The mention of Commissar Cortez was enough to put an end to it, at least temporarily.

Wulfe didn't grudge them their curiosity. It was only natural. But he couldn't reconcile himself with what he'd seen and heard. Borscht was in a hospital bed back in Banphry. There were no two ways about it. On the other hand, Wulfe wasn't about to concede insanity, either.

Metzger's voice sounded over his headset, announcing their proximity to the primary mission objective. Ghotenz was less than an hour away. That helped Wulfe to centre his thoughts a little.

It was mid-afternoon now, and the air inside the turret was stiflingly hot. Wulfe ordered all the hatches open, making an immediate difference. He rode up in the cupola and, as *Last Rites* and the black Chimera approached the low hills that sheltered the town, he watched his tank's shadow gradually lengthen on the road in front of him as the sun moved ever westwards.

Only eight hours left until the first massive impact shook this world. In the global firestorm, every living thing would be blasted to ash. It would be a quick, merciful death for most, but it was no soldier's death. There was no glory in it.

'There's something on the road up ahead, sir,' reported Metzger.

Wulfe scanned the highway and spotted the object in question. Metzger had good eyes. There was something approaching, large and dark, but indistinct. As the two Imperial machines sped closer to it, the shape resolved itself into the form of a great, shaggy boviath, three metres tall at its massive, hunched shoulders and just as broad. Six curving black horns framed its leathery face. It dragged a large cart, filled with people, up the highway towards them. Wulfe counted twenty passengers, most of them adults.

Last Rites pulled up beside the cart and Wulfe ordered its driver to halt. The cart's driver shouted something to his beast and, with a deep, resonating moan, the boviath slowed to a stop. Every man, woman and child in the cart turned their eyes towards Wulfe, but it was a tall, ugly woman in the gaudy robes of the Palmerosi merchant class who addressed him.

'You've come, then,' she said. 'You've come to stop it.'

Wulfe locked eyes with her. 'To stop what, *udoche?*' As was proper here, he used the local term for a woman one doesn't wish to court. A short, bearded man seated beside her, presumably her husband, nodded his approval.

'The madness, of course,' answered the woman. 'Ghotenz is in utter chaos. The riots. The killings. We were lucky to get out alive.' At these words, some of the men in the cart patted old civilian-model laslocks.

So the townsfolk are rioting, thought Wulfe. Great!

'Thank you for your warning, udoche,' he said. 'We'll do what we can. But where are you going?'

'We're going to evacuate. We've heard of vast ships at Banphry and intend to buy our passage off-world.'

Just for a moment, Wulfe considered telling them the truth. They'd never make it to Banphry. Even if they had time, even if there were no orks on the road ahead, no amount of money would help them. They were doomed. But perhaps it was kinder to let their hopes carry them to the end.

'Be careful on the highway,' he told them. 'There may be greenskins in Lugo's Ditch.'

'I've yet to see one of these *green-kin*,' said the woman. 'But the pamphlets say loud shouting is weapon enough against them.' She jabbed her thumb at a barrel-chested man in the back of the cart. 'Brudegar has the loudest voice in Ghotenz. He'll drive the aliens from our path.'

Wulfe gave an involuntary shake of his head. This kind of fatal ignorance was the Imperial propaganda machine at its worst. Citizens rarely knew the danger orks represented until they were bearing down on them roaring 'Waaagh!' and all the shouting in the Imperium wouldn't do a damned thing.

Conscious of the black Chimera idling impatiently behind him, Wulfe waved the locals on, and the cart-driver cracked his whip. The massive boviath brayed and began hauling its burden off up the highway, and the Imperial vehicles resumed their journey.

Black smoke could be seen now, rising into the afternoon sky from just beyond the next hill. Only a few kilometres separated them from their objective.

Riots, the woman had said. And killings.

Wulfe steeled himself, thinking that perhaps the least pleasant phase of this whole fiasco might yet lie ahead.

Ghotenz, East Vestiche,
16.02 local (7 hours 45 minutes to Planetkill)

HE WAS RIGHT.

Ghotenz, when he saw it, was a town lost to anarchy. Bloated corpses lay strewn about the base of the old-fashioned curtain wall, rotting in the afternoon heat. Flocks of floating maldrothids, indigenous carrion-feeders, had descended from the sky to gorge themselves on the reeking dead. These strange creatures floated three metres above the ground, plucking soft gobbets of human flesh from the bodies below. Their tentacles, each tipped with a sharp beak, lifted morsels of meat to obscene pink mouths while fat flies buzzed around them.

The spectacle was stomach-churning, and so was the smell. Fighting the urge to vomit, Wulfe thumbed his laspistol's safety off, took aim, and fired into the nearest flock.

He struck one of the maldrothids dead-centre, his shot igniting the creature's internal gases. Its sac-like body exploded with a pop.

Others nearby immediately began pushing off from the ground with their long tentacles. They rose into the air to drift away in search of a safer meal.

'By the Throne,' voxed Holtz from his sponson. 'They're foul, unholy things!'

Outside the gatehouse, his back resting against a stone wall, there sat an old, sun-browned man with a wounded leg. Beside him lay a battered laslock. Judging by the number of empty green bottles surrounding him, he was about the business of drinking himself to death.

As the mighty form of *Last Rites* loomed over him, the man reached drunkenly for his weapon, missed it twice, and gave up. 'Wha'dya want, stranger?' he asked, squinting up at Wulfe. 'Have y'come here to die with the folks the Emp'ror forsook?'

Wulfe scowled down at him. 'Watch your tongue, citizen. The Emperor only forsakes traitors and heretics.'

The old man made a rude noise and resumed his drinking.

Wulfe cursed him for a fool and ordered *Last Rites* through the town's open gates with Dessembra's vehicle following a steady ten metres behind.

As they passed into the town, Wulfe swept his pintle-mounted heavy stubber from right to left, covering the corners of the streets and alleyways they passed. Then he remembered that Garver was dead and that the tank's right flank was open. 'Stay alert, all of you,' he told his crew. 'Holtz, I want that heavy bolter covering side streets, windows, doors. Viess, same goes for the co-ax. I'll keep an eye on our right.'

Fires still burned in some of the buildings. They passed walls bearing hastily scrawled slogans like *What frakking Emperor?* and *Fine day for an apocalypse!* Most of the stores and stalls had been looted. Rows of squat yellow habs sat silent and still, their windows shattered, their doors splintered. Lifeless bodies hung from blood-stained windowsills and balconies. The streets themselves were dotted with so many corpses that *Last Rites* couldn't avoid them. Wulfe ordered Metzger to drive over them, grimacing every time a wet crunch sounded from underneath the tank. Many of the bodies on the street were women, their clothing shredded. The crack of laslocks and autopistols rang out frequently, sending frightened maldroth-ids up into the air, abandoning the rich pickings until things settled down.

All this carnage, thought Wulfe, is the work of man. There's no sign of an ork hand in any of this.

Only recently, Ghotenz had been a town of dedicated, hard-working Imperial citizens. Foreknowledge of their doom had shattered that. Word of the coming end had unravelled their civilisation faster than any xenos invasion ever could have.

Dessembra's voice broke through the static on the mission channel. 'Turn left at the next corner, sergeant,' she said, 'then take your second right. Our objective awaits us in the church at the end of Procession Street.'

Wulfe relayed the orders to Metzger and the tank rolled on. The sound of gunfire was more frequent now. It was getting closer, too.

As *Last Rites* turned onto Procession Street, Wulfe's jaw dropped. Up ahead, in the square at the end of the street, a violent riot was raging. The focus of the mob's ire was a small Imperial church – a black two-storey structure with a proud golden aquila perched atop its central spire. Wulfe watched in horror as some of the rioters fired at the sacred icon. On the wide stone steps below, people shouted and jeered, and launched rocks and bottles at the building's stained-glass windows.

'They're attacking the church!' snarled Wulfe.

From her Chimera, Dessembra must have seen it too. 'Forward, sergeant,' she ordered. 'They mustn't get inside. Kill every last one of them if you have to.'

Last Rites charged down Procession Street.

The rioters turned. Many who saw her bearing down on them fled screaming into the shadowed side-streets, but others were more foolish. They swung their weapons around and began peppering her hull with small-arms fire.

Shots ricocheted around Wulfe, but he stayed in his cupola, anger galvanizing him. Setting his heavy stubber to full-auto, he swept the barrel from left to right, spraying the mob with enfilading fire. A hailstorm of lead cut through the apostate ranks, ripping into their unprotected bodies. Screams of pain filled the air. Those who weren't killed or wounded leapt for hard cover then leaned out from stone corners to take hopeless pot-shots at the tank.

The left sponson rattled back at them, its heavy bolter chewing apart their inadequate defences, killing them in a blizzard of stone chips.

Behind him, Wulfe heard the rapid cracking of the Chimera's multilaser and the chattering of her hull-mounted gun. Between them, the two Imperial vehicles unleashed an overwhelming barrage on the street and its buildings.

Less than a minute later, Wulfe ordered his men to cease fire. Procession Street was a silent, blood-soaked wasteland. The only think moving was the smoke that curled from the muzzles of Imperial guns.

With the mission clock never far from his mind, he glanced down at his pocket-chronometer. About seven hours left. Whatever the bloody Sororitas have come here to do, he thought, they'd better do it quickly. There was still the return journey to contend with. They couldn't pass through Lugo's Ditch again. That would be suicide.

'Forward,' he voxed to Metzger.

With the immediate threat neutralized, the two vehicles approached the church. Sister Superior Dessembra ordered them to a halt at the bottom of the steps. Seconds later, the Chimera's rear hatch was thrown open and the three sisters hospitaller emerged into the dry afternoon air.

'Secure the area, Sergeant Wulfe,' Dessembra called out as she stepped over a twitching body. Some of the wounded rioters were still alive, but only just. 'Nothing must disturb us.'

Each of the women, Wulfe saw, carried a sealed ceramite case marked with twin insignia: the winged and laurelled Cadian Gate symbol of the 18th Army Group, and the distinctive fleur-de-lys of the Adeptus Sororitas.

'Metzger,' voxed Wulfe, 'get her ready for a hasty exit. Holtz, stay sharp. Viess, use the co-ax. Siegler, get up into this cupola and man the stubber. Cover the blind spots. Nothing gets close enough to threaten the tank or the Chimera. Is that understood?'

With a quick check of the charge-pack in his laspistol, he leapt down from the hull of his tank and strode up the church steps after the three women. Halfway up, he turned to take a quick look at the tank's right sponson. It was a mess of twisted, blackened metal. Wulfe shook his head. If there was anything left of Garver inside, it wouldn't be much.

Loud creaking announced the opening of the church doors. Wulfe continued up the steps, stopped behind Sister Urahlis, and saw a thin, sallow-faced man in a burgundy robe peering out at them from within. Seeing the insignia on Dessembra's robes, the man smiled and opened the door wider, ushering them in.

'Frater Gustav,' said Sister Superior Dessembra. 'Tell me, does the man live?'

'He lives, sister superior,' replied Gustav in a high, scratchy voice. 'I've been ministering to him in the undercroft, but I lack the skills to do much good.'

The sisters moved inside and Wulfe followed, stepping beyond the heavy wooden doors to find the church filled with people. They knelt on low wooden benches facing the glittering golden altar. They were deep in prayer.

The faithful, thought Wulfe. *While the town fell into madness, they took shelter in this sacred house. That, at least, is as it should be.*

On his left, Dessembra and the thin priest were talking as they descended a dark stone stairwell followed by the two sister-acolytes. 'You did a great thing when you reported his whereabouts, frater,'

Dessembra was saying. 'The man is critical to the war effort in this sector.'

Uninvited and unnoticed, Wulfe hurried after them, following them along a short, dark corridor to a gloomy chamber under the church.

There, in a room lit by hundreds of flickering candles, was the answer to a question Wulfe had first asked back in van Droi's command tent: who were they expected to rescue? The man's identity was no longer classified.

Captain Waltur Kurdheim, only surviving son of General Argos Kurdheim, lay groaning and shivering on a makeshift bed.

The captain's aging father was a High Strategos in the Officio Tacticae. He'd been attached to Army Group *Exolon* for years. If anyone had the authority to send Imperial tanks on such a reckless mission for personal reasons, it was the hawk-faced old general.

Dessembra moved swiftly to the captain's bedside and checked his pulse, then gestured sharply at Urahlis and Mellahd. 'Quickly, sisters. Open the cases. I need 10cc's of paralycium and 15cc's of gamalthide.'

Wulfe crossed to the opposite side of the young captain's bed. 'By the Eye, sister superior,' he said. 'He's in bad shape. What's wrong with him?'

Dessembra looked up as if seeing Wulfe for the first time. 'What are you doing here, sergeant? Get out at once. You mustn't be in here. Get out, Throne curse you!'

Before Wulfe could respond, he felt a weak hand grip his forearm. It was Captain Kurdheim's. Wulfe looked down into wide brown eyes filled with fear.

'The frater betrayed me,' rasped Kurdheim. 'Don't leave me to them, soldier. If you've any honour in you…'

Wulfe looked at the pale white hand on his arm. 'Rest easy, captain,' he said. 'These women are sisters hospitaller of the Order of Serenity. Medical specialists. They've come to save you.'

Kurdheim pulled his hand away. 'Fool,' he coughed. 'They're my father's lapdogs. He's the only man they came to save.'

Wulfe looked at Dessembra, his frown communicating his confusion.

'He's badly wounded, sergeant,' she said, pulling back the blood-stained sheets. Wulfe saw a big wet bandage on the captain's side. 'His company was lost four days ago on the far side of the Yucharian Mountains. It's a miracle that he made it here. Now, please, step outside and let us do our work.'

Wulfe trusted Dessembra about as far as he could throw an auroch, and he liked her even less, but he could find no legitimate excuse to stay. He left as ordered, but a nagging voice remained in his head. Something wasn't right. Captain Kurdheim hadn't seemed confused at all. His eyes had been sharp and bright, despite his obvious pain. And the fear in them… Wulfe knew real fear when he saw it.

Rather than return to his tank, he stationed himself on the other side of the undercroft door. The sisters would need help, he rationalised, in carrying the young captain up to the Chimera.

Moments later, the screams began. The first was so sudden and unexpected that Wulfe almost leapt into the air. He burst back into the undercroft with his laspistol drawn, but what he saw stopped him dead.

Captain Kurdheim lay under his sheets as before, only now they were utterly drenched with blood. The whole chamber stank of it. Transparent tubes snaked out from under the sheets to a boxy medical device that sat in an open case on the floor. The young captain was screaming through gritted teeth as some kind of thick, viscous substance was being siphoned from his paralysed body and collected inside the machine.

As Wulfe stood stunned and horrified, following the flow of the grey-pink fluid down the transparent tubes, he saw four pale shapes in the shadows by the foot of the bed.

It can't be, he thought. Throne above, it can't!

It was difficult to tell in the low light, but they looked uncomfortably like severed hands and feet.

Wulfe raised his pistol towards the ceiling and fired off a shot. The crack of ionised air was deafening in the small chamber. The women started. Frater Gustav let out a frightened whimper.

Dessembra spun to face Wulfe, anger twisting her fleshy features. 'I told you to stay outside, you dolt. Don't interfere!'

'Ball-rot, sister,' Wulfe spat back. 'That man is a Cadian officer and, from the sounds of it, you're torturing him to death. You'd better have a damned fine explanation for this.'

'You're out of your depth, sergeant. I was assured by your superiors that you'd comply.' Dessembra turned to Sister Mellahd. 'Show him our orders.'

'But they're classified, sister superior,' protested Mellahd.

'Do it, blast you, girl!'

The shapely young Sororitas bowed to her superior, then lifted a rolled parchment from one of the ceramite cases and held it out to Wulfe. 'It's all here, sergeant,' she said. 'See for yourself.'

Without lowering his weapon, Wulfe looked over the scroll. What he read filled him with outrage. The young captain was right – these women hadn't come to save him at all.

They'd come to save his father.

The scroll avoided naming General Kurdheim's particular condition – perhaps it was a source of some embarrassment – but it was very specific about the nature of the cure. Fresh marrow had to be extracted from his son's living body. The scroll listed drugs approved for the procedure, but Wulfe couldn't find any anaesthetics among them. A line in bold red script said something about anaesthesium denaturing important elements of the extracted marrow, but the medical jargon was far too deep for Wulfe to tackle. It was clear, however, that *Exolon* High Command had given full authorisation to this horrific operation. Penalties for failure were listed at the bottom. Anyone interfering in the retrieval of the young captain's bone marrow would be executed publicly as a traitor.

'This is sick,' said Wulfe. 'He's conscious, for Throne's sake.'

Dessembra spoke without turning. 'The captain will make this sacrifice for his father, whether he wishes to or not. General Kurdheim is an important man. His survival is critical to our success in this sector. His son, on the other hand, is expendable. Think logically, sergeant, and you'll see that it makes perfect sense.'

Thick fluids continued to drain from Kurdheim's body, sliding down the transparent tubing and into the humming machine. Something clogged one of the tubes and Sister Urahlis moved forward to adjust it. As she did so, the captain howled in agony.

Wulfe's face was twisted with pity and rage. This was too much. He pointed the barrel of his laspistol straight at the captain's head and said, 'I can free you from your misery, sir. Just say the word! Order it!'

In the blink of an eye, Dessembra had positioned herself between the pistol and the paralysed officer, blocking Wulfe's shot. 'The marrow must be taken from a living body,' she said, her eyes boring into Wulfe's. 'Do you want to give him peace, sergeant? Do you really want to cut this operation short prematurely? Think about it. You're gambling with the lives of your crew. You saw the paper. If we don't get back to Banphry before that first rock hits, we die. If we return without the marrow, we die. And if you return without me, I can promise you that the Commissariat will be waiting for you. And you will die.'

Wulfe's hand was shaking. He itched to kill this woman. How could such a monster claim to serve the righteous Golden Throne? Do it, his conscience urged. Kill her. End this man's agony and punish this dreadful woman for the lives she's already cost Gossefried's Gunheads.

But Wulfe knew he couldn't condemn his crew. To kill Dessembra was to kill all of them. And, as

Dessembra watched the realisation show on his face, she knew she had him. With an infuriating grin, she said, 'Leave this chamber now, sergeant. We'll be finished shortly. Have the vehicles ready to move out on my word.'

Hating himself for it, Wulfe holstered his pistol and turned from the room. As he walked stiffly up the stone stairs, he tried to block out the captain's screams, but it was hard. The young man was yelling Wulfe's name over and over, cursing him to the darkest corners of the warp.

Ghotenz, East Vestiche,
17.17 local (6 hours 30 minutes to Planetkill)

WULFE EMERGED FROM the church to find the sun low on the western horizon. The sky was filled with a watery glow, casting the ravaged town in hues of reddish gold. In front of *Last Rites*, dozens of townsfolk had gathered, kneeling with their hands on top of their heads while Siegler covered them with the pintle-mounted heavy stubber.

Wulfe climbed his tank to stand on the engine decking, just behind the turret, and said, 'What's going on here?'

'Locals, sir,' said Siegler. 'They presented themselves while you were inside. Waving white flags, they were. They've come to ask for help.'

'After the attack on the church?'

'They say they had nothing to do with the riots, sir. Busy defending their homes.'

A dark-skinned man kneeling at the front of the group eyed Wulfe, spotted the silver pips on his lapels and said, 'Forgive me, sir, but would you be the officer in charge?' He was middle-aged, muscular and wore the uniform of a town custodian.

Law enforcement, thought Wulfe. Where was *he* during the riot?

'I'm no officer,' he replied. 'But I'm in charge, after a fashion.'

'Then, may we stand?' asked the custodian. 'There are elders among us. We've not come to threaten you or your men.'

Without lowering his voice, Wulfe said, 'Keep them covered, Siegler.' Then to the crowd he said, 'Stand if you wish.'

Slowly, they got to their feet. Some needed help to rise. The custodian took a step closer to Wulfe's tank and said, 'Ships have been crossing the sky in greater numbers than usual today. Some of the merchants fled west, talking about evacuation, and we've all heard about the asteroids and the coming end. We thought…. Have you come to help us?'

Wulfe had to lie. He knew that much. *Last Rites* still had to make it out of here in one piece. Let these people believe whatever they wanted if it served that purpose. False hope was better than genuine despair, wasn't it?

'We've come to Ghotenz on other business,' said Wulfe, 'but I can tell you that a Naval lifter is scheduled to arrive here later this evening. Have no fear. The ship will come in plenty of time. But you must be ready to leave.'

Excited muttering swept through the crowd. Wulfe tried not to look at them for fear of seeing relief on their faces. In the last twelve hours, his self-respect had been eroded almost to nothing.

He had begun to hate himself, and there was more to come.

'You'll each have a personal cargo allowance of twelve kilograms,' he told them, cementing the lie. 'It's not much, I know, but it's better than nothing. No weapons of any kind may be taken aboard. No plants or animals are permitted.'

'Where should we gather?' asked a woman on the right. 'We don't want to waste any time.'

'The bhakra fields south-west of the town seem best suited to a landing,' said Wulfe. 'I recommend that you assemble there.'

'This is wonderful news,' said another woman behind the custodian. 'Praise the Emperor!'

The rest of the crowd took up the cheer.

Automatically, Wulfe did the same, but there was a bitter taste in his mouth. 'You should return to your homes now,' he called down to them. 'Our vehicles will be leaving momentarily and our way must be clear.'

'Why don't you wait to be lifted out with us?' asked the custodian. 'Your men must be tired and hungry.'

'Thank you,' said Wulfe. 'But our work isn't finished. We have another stop to make before we can evacuate.'

More mutters rippled through the crowd, this time filled with respect and sympathy.

The custodian turned to the townsfolk and said, 'Let's disperse, people. Back to your homes, now. We must all pack for the evacuation.'

After saluting Wulfe with something like parade-ground pomp, the custodian led the crowd away from the square. Their excited chatter filled the street until they disappeared from view.

Siegler turned to Wulfe and asked, 'Are we ready to move out, sir?'

Wulfe looked for it, but Siegler's expression was void of any criticism.

'We're just waiting on–'

The old church doors creaked loudly behind him, and the sisters hospitaller emerged into the fading sunlight. Frater Gustav followed them out. Screams and curses, barely discernable over the noise of the idling tank, still issued from within the church. Wulfe leapt down from the rear decking and climbed the church stairs once more.

Dessembra turned at the door and took the thin priest's hands in her own. 'The Emperor will reward you soon, frater,' she said. 'But one last thing, please. Lugo's Ditch is held by the foe, and we must reach The Gold Road some other way.'

Gustav nodded. 'There is an old trade route, sister superior, that we used before the highway was built. Follow the dirt track north at first. A series of switchbacks will take you up into the highlands, ending just east of Gormann's Point. You can rejoin The Gold Road there.'

'How long will it take?' Dessembra asked.

'From what you've told me, sister superior, you'll be cutting it fine, but it will save you the trouble of the canyon.'

Wulfe stormed over to the small group and thrust his face in front of Dessembra's. 'Finished mutilating Cadian officers, are we?'

Dessembra's expression hardened in a flash. 'Watch your tongue, sergeant. We have what we came for, if that's what you mean.'

'Then why in the warp is the man still screaming?'

Dessembra tried to push past him, but Wulfe's hand flashed out and grasped her wrist. She struggled for a moment, but the sergeant's grip was like iron. The sister-acolytes stepped forward to intervene, but the cold fire in Wulfe's eyes made them hesitate.

'Unhand me, damn you,' spat Dessembra. 'Not that it's any of your business, sergeant, but General Kurdheim was quite clear on the matter. His son will be allowed the honour of dying with this planet and its many faithful martyrs.'

Wulfe felt like striking the woman in her fat face. 'The honour of what? He's in absolute hell. Can't you hear that?'

Echoing up from the below the church, the captain's screams were gut-wrenching. 'His suffering will atone for his unwillingness to do his duty,' said Dessembra. 'He'll go before the Emperor with a clear conscience.'

Maybe it was Dessembra's voicing of the word, but Wulfe found he couldn't suppress his own conscience any longer. He'd done far too much of that already today. Releasing Dessembra and shoving Frater Gustav violently aside, he marched back into the church, drawing his laspistol as he moved.

'Get back here, sergeant,' screeched Dessembra. 'The general's orders were very specific. You'll face a court martial for this!'

Wulfe didn't stop. Looking over his shoulder, he called out, 'This is supposed to be a mercy run, you fat grox. And mercy is what I intend to give him.'

Moments later, the sharp crack of a laspistol rang out from the undercroft.

* * *

26 kilometres north of Ghotenz, East Vestiche, 17.53 local (5 hours 54 minutes to Planetkill)

THEY FOLLOWED THE frater's suggested route back to the highway without encountering the enemy, but the sky was darkening quickly, and Wulfe felt time slipping away from him like water through his fingers. The road up into the highlands was hard, and lesser vehicles would have struggled – sure-footed boviaths were far better suited to it – but the muscular engines of the Imperial war-machines had enough grunt for the job. There were some hair-raising moments. Twice, while turning hairpin bends, *Last Rites* almost slid from the steep, narrow trail. She would have plummeted, smashing her crew to death inside her, had Metzger not demonstrated remarkable skills. Even Holtz, still convinced that the new man was a doombringer, felt compelled to pay him a terse compliment.

To Wulfe's great relief, the land soon flattened out. They turned westward just six kilometres south of the old outpost under a night sky dusted with bright, winking stars. Some of those stars were moving – naval transports and escort ships leaving orbit with all haste.

Emperor above, thought Wulfe as he gazed up through his open hatch, let the last ship wait for us.

The vox was quiet. Wulfe watched the other men in the turret struggle with their growing sense of desperation. Siegler was rocking back and forth in his chair, muttering mathematical problems in an attempt to divert his mind. Viess was patting the turret wall beside him and cooing, 'Faster, old girl! You can do it!'

Wulfe watched the second hand spinning on his chronometer, willing it to slow down, but it seemed to get faster instead. The background static of the tank's intercom hissed in his ear, broken only by affirmations when he issued occasional orders to Metzger or general reminders to stay on the lookout for any signs of a firefight out there in the dark. The only orks they spotted, however, were the occasional green bodies on the road. They were surrounded by human corpses. Wulfe guessed a warband had swept north towards Zimmamar, slaughtering any refugees caught in its path.

The tank's headlamps occasionally picked out flocks of maldrothids floating silently in the dark, feasting on the recently deceased. Holtz and Viess, either offended by the sight or just eager to distract themselves, requested permission to fire on the eerie scavengers, but Wulfe wouldn't have it. Gunfire and muzzle flashes might draw unwanted attention. He imagined orks crouched by the roadside in the dark, just waiting for a target to come along.

About halfway between Gormann's Point and Ban-phry, with a little over seventy kilometres still to go, Dessembra voxed him. 'You must realise, sergeant,' she said, 'that at this speed, there's no hope of catch-ing our ride out.'

'I hope you're not suggesting we give up,' replied Wulfe sourly. 'She's not built for speed, but my man is squeezing everything he can out of her.'

'I'm sure he is, but I think you're missing my point. My Chimera is lighter and capable of far higher speeds than your tank. Since I believe we're no longer under direct threat from orks, and no longer require your protection, I'm ordering my driver to break formation and pull ahead of you. It's imperative that our cargo reaches General Kurdheim. I'm sure you understand.'

There we have it, thought Wulfe. I should have expected no less from you, Dessembra.

'Emperor's speed to you, then,' he voxed back coldly.

The Chimera pulled out of *Last Rites*'s slipstream, charged past her on the right, and pulled back in directly ahead of her. Contrary to Wulfe's expectations, however, the black transport didn't accelerate away.

'Stop your tank,' ordered Dessembra.

'What?'

'I said stop your tank, sergeant. Order your man to pull up at once.'

Wulfe did as he was told. Viess and Siegler turned to give him nervous looks. The last thing they could afford to do right now was to lose forward momentum.

The Chimera slid to a halt on the road ahead, starkly illuminated by *Last Rites*'s headlamps. A heartbeat later, the rear hatch opened. Dessembra appeared in the glaring white light, gesturing impatiently.

'Get a move on, sergeant,' she voxed. 'If you and your men aren't onboard in less than a minute…'

Wulfe could hardly believe his ears. 'Everybody out on the double,' he ordered. 'Into the Chimera, damn you. Don't stop to take anything!'

Hatch doors clanged as they were flung open. Wulfe hauled himself up and out of his cupola in time to see Metzger scramble from his hatch at the front of the tank. Holtz launched himself backwards through his sponson hatch and landed on his back with a grunt. No time for graceful exits.

Wulfe raced over to the Chimera's rear door and stood there, yelling at his men to double-time it. Only when they were all inside did he enter, slamming the hatch shut and locking it. He heard Dessembra say, 'Full-ahead please, Corporal Fichtner!' and the vehicle leapt forward with a sudden burst of acceleration.

Dessembra moved through the cramped passenger compartment until she was standing before Wulfe. She nodded to him once, then, without breaking eye contact, lowered herself into the seat opposite him. 'You see sergeant?' she said. 'Perhaps I'm not the monster you think I am, especially when circumstances allow a certain latitude.'

Wulfe wouldn't let her off that easily. He doubted he'd ever be completely free from his terrible memories of the church undercroft. Wordlessly, he looked along the compartment at the rest of his crew and saw his own mixed feelings mirrored on their faces. Even Metzger, with them for less than a full day, looked glum.

Dessembra followed his gaze. 'What's wrong with you all? You should be grateful. Your chances of survival are now markedly improved.'

A sad smile tugged at the corners of Wulfe's mouth. 'We *are* grateful, sister superior, but we're grieving, too.' Speaking for the attention of his crew, he added, '*Last Rites* was the very finest tank I've had the pleasure to command. She was reliable and responsive, accurate and unstoppable.' His men nodded in silent assent. 'With the Emperor's blessing, her indomitable spirit will infuse another great war-machine. May she be reborn to fight on for the glory of the Imperium.'

'Ave Imperator,' the men intoned.

Dessembra nodded. 'Ave Imperator,' she said, then called to the driver's compartment where the youngest of her acolytes rode beside Corporal Fichtner. 'Sister Mellahd? A hymn if you please. Something to speed our journey back.'

The acolyte's beautiful, oval face appeared at the forward end of the compartment. 'What shall I sing, sister superior?'

With the hint of a grin, Dessembra said, '*Sunder All, His Shining Hammer.*'

It was a well-known favourite of the Cadian tank regiments.

As Mellahd's clear, high voice filled the compartment, lifting the tankers' hearts, Wulfe stared numbly at his chronometer, mesmerized by the inexorable clockwise motion of the hands as the minutes bled away.

58,000 kilometres from Palmeros, Darros III System, Segmentum Solar, 11.31 ship's time (0 hours 0 minutes to Planetkill)

THE MASSIVE IMPERIAL Navy starship *Hand of Radiance* swung away from Palmeros, filled to capacity with rescued men and materiel. Most of those onboard crowded into the ship's vast windowed galleries where, together, they bore witness to the death of an Imperial world. For some, the horrific, violent beauty of it was too much. Dozens fainted.

Wulfe opted not to watch, though the rest of his crew did.

When the first of Ghazghkull Thraka's accursed asteroids punched a hole in the planet's surface and ignited the global firestorm, he was alone in one of the starship's many small chapels, kneeling on a cold wooden bench, praying to the Emperor for the souls of dead men.

He prayed for Kohl, for Strieber and for the crews of their tanks. For Jans Garver, who had died well in faithful service to the Golden Throne. And for Dolphus Borscht – tank driver and friend – who had passed away in his hospital bed during the day.

A shiver ran the length of his spine as he remembered reading Boscht's death certificate. The time of his old friend's passing coincided, almost to the minute, with his inexplicable appearance in the canyon.

Wulfe had opted not to mention the chilling apparition in his report. People who spoke of such things tended to disappear without explanation.

Finally, he prayed for Captain Waltur Kurdheim – tormented and sacrificed to prolong the life of his powerful, uncaring father. A mercy run, Dessembra had called it. More like a sick joke. Wulfe hoped the young officer's soul was at peace in the presence of the undying Emperor.

He rose from his knees and sat back on a wooden pew, turning his thoughts to the future. The 18th Army Group was already en route to their next theatre of war. High Command was talking of a major operation on *Planet G*. They wouldn't disclose the true name of their destination until *Hand of Radiance* arrived in-system to rendezvous with the rest of the fleet, but rumours ran that Commissar Yarrick was somehow involved. And that meant orks.

The fighting, the killing, the losses, thought Wulfe. Endless war.

Despite his melancholy mood, his face betrayed the ghost of a smile.

Last Rites II, he'd been told, would be waiting for him when he got there.

ABOUT THE AUTHORS

HENRY ZOU

H.T.R Zou lives in Sydney, Australia. He joined the Army to hone his skills in case of a zombie outbreak and has been there ever since. Despite this, he would much rather be working in a bookstore, or basking in the quiet comforts of some other book-related occupation. One day he hopes to retire and live in a remote lighthouse with his lady and her many cats, completely zombie-free.

RICHARD WILLIAMS

Richard Williams was born in Nottingham, UK and was first published in 2000. He has written fiction for publications ranging from *Inferno!* to the *Oxford & Cambridge May Anthologies*, on topics as diverse as gang initiation, medieval highwaymen and arcane religions. In his spare time he is a theatre director and actor. *Relentless*, his first full-length novel, was published in 2008.

Visit his official website at
www.richard-williams.com

GRAHAM MCNEILL

Hailing from Scotland, Graham McNeill worked for over six years as a Games Developer in Games Workshop's Design Studio before taking the plunge to become a full-time writer. In addition to many previous novels, including bestsellers *False Gods* and *Fulgrim*, Graham has written a host of SF and Fantasy stories and comics. Graham lives and works in Nottingham and you can keep up to date with where he'll be and what he's working on by visiting his website.

Join the ranks of the 4th Company at
www.graham-mcneill.com

SIMON DYTON

After reading too many Fighting Fantasy gamebooks as a child, Simon's adventures led him to live and work in New York City. Interested in all kinds of literature and history, he spends much of his spare time relieved that he doesn't live in the grim darkness of the 41st millennium, and the rest of it glad that he lives in a place and time that has amazing Chinese takeaway at 2am.

ROBEY JENKINS

A Public School-educated, Oxford-graduate, retired Army officer, Robey Jenkins likes defying stereotypes. Having left the beaten career track, he divides his time between parenting his children, writing science fiction, designing jigsaws, composing Christian music and finishing his 3,000 point Space Marine army. He can often be found organising wargaming events at Warhammer World and has a mild obsession with the narrative skirmish game, *Inquisitor*. Married to Jenny, he lives in York, UK. *Phobos Worked in Adamant* is his first published work.

MATTHEW FARRER

Matthew Farrer lives in Australia, and is a member of the Canberra Speculative Fiction Guild. He has been writing since his teens, and has a number of novels and short stories to his name, including the popular Shira Calpurnia novels for the Black Library.

STEVE PARKER
Born and raised in Edinburgh, Scotland, Steve Parker now lives and works in Tokyo, Japan. As a video-game writer/designer, he has worked on titles for various platforms. In 2005, his short fiction started appearing in American SF/fantasy/horror magazines. In 2006, his story 'The Falls of Marakross' was published in the Black Library's *Tales from the Dark Millennium* anthology. His first novel, *Rebel Winter*, was published in 2007.

Aside from writing, his interests include weight-training, non-traditional martial arts and wildlife conservation.

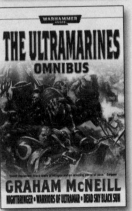